UNCLE DYNAMITE

ABOUT THE AUTHOR

P. G. Wodehouse (1881–1975) is widely regarded as the greatest comic writer of the twentieth century. Wodehouse wrote more than 70 novels and 200 short stories, creating numerous much-loved characters – the inimitable Jeeves and Wooster, Lord Emsworth and his beloved Empress of Blandings, Mr Mulliner, Ukridge, and Psmith. His humorous articles were published in more than 80 magazines, including *Punch,* over six decades. He was also a highly successful music lyricist, once with over five musicals running on Broadway simultaneously. P. G. Wodehouse was awarded the Mark Twain Prize for 'an outstanding and lasting contribution to the happiness of the world'.

Also By P. G. Wodehouse

Jeeves and Wooster

The Inimitable Jeeves
Carry On, Jeeves
Very Good, Jeeves
Thank You, Jeeves
Right Ho, Jeeves
The Code of the Woosters
Joy in the Morning
The Mating Season
Ring for Jeeves
Jeeves and the Feudal Spirit
Jeeves in the Offing
Stiff Upper Lip, Jeeves
Much Obliged, Jeeves
Aunts Aren't Gentlemen

Blandings Castle

Something Fresh
Leave it to Psmith
Summer Lightning
Full Moon
Pigs Have Wings
A Pelican at Blandings
Sunset at Blandings

Uncle Fred

Uncle Fred in the Springtime
Cocktail Time
Service with a Smile

Monty Bodkin

The Luck of the Bodkins

Standalone novels

The Pothunters
Piccadilly Jim
A Damsel in Distress
The Adventures of Sally
The Small Bachelor
Money for Nothing
Big Money
Hot Water
Laughing Gas
Summer Moonshine
The Girl in Blue

UNCLE DYNAMITE

P. G. Wodehouse

PENGUIN BOOKS

PENGUIN BOOKS

UK | USA | Canada | Ireland | Australia
India | New Zealand | South Africa

Penguin Books is part of the Penguin Random House group of companies
whose addresses can be found at global.penguinrandomhouse.com

Penguin
Random House
UK

First published in the UK by Herbert Jenkins Ltd in 1948
Reissued by Hutchinson Heinemann in 2023
Published in Penguin Books in 2024

001

Please be aware that this book was originally published in the 1940s and contains
language, themes or characterisations which you may find outdated.

Typeset in 11.75 pt/14.25 pt Garamond MT Std by Jouve (UK), Milton Keynes
Printed and bound in Great Britain by Clays Ltd, Elcograf S.p.A.

The authorised representative in the EEA is Penguin Random House Ireland,
Morrison Chambers, 32 Nassau Street, Dublin D02 YH68

A CIP catalogue record for this book is available from the British Library

ISBN: 978–1–529–15711–6

www.greenpenguin.co.uk

Introduction

I recently picked up a classic novel, and found it contained an introduction by a very well-known writer. I read it eagerly, before quickly realising that in fact, the condescending tone was putting me off actually starting the book. I was so cross, it almost ruined the enjoyment of it. 'What's the point of introductions?!' I thought to myself. So when I was asked to put finger to button and carve out a few hundred words at the start of a work by, in my opinion, the funniest writer that has ever lived, I almost fled the country in panic. How can anyone be worthy enough to have their words before Pelham Grenville Wodehouse's? In truth, no one is. But nonetheless, it's the greatest of honours to be asked to introduce you, dear bookholder, to one of the greatest and silliest stories ever told.

The problem I had with the aforementioned introduction was that it set out to make the reader believe that the novel in question 'wasn't for everyone' and that you had to be of supreme intellect to truly 'get it'. Well, I thought that was tosh. I consider myself to be of fairly low intellect, and *I* got it. And it was . . . fine. Two out of five. I have always been very keen to say that reading is for everyone. You should never try to put someone *off* reading – you can't know what they might get out of it. Luckily, this book you're holding, well, this book is for *everyone*. The only thing you need to bring to the party is a willingness to laugh.

Why me, then? Well, it's a fair question. As well as blabbering on the radio, I also write books – children's books. Big, fun, daft adventures that have been partly inspired by Wodehouse himself. I love playing with words and worlds, creating new ones and inventing new similes. There's nothing better than conjuring up a new, colourful character that leaps purposefully off the page like a toad who's just remembered he's late for a slug hunt. Wodehouse's books are my favourite things to read, bar anything except maybe the cricket scores. And when England are playing, P. G. still often wins anyway, because England often don't. If you're new to the world of P. G. Wodehouse: I am completely and utterly jealous. You're about to enjoy a brilliantly batty array of characters, the wittiest dialogue and the most inventive wordplay ever. If you're familiar with the series: 'What ho, old bean!' Lovely new cover, isn't it? And isn't the flap jolly! As jolly as a jolly bird!

I read somewhere that Wodehouse used to write each of his sentences ten times to make sure they were absolutely perfect. Pretty astounding when you think about how long that would take. Such dedication to his craft is one of the reasons he's so highly regarded. It's also fairly devastating to us mere mortals, isn't it? I imagine most of us have spent our lives writing sentences that we've barely even re-read once.

But that's how P. G. Wodehouse created comedic and literary perfection. You can tell he enjoyed honing each joke, trying out new phrases and experimenting with language. This is probably the most valuable lesson I've learned reading his books over the years. If you're not having fun making something, how can you expect others to enjoy it?

Wodehouse once said that his primary aim was 'to spread sweetness and light'. Isn't that magical? No other agenda but to make people laugh and give them a good time. It's pure escapism, and that's what I've always loved the most about his stories. They've been with me through school, university, family sadness, embarrassing breakups, work stresses, global pandemics and . . . well, you'd be a fool to try and predict what's next. What I *can* predict is that whatever it is, I'll be able to rely on one of his imagined friends to get me out of a funk. Incidentally the Earl of Ickenham, who you'll meet shortly, is one of the best de-funkers going.

My first encounter with Wodehouse was at school, although frustratingly, he was never formally taught. Why *is* he never taught? Strangely, it was a deep-voiced, bespectacled Physics teacher (and Wodehouse fanatic) by the name of Mr Hows who opened the door for me to this literary wonderland. Books I'd experienced in school up until this point had been dealt with very seriously. They must be FULLY annotated. You must look for hidden meaning. Read it and read it and read it again until it's not fun any more. Despite this, when Mr Hows boomed out one day in assembly that he was going to stage a dramatic reading of Jeeves and Wooster, I shyly enquired about it. I loved drama and farting around on stage and it was something I wanted to get better at. I was vaguely aware of the Fry and Laurie TV adaptation, but being fifteen years old and attending a state school in Bishop's Stortford in the early 2000s, I was more concerned with who The Rock was fighting at Wrestlemania than how Bertie was going to avoid marrying Honoria Glossop. (Spoiler alert, he does avoid it. Oh, and The Rock lost to Triple H, if you're interested. A great injustice.) So, I took to the stage to be on the stage, rather than out of a love of P. G.'s comic characters.

All this changed the moment I was cast as Mr Hows's Jeeves. A whole new world of entertainment opened up. I entered a colourful universe of aristocratic buffoonery and public school nonsense that I had previously known nothing about. I found it all ridiculous, charming and, most importantly of all, funny. So very funny. Like most of us, I wasn't the most confident teenager and I'm glad of that now. I've found it important to be wary of over-confident fifteen-year-olds. And I hadn't really found my 'thing'. But along came Bertie and Jeeves, and it started to dawn on me that this was it.

As Jeeves, I sauntered across the stage delivering the most perfectly polite and tempered putdowns to my employer, the blundering Bertie Wooster, played delightfully by my mate Bruce. And, as the play went on, I realised the true joy of Wodehouse's words. I wore an old suit of my dad's, gelled my hair down and learned how to walk and talk like the infamous valet. My confidence both in life and onstage rocketed. I loved being in front of an audience, I liked making people laugh. From there, I dived into all things silly. Old Radio 4 comedies like *Round the Horne*, Mel Brooks movies, Monty Python and, of course, the Wodehouse back catalogue. Every time I saw one in a bookshop, I added it to my collection. All of these silly things have a thread running through them. Just be funny and make sure the audience has the best time with you. This message has led me to what I'm doing today, and Mr Hows is the reason I'm writing this now. He was a disciple of Wodehouse, one of the 'Drones', if you will (a little joke for the fans there).

The most wonderful thing about Wodehouse's work is that it's truly funny, in the sense that there's no need to even try and look for deeper meaning. It's fun for the sake of fun, and there really isn't enough of that in the world. No need to overthink it, and certainly no need to annotate it either. Delightfully, I've ended up re-reading them. Lord Ickenham is said to be one of P. G.'s favourite creations. His frenetic, chaotic and mischievous energy ensures the stories he features in bound along gleefully. As a reader, he's a joy to spend time with. Regardless of the sticky situation he finds himself in, you always know he'll unstick himself . . . somehow. The real magic is finding out how. Every work by Wodehouse is a 'page-turner', but the presence of Frederick Twistleton, 5th Earl of Ickenham, in any of his stories means you'll not just turn the pages but find yourself polishing off the paragraphs and chomping through the chapters at an alarming rate.

Wodehouse novels offer up the chance to read for pleasure in its purest form, one of the best things you can do for your brain. As Stephen 'Jeeves' Fry once said, 'You don't analyse such sunlit perfection, you just bask in its warmth and splendour.' Warmth and kindness run throughout Wodehouse's work. There's never a suggestion of him wanting to skewer a particular section of society, but he is incredibly playful. Some of the characters he writes may well be flawed, bumbling, wealthy ninnies but I always get the impression that he rather likes them. He finds them fascinating, and he thinks that people are essentially good. Uncle Fred, for example, only ever wants the very best for the mismatched young lovers in the story, no matter how farcical his methods may be. Yes, he enjoys creating mischief, but it's always well intentioned. My favourite type of mischief! The great comic writer Ben Elton said in an interview that P. G. Wodehouse 'loved being alive'. I adore that description. I feel at my most alive when I'm visiting Aunt Dahlia at Brinkley Court, wondering how Jeeves will extricate Bertie from his next scrape or how Uncle Fred will get away with pretending to be three people at once. 'For anyone that's tired of cynicism,' said Elton, 'I recommend a trip to P. G. Wodehouse's world – it will refresh you enormously.'

Right, that's quite enough from me now. Shall I summarise the plot? Explain what you're about to read? Absolutely not.

No one could do it justice. Pour yourself a snifter of something tasty, loosen your breeches and let it all play out. Expect blustering Bostocks, bonnie babies, a blue Bill, a bouncy Bean, a booming Brabazon-Plank and bountiful busts. Come on then, let's dive head first into Wodehouse's world. Be careful to not get too oiled, though – you don't want to miss a single word. Remember, each sentence was checked ten times for your reading pleasure . . . each deserves your attention. Here come 300 pages of pure joy. If it's laughter you're after, you've picked just the right book. In the words of Uncle Dynamite, Lord Ickenham himself: 'Expect sensational results shortly!'

Greg James, 2023

PART ONE

I

On the little branch line which starts at Wockley Junction and conveys passengers to Eggmarsh St John, Ashenden Oakshott, Bishop's Ickenham and other small and somnolent hamlets of the south of England the early afternoon train had just begun its leisurely journey.

It was a train whose patrons, sturdy sons of the soil who did not intend to let a railway company trouser more of their money than they could help, had for the most part purchased third-class tickets. But a first-class compartment had been provided for the rich and thriftless, and today it had two occupants, a large youth of open and ingenuous countenance, much sunburned, and a tall, slim, distinguished-looking man some thirty years his senior with a jaunty grey moustache and a bright and enterprising eye, whose air was that of one who has lived to the full every minute of an enjoyable life and intends to go on doing so till further notice. His hat was on the side of his head, and he bore his cigar like a banner.

For some ten minutes after the train had started, the usual decent silence of the travelling Englishman prevailed in the compartment. Then the young man, who had been casting covert glances at his companion, cleared his throat and said, 'Er.'

The elderly gentleman looked up inquiringly. Deepening in colour, for he was of bashful temperament and was already wondering why he had been ass enough to start this, the sunburned youth proceeded.

'I say, excuse me. Aren't you Lord Ickenham?'

'I am.'

'Fine.'

The elderly gentleman seemed puzzled.

'I'm pretty pleased about it myself,' he admitted. 'But why do you rejoice?'

'Well, if you hadn't been –' said the young man, and paused aghast at the thought of what horrors might not have resulted from the wanton addressing of a perfect stranger. 'What I mean is, I used to know you. Years ago. Sort of. I was a pal of your nephew Pongo, and I came over to your place for tennis sometimes. You once tipped me five bob.'

'That's how the money goes.'

'I don't suppose you remember me. Bill Oakshott.'

'Of course I remember you, my dear fellow,' said Lord Ickenham heartily and quite untruthfully. 'I wish I had a tenner for every time I've said to my wife, "Whatever became of Bill Oakshott?"'

'No, really? Fine. How is Lady Ickenham?'

'Fine.'

'Fine. She once tipped me half a crown.'

'You will generally find women loosen up less lavishly than men. It's something to do with the bone structure of the head. Yes, my dear wife, I am glad to say, continues in the pink. I've just been seeing her off on the boat at Southampton. She is taking a trip to the West Indies.'

'Jamaica?'

'No, she went of her own free will.'

The human tomato digested this for a moment in silence, seemed on the point of saying 'Fine,' then changed his mind, and enquired after Pongo.

'Pongo,' said Lord Ickenham, 'is in terrific form. He bestrides the world like a Colossus. It would not be too much to say that

'Moab is his washpot and over what's-its-name has he cast his shoe. He came into the deuce of a lot of money the other day from a deceased godfather in America, and can now face his tailor without a tremor. He is also engaged to be married.'

'Good.'

'Yes,' said Lord Ickenham, rather startled by this evidence of an unexpectedly wide vocabulary. 'Yes, he seems fairly radiant about it. I myself, I must confess, am less enthusiastic. I don't know if you have noticed it, Bill Oakshott, but nothing in this world ever works out one hundred per cent satisfactorily for all parties. Thus, while A is waving his hat and giving a series of rousing cheers, we see B frowning dubiously. And the same is true of X and Z. Take this romance of Pongo's, for instance. I was hoping that he would marry another girl, a particular protégée of mine whom I have watched grow from a child, and a singularly fascinating child, at that, to a young woman of grace, charm and strength of character who in my opinion has everything. Among other advantages which she possesses is sense enough for two, which, it seems to me, is just the amount the wife of Reginald ("Pongo") Twistleton will require. But it was not to be. However, let us look on the bright side. Shall we?'

'Oh, rather.'

'Fine. Well, looking on the bright side, I haven't met this new girl, but she sounds all right. And of course the great thing is to get the young blighter safely married and settled down, thus avoiding the risk of his coming in one day and laying on the mat something with a platinum head and an Oxford accent which he picked up on the pier at Blackpool. You remember what a pushover he always was for the gentle sex.'

'I haven't seen Pongo since we were kids.'

'Even then he was flitting from flower to flower like a

willowy butterfly. He was the Don Juan of his dancing class when he wore Little Lord Fauntleroy suits, his heart an open door with "Welcome" on the mat.'

'He'll chuck all that sort of thing now.'

'Let us hope so. But you remember what the fellow said. Can the leopard change his spots, or the Ethiopian his hue? Or is it skin? And talking of Ethiopians,' said Lord Ickenham, allowing himself to become personal, 'has someone been cooking you over a slow fire, or did you sit in the sun without your parasol?'

Bill Oakshott grinned sheepishly.

'I am a bit sunburned, aren't I? I've been in Brazil. I'm on my way home from the boat.'

'You reside in this neighbourhood?'

'At Ashenden Manor.'

'Married?'

'No. I live with my uncle. Or, rather, he lives with me.'

'What is the distinction?'

'Well, what I mean is, Ashenden really belongs to me, but I was only about sixteen when my father died, and my uncle came barging over from Cheltenham and took charge. He dug in, and has been there ever since. Running the whole show. You'd think from the way he goes on,' said Bill, stirred to unwonted loquacity by the recollection of his wrongs, 'that he owned the bally place. Well, to give you an instance, he's pinched the best room in the house for his damned collection of African curios.'

'Does he collect African curios? God help him.'

'And that's not all. Who has the star bedroom? Me? No! Uncle Aylmer. Who collars the morning paper? Me? No! Uncle Aylmer. Who gets the brown egg at breakfast?'

'Don't tell me. Let me guess. Uncle Aylmer?'

'Yes. Blast him!'

Lord Ickenham stroked his moustache.

'A certain guarded something in your manner, Bill Oakshott,' he said, 'suggests to me that you do not like having your Uncle Aylmer living at Ashenden Manor. Am I correct?'

'Yes.'

'Then why not bung him out?'

The truculence faded from Bill Oakshott's demeanour, leaving in its place embarrassment. He could have answered the question, but to do so would have involved revealing his great love for his uncle's daughter, Hermione, and agreeable old bird though Lord Ickenham was, he did not feel that he knew him intimately enough.

'Oh, well,' he said, and coyly scraped a shoe like a violin case along the floor of the compartment. 'No, I don't quite see how I could do that.'

'There are complications?'

'Yes. Complications.'

'I understand.'

It was plain to Lord Ickenham that he had stumbled upon a delicate domestic situation, and he tactfully forbore to probe into it. Picking up his *Times*, he turned to the crossword puzzle, and Bill Oakshott sat gazing out of the window at the passing scenery.

But he did not see the familiar fields and spinneys, only the lovely face of his cousin Hermione. It rose before him like some radiant vision, and soon, he reflected, he would be beholding it not merely with the eye of imagination. Yes, at any moment, now that he was back in England again, he was liable to find himself gazing into her beautiful eyes or, if she happened to be standing sideways, staring at her pure, perfect profile.

7

In which event, what would the procedure be? Would he, as before, just gape and shuffle his feet? Or would he, fortified by three months in bracing Brazil, at last be able to shake off his distressing timidity and bring himself to reveal a silent passion which had been functioning uninterruptedly for some nine years?

He hoped so, but at the same time was compelled to recognise the point as a very moot one.

A tap on the knee interrupted his meditations.

'Next stop, Ashenden Oakshott,' Lord Ickenham reminded him.

'Eh? Oh, yes. That's right, so it is.'

'You had better be girding up your loins.'

'Yes,' said Bill, and rose and hauled down his suitcase from the rack. Then, as the train puffed out of the tunnel, he gave a sudden sharp cry and stood staring. As if unable to believe his eyes, he blinked them twice with great rapidity. But they had not deceived him. He still saw what he thought he had seen.

Under normal conditions there is about the station of Ashenden Oakshott little or nothing to rouse the emotions and purge the soul with pity and terror. Once you have seen the stationmaster's whiskers, which are of a Victorian bushiness and give the impression of having been grown under glass, you have drained it of all it has to offer in the way of thrills, unless you are one of those easily excited persons who can find drama in the spectacle of a small porter wrestling with a series of large milk cans. 'Placid' is the word that springs to the lips.

But today all this was changed, and it was obvious at a glance that Ashenden Oakshott was stepping out. From the penny-in-the-slot machine at the far end to the shed where the porter kept his brooms and buckets the platform was dark with what practically amounted to a sea of humanity. At least forty persons must have been present.

Two, selected for their muscle and endurance, were holding aloft on poles a streamer on which some loving hand, which had not left itself quite enough room, had inscribed the words:

WELCOME HOME, MR WILLm

and in addition to these the eye noted a Silver Band, some Boy Scouts, a policeman, a clergyman, a mixed assortment of villagers of both sexes, what looked like an Infants' Bible Class (with bouquets) and an impressive personage with a large white moustache, who seemed to be directing the proceedings.

From his post by the window Bill Oakshott continued to stand rigid and open-mouthed, like some character in a fairy story on whom a spell has been cast, and so limpid was his countenance that Lord Ickenham had no difficulty in analysing the situation.

Here, he perceived, was a young man of diffident and retiring disposition, one who shrank from the public eye and quailed at the thought of being conspicuous, and for some reason somebody had organised this stupendous reception for him. That was why he was now looking like a stag at bay.

Publicity was a thing from which Lord Ickenham himself had never been averse. He frankly enjoyed it. If Silver Bands and Boy Scouts had come to welcome him at a station, he would have leaped to meet them with a whoop and a holler, and would have been out taking bows almost before the train had stopped. But it was plain that this young friend of his was differently constituted, and his heart was moved by his distress.

The kindly peer had always been a practical man. He did not, as others might have done, content himself in this crisis with a pitying glance or a silent hand-clasp.

9

'Nip under the seat,' he advised.

To Bill it seemed like a voice from heaven. It was as if in the hour of deadly peril his guardian angel had suddenly come through with something constructive. He followed the counsel without delay, and presently there was a lurch and a heave and the train resumed its journey.

When he crawled out, dusting his hands, he found his companion regarding him with open admiration.

'As neat a vanishing act as I have ever witnessed,' said Lord Ickenham cordially. 'It was like a performing seal going after a slice of fish. You've done this sort of thing before, Bill Oakshott. No? You amaze me. I would have sworn that you had had years of practice on race trains. Well, you certainly baffled them. I don't think I have ever seen a Silver Band so nonplussed. It was as though a bevy of expectant wolves had overtaken a sleigh and found no Russian peasant aboard, than which I can imagine nothing more sickening. For the wolves, of course.'

Bill Oakshott was still quivering. He gazed gratefully at his benefactor and in broken words thanked him for his inspired counsel.

'Not at all,' said Lord Ickenham. 'My dear fellow, don't mention it. I am like the chap in Damon Runyan's story, who always figured that if he could bring a little joy into any life, no matter how, he was doing a wonderful deed. It all comes under the head of spreading sweetness and light, which is my constant aim.'

'Well, I shall never forget it, never,' said Bill earnestly. 'Do you realise that I should have had to make a speech, besides probably kissing all those ghastly children with the flowers?' He shuddered strongly. 'Did you see them? About a million of them, each with a posy.'

'I did, indeed. And the sight confirmed me in my view that

since the days when you used to play tennis at my place you must have become pretty illustrious. I have knocked about the world long enough to know that infants with bouquets don't turn out for every Tom, Dick and Harry. I myself am a hell of a fellow – a first-class Earl who keeps his carriage – but have infants ever offered me bouquets? What have you been doing, Bill Oakshott, to merit this reception – nay, this Durbar?'

'I haven't done a thing.'

'Well, it's all very odd. I suppose it *was* in your honour that the affair was arranged? They would hardly have said "Mr Willm", if they had meant someone else.'

'No, that's true.'

'Have you any suspicions as to the ringleaders?'

'I suppose my uncle was at the bottom of it.'

'Was he the impressive citizen with the moustache, who looked like Clemenceau?'

'Yes. He must have got the thing up.'

'But why?'

'I don't know.'

'Search your memory. Can you think of nothing you have done recently which could have put you in the Silver Band and Boy Scout class?'

'Well, I went on this expedition up the Amazon.'

'Oh, you went on an expedition, did you, and up the Amazon, to boot. I didn't realise that. I assumed that you had merely been connected with the Brazil nut industry or something. That might account for it, of course. And why did you commit this rash act? Wanted to get some girl out of your system, I suppose?'

Bill blushed. It had indeed been the seeming hopelessness of his love for his cousin Hermione that had driven him to try a cure which, as he might have foreseen, had proved quite ineffective.

'Why, yes. Something of the sort.'

'In my day we used to go to the Rocky Mountains and shoot grizzlies. What made you choose Brazil?'

'I happened to see an advertisement in *The Times* about an expedition that was starting off for the Lower Amazon, run by a chap called Major Plank, and I thought it might be a good idea to sign on.'

'I see. Well, I wish I had known of this before. I could have stuck on a lot of dog on the strength of having met you as a boy. But we shall be at Bishop's Ickenham in a minute or two, and the question arises, what do you propose to do? Wait for a train back? Or shall I take you to my place and give you a drink and send you home in the car?'

'Wouldn't that be a nuisance?'

'On the contrary. Nothing could suit my book better. That's settled then. We now come to a matter to which I think we ought to devote some little attention. What story are you going to tell your uncle, to account for your non-appearance at the revels?'

A thoughtful look came into Bill Oakshott's face. He winced slightly, as if a Brazilian alligator had attached itself to the fleshy part of his leg.

'I was rather wondering about that,' he confessed.

'A good, coherent story will undoubtedly be required. He will be feeling chagrined at your failure to materialise, and he looked a dangerous specimen, the sort of man whose bite spells death. What is he? An all-in wrestler? A chap who kills rats with his teeth?'

'He used to be Governor of one of those Crown colonies.'

'Then we must strain every nerve to pacify him. I know these ex-Governors. Tough nuts. You didn't mention his name, by the way.'

'Bostock. Sir Aylmer Bostock.'

'What? Is that who he is? Well, I'll be dashed.'

'You know him?'

'I have not seen him for more than forty years, but at one time I knew him well. We were at school together.'

'Oh, really?'

'Mugsy we used to call him. He was younger than me by some three years, one of those tough, chunky, beetle-browed kids who scowl at their seniors and bully their juniors. I once gave him six of the juiciest with a fives bat in the hope of correcting this latter tendency. Well, the mystery of that civic welcome is now explained. Mugsy is to stand for Parliament shortly, my paper informs me, and no doubt he thought it would give him a leg up. Like me, he hopes to trade on his connection with a man who has extended the bounds of Civilisation.'

'I didn't extend the bounds of Civilisation.'

'Nonsense. I'll bet you extended them like elastic. But we are getting away from our discussion of what story you are to tell. How would it be to say that the warmth of the day caused you to drop off into a light slumber, and when you woke up blowed if you weren't at Bishop's Ickenham?'

'Fine.'

'You like it? I don't think it's so bad myself. Simple, which is always good. Impossible to disprove, which is better. And with the added advantage of having a historic precedent; the case, if you remember, of the lady who wanted to go to Birmingham and they were taking her on to Crewe. Yes, I fancy it ought to get by. So that was young Mugsy, was it?' said Lord Ickenham. 'I must say I'm surprised that he should have finished up as anything so comparatively respectable as Governor of a Crown colony. It just shows you never can tell.'

'How long did you say it was since you had met him?'

'Forty-two years come Lammas Eve. Why?'

'I was only wondering why you hadn't run across him. Living so close, I mean.'

'Well, I'll tell you, Bill Oakshott. It is my settled policy to steer pretty clear of the neighbours. You have probably noticed yourself that the British Gawd-help-us seems to flourish particularly luxuriantly in the rural districts. My wife tries to drag me to routs and revels from time to time, but I toss my curls at her and refuse to stir. I often think that the ideal life would be to have plenty of tobacco and be cut by the County. And as regards your uncle, I look back across the years at Mugsy, the boy, and I see nothing that encourages me to fraternise with Mugsy, the man.'

'Something in that.'

'Not an elfin personality, Mugsy's. I'm afraid Pongo doesn't realise what he's up against in taking on such a father-in-law. It's his daughter Hermione that he's gone and got engaged to, and I see a sticky future ahead of the unhappy lad. Ah, here we are,' said Lord Ickenham, as the train slowed down. 'Let's go and get that drink. It's just possible that we may find Pongo at the old shack. He rang me up this morning, saying he was coming to spend the night. He is about to visit Ashenden Manor, to show the old folks what they've got.'

He hopped nimbly on to the platform, prattling gaily, quite unaware that he had to all intents and purposes just struck an estimable young man behind the ear with a sock full of wet sand. The short, quick, gulping grunt, like that of a bulldog kicked in the ribs while eating a mutton chop, which had escaped Bill Oakshott on the cue 'got engaged to', he had mistaken for a hiccough.

II

The summer afternoon had mellowed into twilight and Bill Oakshott had long since taken his bruised heart off the premises before Pongo Twistleton fetched up at the home of his ancestors. One of those mysterious breakdowns which affect two-seater cars had delayed him on the road. He arrived just in time to dress for dinner, and the hour of eight found him seated opposite his uncle in the oak-panelled dining room, restoring his tissues after a trying day.

Lord Ickenham, delighted to see him, was a gay and effervescent host, but during the meal the presence of a hovering butler made conversation of a really intimate nature impossible, and the talk confined itself to matters of general interest. Pongo spoke of New York, whence he had recently returned from a visit connected with the winding up of his godfather's estate, and Lord Ickenham mentioned that Lady Ickenham was on her way to Trinidad to attend the wedding of the daughter of an old friend. Lord Ickenham alluded to his meeting with Pongo's former crony, Bill Oakshott, and Pongo, though confessing that he remembered Bill only imperfectly – 'Beefy stripling with a pink face, unless I'm thinking of someone else' – said that he looked forward to renewing their old friendship when he hit Ashenden Manor.

They also touched on such topics as the weather, dogs, two-seater cars (their treatment in sickness and in health), the foreign policy of the Government, the chances of Jujube for the Goodwood Cup, and what you would do – this subject arising from Pongo's recent literary studies – if you found a dead body in your bath one morning with nothing on but pince-nez and a pair of spats.

It was only when the coffee had been served and the cigars lighted that Lord Ickenham prepared to become more expansive.

'Now we're nice and cosy,' he said contentedly. 'What a relief it always is when the butler pops off. It makes you realise the full meaning of that beautiful line in the hymn book – "Peace, perfect peace, with loved ones far away." Not that I actually love Coggs. A distant affection, rather, tempered with awe. Well, Pongo, I'm extraordinarily glad you blew in. I was wanting a quiet chat with you about your plans and what not.'

'Ah,' said Pongo.

He spoke reservedly. He was a slender, personable young man with lemon-coloured hair and an attractive face, and on this face a close observer would have noted at the moment an austere, wary look, such as might have appeared on that of St Anthony just before the temptations began. He had a strong suspicion that now that they were alone together, it was going to be necessary for him to be very firm with this uncle of his and to maintain an iron front against his insidious wiles.

Watching the head of the family closely during dinner, he had not failed to detect in his eyes, while he was speaking of his wife's voyage to the West Indies, a lurking gleam such as one might discern in the eye of a small boy who has been left alone in the house and knows where the key of the jam cupboard is. He had seen that gleam before, and it had always heralded trouble of a major kind. Noticeable even as early as the soup course, it had become, as its proprietor puffed at his cigar, more marked than ever, and Pongo waited coldly for him to proceed.

'How long are you proposing to inflict yourself on these Bostocks of yours?'

'About a week.'

'And after that?'

'Back to London, I suppose.'

'Good,' said Lord Ickenham heartily. 'That was what I wanted to know. That was what I wished to ascertain. You will return to London. Excellent. I will join you there, and we will have one of our pleasant and instructive afternoons.'

Pongo stiffened. He did not actually say 'Ha!' but the exclamation was implicit in the keen glance which he shot across the table. His suspicions had been correct. His wife's loving surveillance having been temporarily removed, Frederick Altamont Cornwallis, fifth Earl of Ickenham, was planning to be out and about again.

'You ask me,' a thoughtful Crumpet had once said in the smoking room of the Drones Club, 'why it is that at the mention of his Uncle Fred's name Pongo Twistleton blenches to the core and calls for a couple of quick ones. I will tell you. It is because this uncle is pure dynamite. Every time he is in Pongo's midst, with the sap running strongly in his veins, he subjects the unfortunate young egg to some soul-testing experience, luring him out into the open and there, right in the public eye, proceeding to step high, wide and plentiful. For though well stricken in years the old blister becomes on these occasions as young as he feels, which seems to be about twenty-two. I don't know if you happen to know what the word "excesses" means, but those are what he invariably commits, when on the loose. Get Pongo to tell you some time about that day they had together at the dog races.'

It was a critique of which, had he heard it, Lord Ickenham would have been the first to admit the essential justice.

From boyhood up his had always been a gay and happy disposition, and in the evening of his life he still retained, together with a juvenile waistline, the bright enthusiasms and the fresh, unspoiled mental outlook of a slightly inebriated undergraduate. He had enjoyed a number of exceedingly agreeable outings in his nephew's society in the course of the last few years, and was pleasantly conscious of having stepped on these occasions as high, wide and plentiful as a man could wish, particularly during that day at the dog races. Though there, he had always maintained, a wiser policeman would have been content with a mere reprimand.

'As you are aware, if you were not asleep while I was talking at dinner,' he said, resuming his remarks, 'your aunt has left me for a few weeks and, as you can well imagine, I am suffering agonies. I feel like one of those fellows in the early nineteenth-century poems who used to go about losing dear gazelles. Still—'

'Now listen,' said Pongo.

'Still, in practically every cloud wrack the knowledgeable eye, if it peers closely enough, can detect some sort of a silver lining, however small, and the horror of my predicament is to a certain extent mitigated by the thought that I now become a mobile force again. Your aunt is the dearest woman in the world, and nobody could be fonder of her than I am, but I sometimes find her presence . . . what is the word I want . . . restrictive. She holds, as you know, peculiar views on the subject of my running around loose in London, as she puts it, and this prevents me fulfilling myself. It is a pity. Living in a rural morgue like Bishop's Ickenham all the time, one gets rusty and out of touch with modern thought. I don't suppose these days I could tell you the name of a single chucker-out in the whole of the West End area, and I used to know them all. That is why—'

'Now listen.'

'That is why the fact of her having packed a toothbrush and popped off to Trinidad, though it blots the sunshine from my life, is not an unrelieved tragedy. Existence may have become for me an arid waste, but let us not forget that I can now be up and doing with a heart for any fate. Notify me when you return to London, and I will be with you with my hair in a braid. Bless my soul, how young I'm feeling these days! It must be the weather.'

Pongo knocked the ash off his cigar and took a sip of brandy. There was a cold, stern look on his face.

'Now listen, Uncle Fred,' he said, and his voice was like music to the ears of the Recording Angel, who felt that this was going to be good. 'All that stuff is out.'

'Out?'

'Right out. You don't get me to the dog races again.'

'I did not specify the dog races. Though they provide an admirable means of studying the soul of the people.'

'Or on any other frightful binge of yours. Get thou behind me, about sums it up. If you come to see me in London, you will get lunch at my flat and afterwards a good book. Nothing more.'

Lord Ickenham sighed, and was silent for a space. He was musing on the curse of wealth. In the old days, when Pongo had been an impecunious young fellow reading for the Bar and attempting at intervals to get into an uncle's ribs for an occasional much-needed fiver, nobody could have been a more sympathetic companion along the primrose path. But coming into money seemed to have changed him completely. The old, old story, felt Lord Ickenham.

'Oh, very well,' he said. 'If that is how you feel —'

'It is,' Pongo assured him. 'Make a note of it on your cuff.

And it's no good saying "Ichabod", because I intend to stick to my position with iron resolution. My standing with Hermione is none too secure as it is – she looks askance at my belonging to the Drones – and the faintest breath of scandal would dish me properly. And most unfortunately she knows all about you.'

'My life is an open book.'

'She has heard what a loony you are, and she seems to think it may be hereditary. "I hope you are not like your uncle," she keeps saying, with a sort of brooding look in her eye.'

'You must have misunderstood her. "I hope you *are* like your uncle," she probably said. Or "Do try, darling, to be more like your uncle."'

'Consequently I shall have to watch my step like a ruddy hawk. Let her get the slightest suspicion into her nut that I am not one hundred per cent steady and serious, and bim will go my chances of putting on the sponge-bag trousers and walking down the aisle with her.'

'Then you would not consider the idea of my coming to Ashenden as your valet, and seeing what innocent fun we could whack out of the deception?'

'My God!'

'Merely a suggestion. And it couldn't be done, anyway. It would involve shaving off my moustache, to which I am greatly attached. When a man has neither chick nor child, he gets very fond of a moustache. So she's that sort of girl, is she?'

'What do you mean, that sort of girl?'

'Noble-minded. High principled. A credit to British womanhood.'

'Oh, rather. Yes, she's terrific. Must be seen to be believed.'

'I look forward to seeing her.'

'I have a photograph here, if you would care to take a

dekko,' said Pongo, producing one of cabinet size from his breast pocket like a conjurer extracting a rabbit from a top hat.

Lord Ickenham took the photograph, and studied it for some moments.

'A striking face.'

'Don't miss the eyes.'

'I've got 'em.'

'The nose, also.'

'I've got that, too. She looks intelligent.'

'And how. Writes novels.'

'Good God!'

A monstrous suspicion had germinated in Pongo's mind.

'Don't you like her?' he asked incredulously.

'Well, I'll tell you,' said Lord Ickenham, feeling his way carefully. 'I can see she's a remarkable girl, but I wouldn't say she was the wife for you.'

'Why not?'

'In my opinion you will be giving away too much weight. Have you studied these features? That chin is a determined chin. Those eyes are flashing eyes.'

'What's the matter with flashing eyes?'

'Dashed unpleasant things to have about the home. To cope with flashing eyes, you have to be a man of steel and ginger. Are you a man of steel and ginger? No. You're like me, a gentle coffee-caddie.'

'A how much?'

'By a coffee-caddie I mean a man – and there is no higher type – whose instinct it is to carry his wife's breakfast up to her room on a tray each morning and bill and coo with her as she wades into it. And what the coffee-caddie needs is not a female novelist with a firm chin and flashing eyes, but a jolly little soul who, when he bills, will herself bill like billy-o, and

21

who will be right there with bells on when he starts to coo. The advice I give to every young man starting out to seek a life partner is to find a girl whom he can tickle. Can you see yourself tickling Hermione Bostock? She would draw herself to her full height and say "Sir!" The ideal wife for you, of course, would have been Sally Painter.'

At the mention of this name, as so often happens when names from the dead past bob up in conversation, Pongo's face became mask-like and a thin coating of ice seemed to form around him. A more sensitive man than Lord Ickenham would have sent for his winter woollies.

'Does Coggs suffer from bunions?' he said distantly. 'I thought he was walking as if he had trouble with his feet.'

'Ever since she came to England,' proceeded Lord Ickenham, refusing to be lured from the subject into realms of speculation, however fascinating, 'I have always hoped that you and Sally would eventually form a merger. And came a day when you apprised me that the thing was on. And then, dammit,' he went on, raising his voice a little in his emotion, 'came another day when you apprised me that it was off. And why, having succeeded in getting engaged to a girl like Sally Painter, you were mad enough to sever relations, is more than I can understand. It was all your fault, I suppose?'

Pongo had intended to maintain a frigid silence until the distasteful subject should have blown over, but this unjust charge shook him out of his proud reserve.

'It wasn't anything of the bally kind. Perhaps you will allow me to place the facts before you.'

'I wish you would. It's about time someone did. I could get nothing out of Sally.'

'You've seen her, then?'

'She came down here with Otis a couple of weeks ago and

left one of her busts in my charge. I don't know why. That's it, over there in the corner.'

Pongo gave the bust a brief and uninterested glance.

'And she didn't place the facts before you?'

'She said the engagement was off, which I knew already, but nothing more.'

'Oh? Well,' said Pongo, breathing heavily through the nostrils as he viewed the body of the dead past, 'what happened was this. Just because I wouldn't do something she wanted me to do, she called me a lily-livered poltroon.'

'She probably meant it as a compliment. A lily liver must be very pretty.'

'High words ensued. I said so-and-so, and she said such-and-such. And later that evening ring, letters and all the fixings were returned by district messenger boy.'

'A mere lovers' tiff. I should have thought you would have made it up next day.'

'Well, we jolly well didn't. As a matter of fact, that lily-livered sequence was simply what put the lid on it. We had been getting in each other's hair for some time before that and there was bound to be a smash-up sooner or later.'

'What were the principal subjects of disagreement?'

'For one thing, that damned brother of hers. He makes me sick.'

'Otis isn't everybody's money, I admit. He's a publisher now, Sally tells me. I suppose he will make as big a mess of that as he did of his antique shop. Did you tell her he made you sick?'

'Yes. She got a bit steamed up about it. And then there was more trouble because I wanted her to chuck being a sculptress.'

'Why didn't you like her being a sculptress?'

'I hated her mixing with all that seedy crowd in Chelsea. Bounders with beards,' said Pongo, with an austere shudder.

'I've been in her studio sometimes, and the blighters were crawling out of the woodwork in hundreds, bearded to the eyebrows.'

Lord Ickenham drew thoughtfully at his cigar.

'I was mistaken in saying that you were not a man of steel and ginger. You appear to have thrown your weight about like a sheikh.'

'Well, she threw her weight about with me. She was always trying to boss me.'

'Girls do. Especially American girls. I know, because I married one. It's part of their charm.'

'Well, there's a limit.'

'And with you that was reached – how? You had started to tell me. What was it she wanted you to do?'

'Take some jewellery with me when I went to New York and smuggle it through the customs.'

'Bless her heart, what an enterprising little soul she is. But since when has Sally possessed jewellery?'

'It wasn't for her, it was for one of her rich American pals, a girl named Alice something. This ass of a female had been loading herself up with the stuff in and around Bond Street and didn't like the idea of paying duty on it when she got back to New York, and Sally wanted me to run it through for her.'

'A kindly thought.'

'A fat-headed thought. And so I told her. A nice chump I should have looked, being disembowelled by port officials.'

Lord Ickenham sighed.

'I see. Well, I'm sorry. A wealthy husband like you would have come in very handy for Sally. I'm afraid that girl is on the rocks.'

Pongo's lower jaw dropped a notch. Love might be dead, but he had a feeling heart.

'Oh, I say!'

'I don't believe she gets enough to eat.'

'What rot!'

'It isn't rot. She seemed thin to me, and I didn't like the way she tucked into the lamb and green peas, as if she hadn't had a square meal for weeks. There can't be a fortune in sculping, if that's the right verb. Who the dickens buys clay busts?'

'Oh, that's all right,' said Pongo, relieved. 'She doesn't depend on her sculping. She's got a little bit of money an aunt in Kansas City left her.'

'I know. But I'm wondering whether something hasn't gone wrong with that sheet anchor. It's two years since she came to London to join Otis. He may have wheedled it out of her. A chap like Otis can do a lot in two years.'

'Sally's got too much sense.'

'The most level-headed girls often prove perfect mugs where a loved brother is concerned. At any rate, in answer to a recent communication of mine telling her that I hoped shortly to be in London and would like her to keep an evening free for dinner I got a letter saying she was glad I was coming up, because she wanted to see me on a very urgent matter. She underlined the "very". I didn't like the ring of that statement. It was the sort of thing you used to write to me in the old days, when you were having a passing unpleasantness with your bookie and hoped to float a small loan. Well, I shall be seeing her tomorrow, and I will institute a probe. Poor little Sally, I hope to God she's all right. What an admirable girl she is.'

'Yes.'

'You still feel that, do you?'

'Oh, rather. I'm frightfully fond of Sally. I tried to do her a bit of good just before I left for America. Hermione told me old Bostock wanted a bust of himself, to present to the village club, and I got her to put him on to Sally. I thought she might be glad of the commish.'

'Well, well. An impulsive girl would be touched by a thing like that. Yes, indeed. "The whitest man I know," one can hear her saying. I believe, if you played your cards right, you could still marry her, Pongo.'

'Aren't you overlooking the trifling fact that I happen to be engaged to Hermione?'

'Slide out of it.'

'Ha!'

'It is what your best friends would advise. You are a moody, introspective young man, all too prone to look on the dark side of things. I shall never forget you that day at the dog races. Sombre is the only word to describe your attitude as the cop's fingers closed on your coat collar. You reminded me of Hamlet. What you need is a jolly, lively wife to take you out of yourself, the sort of wife who would set booby traps for the Bishop when he came to spend the night. I don't suppose this Hermione Bostock of yours ever made so much as an apple-pie bed in her life. I'd give her a miss. Send her an affectionate telegram saying you've changed your mind and it's all off. I have a telegraph form in my study.'

A look of intense devoutness came over Pongo's face.

'For your information, Uncle Fred, wild horses wouldn't make me break my engagement.'

'Most unlikely they'll ever try.'

'I worship that girl. There's nothing I wouldn't do for her. Well, to give you a rough idea, I told her I was a teetotaller. And why? Purely because she happened one day to express the hope that I wasn't like so many of these modern young suction pumps, always dropping in at bars and lowering a couple for the tonsils. "Me?" I said. "Good Lord, no. I never touch the stuff." That'll show you.'

'So when you get to Ashenden —'

'— They'll uncork the barley water and bring on the lemonade. I know. I've foreseen that. It'll be agony, but I can take it. For her sake. I worship her, I tell you. If H. Bostock isn't an angel in human shape, then I don't know an angel in human shape when I see one. Until now I have never known what love was.'

'Well, you have had ample opportunity of finding out. I have watched you with the tender solicitude through about fifty-seven romances, starting with that freckled child with the missing front tooth at the dancing class, who blacked your eye with a wooden dumb-bell when you kissed her in the cloak-room, and ending with this —'

Lord Ickenham paused, and Pongo eyed him narrowly.

'Well? This what?'

'This gruesome combination of George Eliot, Boadicea and the late Mrs Carrie Nation,' said Lord Ickenham. 'This flashing-eyed governess. This twenty-minute egg with whom no prudent man would allow himself to walk alone down a dark alley.'

It was enough. Pongo rose, a dignified figure.

'Shall we join the ladies?' he said coldly.

'There aren't any,' said Lord Ickenham.

'I don't know why I said that,' said Pongo, annoyed. 'What I meant was, let's stop talking bally rot and go and have a game of billiards.'

III

It was with a light heart and a gay tra-la-la on his lips that Pongo Twistleton set out for Ashenden Manor on the following afternoon, leaving Lord Ickenham, who was not embarking on his metropolitan jaunt till a few hours later, waving benevolently from the front steps.

Nothing so braces a young man in love as the consciousness of having successfully resisted a Tempter who has tried to lure him into a course of action of which the adored object would not approve: and as he recalled the splendid firmness with which he had tied the can to his Uncle Fred's suggestion of a pleasant and instructive afternoon in London, Pongo felt spiritually uplifted.

Pleasant and instructive afternoon, forsooth! Few people have ever come nearer to saying 'Faugh!' than did Pongo as Lord Ickenham's phrase shot through his wincing mind like some loathsome serpent. The crust of the old buster, daring to suggest pleasant and instructive afternoons to a man who had put that sort of thing behind him once and for all. With a shudder of distaste he thrust the whole degrading episode into the hinterland of his consciousness, and turned his thoughts to a more agreeable theme, the coming meeting with Hermione's parents.

This, he was convinced, was going to be a riot from the word Go. He had little data about these two old geezers, of course, but he presumed that they were intelligent old geezers, able to spot a good man when they saw one, and it seemed, accordingly, pretty obvious that a fellow like himself – steady, upright, impervious to avuncular wheedlings and true blue from soup to nuts – would have them eating out of his hand in the first minute. 'My dear, he's *charming*!' they would write to Hermione, and bluff Sir Aylmer, whom he pictured as a sort of modern Cheeryble Brother, would say to Lady Bostock (gentle, sweet-faced, motherly), as they toddled up to bed at the conclusion of a delightful first evening, 'Gad, my dear, nothing much wrong with *that* young chap, what?' – or possibly 'What, what?' He looked forward with bright confidence to grappling them to his soul with hoops of steel.

It was consequently with some annoyance that he found on reaching his destination that there was going to be a slight delay before this desirable state of affairs could be consummated. The first essential preliminary to grappling a householder and his wife to your soul with hoops of steel is that you should be able to get into the house they are holding, and this, he discovered, presented unforeseen difficulties.

Ashenden Manor was one of those solidly built edifices which date from the days when a home was not so much a place for putting on the old slippers and lighting the pipe, as a fortress to be defended against uncouth intruders with battering rams. Its front door was stout and massive, and at the moment tightly closed. Furthermore, the bell appeared to be out of order. He leaned against the button with his full weight for a while, but it soon became clear that this was going to get him nowhere, and the necessity of taking alternative action presented itself.

It was at this point that he observed not far from where he stood an open French window, and it seemed to him that he had found a formula. A bit irregular, perhaps, to start your first visit to a place by strolling in through windows, but a kindly, hearty old boy like Sir Aylmer Bostock would overlook that. Abandoning the front door, accordingly, as a lost cause, he stepped through, and an instant later was experiencing the unpleasant shock which always came to people who found themselves for the first time in the room where the ex-Governor kept the African curios which he had collected during his years of honourable exile. Sir Aylmer Bostock's collection of African curios was probably the most hideous, futile and valueless that even an ex-Governor had ever brought home with him, and many of its items seemed to take Pongo into a different and a dreadful world.

And he had picked up and started to scrutinise the nearest to hand, a peculiar sort of whatnot executed in red mud by an artist apparently under the influence of trade gin, and was wondering why even an untutored African should have been chump enough to waste on an effort like this hours which might have been more profitably employed in chasing crocodiles or beaning the neighbours with his knobkerrie, when a voice, having in it many of the qualities of the Last Trump, suddenly split the air.

'REGINALD!'

Starting violently, Pongo dropped the whatnot. It crashed to the floor and became a mere *macédoine*. A moment later, a burly figure appeared in the doorway, preceded by a large white moustache.

2

At about the moment when Pongo at Ickenham Hall was springing to the wheel of his Buffy-Porson and pressing a shapely foot on the self-starter, Sir Aylmer Bostock had gone to his wife's bedroom on the first floor of Ashenden Manor to mend a broken slat in the Venetian blind. He was a man who liked to attend to these little domestic chores himself, and he wanted to have it ready when the midday train brought Lady Bostock back from London, where she had been spending a week with her daughter Hermione.

In predicting that this old schoolmate of his would feel chagrined at Bill Oakshott's failure to co-operate in the civic welcome which he had gone to such trouble to arrange for him, Lord Ickenham had shown sound judgment of character. When an ex-Governor, accustomed for years to seeing his official receptions go like clockwork, tastes in a black hour the bitterness of failure and anti-climax, pique is bound to supervene. Fists will be clenched, oaths breathed, lower lips bitten. And this is particularly so if the ex-Governor is one whose mental attitude, even under the most favourable conditions, resembles, as did Sir Aylmer Bostock's, that of a trapped cinnamon bear. As he worked, his brow was dark, his moustache bristling, and from time to time he snorted in a quiet undertone.

He yearned for his wife's company, so that he could pour into her always receptive ear the story of his wrongs, and soon after he had put the finishing touches to the broken slat he got it. A cab drove up to the front door, and presently Lady Bostock appeared, a woman in the late forties who looked like a horse.

'Oh, there you are, dear,' she said brightly. In conversation with her consort she was nearly always obliged to provide brightness enough for both of them. She paused, sniffing. 'What a curious smell there is in here.'

Sir Aylmer frowned. He resented criticism, even of his smells.

'Glue,' he said briefly. 'I've been mending the blind.'

'Oh, how clever of you, darling. Thank you so much,' said

Lady Bostock, brighter than ever. 'Well, I suppose you thought I was never coming back. It's lovely to be home again. London was terribly stuffy. I thought Hermione was looking very well. She sent all sorts of messages to you and Reginald. Has he arrived yet?'

On the point of asking who the devil Reginald was, Sir Aylmer remembered that his daughter had recently become betrothed to some young pot of cyanide answering to that name. He replied that Reginald had not yet arrived.

'Hermione said he was coming today.'

'Well, he hasn't.'

'Has he wired?'

'No.'

'I suppose he forgot.'

'Silly fat-headed young poop,' said Sir Aylmer.

Lady Bostock regarded him anxiously. She seemed to sense in his manner an anti-Reginald bias, and she knew his work. He was capable, she was aware, when in anything like shape, of reducing young men who had failed to arouse his enthusiasm to spots of grease in a matter of minutes, and she was intensely desirous that no such disaster should occur on the present occasion. Hermione, seeing her off at Waterloo, had issued definite instructions that her loved one, while at Ashenden Manor, was to enjoy the status of an ewe lamb, and Hermione was a girl whom it did not do to cross. She expected people to carry out her wishes, and those who knew what was good for them invariably did so.

Recalling all the timid young aides-de-camp whom she had seen curling up at the edges like scorched paper beneath his glare during those long and happy years in Lower Barnatoland, she gazed at her husband pleadingly.

'You will be nice to Reginald, dear, won't you?'

'I am always nice.'

'I don't want him to complain to Hermione about his unwelcome. You know what she is like.'

A thoughtful silence fell, as they allowed their minds to dwell on what Hermione was like. Lady Bostock broke it on a note of hope.

'You may become the greatest friends.'

'Bah!'

'Hermione says he is delightful.'

'Probably the usual young pest with brilliantined hair and a giggle,' said Sir Aylmer morosely, refusing to look for the silver lining and try to find the sunny side of life. 'It's bad enough having William around. Add Reginald, and existence will become a hell.'

His words reminded Lady Bostock that there was a topic on which an affectionate aunt ought to have touched earlier.

'William has arrived, then?'

'Yes. Oh, yes, he's arrived.'

'I hope the reception went off well. Such a good idea, I thought, when you told me about it. How surprised he must have been. It's so fortunate that he should have come back in good time for the fete. He is always so useful, looking after the sports. Where is he?'

'I don't know. Dead, I hope . . .'

'Aylmer! What do you mean?'

Sir Aylmer had not snorted since his wife's return and now it was as if all the snorts he might have been snorting had coalesced into one stupendous burst of sound. It was surprising that Pongo, at that moment driving in through the main gates, did not hear it and think one of his tyres had gone.

'I'll tell you what I mean. Do you know what that young hound did? Didn't get out at Ashenden Oakshott. Remained skulking in the train, went on to Bishop's Ickenham and turned up hours later in a car belonging to Lord Ickenham, stewed to the gills.'

One hastens to protest that this was a complete misstatement, attributable solely to prejudice and bitterness of spirit. Considering that he had arrived there reeling beneath the blow of the discovery that the girl he loved was betrothed to another, Bill Oakshott had comported himself at Lord Ickenham's residence with the most exemplary abstemiousness. In a situation where many men would have started lowering the stuff by the pailful, this splendid young fellow had exercised an iron self-control. One fairly quick, followed by another rather slower, and he had been through.

It is true that on encountering his uncle his manner had been such as to give rise to misunderstanding, but something of this kind is bound to happen when a nervous young man meets an incandescent senior, of whom he has always stood in awe, knowing that it is he who has brought him to the boil. In such circumstances the face inevitably becomes suffused and the limbs start twitching, even if the subject is a lifelong abstainer.

So much for this monstrous charge.

Lady Bostock made that clicking noise, like a wet finger touching hot iron, which women use as a substitute for the masculine 'Well, I'll be damned!'

'A car belonging to Lord Ickenham?'

'Yes.'

'But how did he come to be in a car belonging to Lord Ickenham?'

'They appear to have met on the train.'

'Oh, I see. I was wondering, because we don't know him.'

'I used to, forty years ago. We were at school together. Haven't seen him since, thank God. He's a lunatic.'

'I have always heard that he was very eccentric.' Lady

Bostock paused, listening. 'Hark. There's a car driving up. It must be Reginald. You had better go down.'

'I won't go down,' said Sir Aylmer explosively. 'Blast Reginald. Let him cool his heels for a bit. I'm going to finish telling you about William.'

'Yes, dear. Do, dear. He does seem to have behaved most oddly. Had he any explanation?'

'Oh, he had his story all ready, trust him for that. Said he went to sleep and woke up to find himself at Bishop's Ickenham. I didn't swallow a word of it. What happened, obviously, was that on seeing the preparations made for his reception he lost his nerve and remained in the train, the young toad, leaving me to get the vicar, his wife, a Silver Band, ten Boy Scouts and fourteen members of the Infants' Bible Class back to their homes without any of them starting a riot. And let me tell you it was a very near thing once or twice. Those Bible Class infants were in ugly mood.'

'It must have been dreadfully disappointing for you all.'

'That's not the worst of it. It has probably lost me hundreds of votes.'

'Oh, but, dear, why? It wasn't your fault.'

'What does that matter? People don't reason. The news of a fiasco like that flies all over the county. One man tells another, it gets about that I have been placed in a ridiculous position, and the voters lose confidence in me. And nothing to be done about it. That is the bitter thought. You can't put a fellow of William's age and size across your knee and get at him with the back of a hairbrush . . . COME IN.'

There had been a knock on the door. It was followed by the entry of Jane, the parlourmaid.

'Your ladyship is wanted on the telephone, m'lady,' said Jane, who believed in respect to the titled. 'It's the vicar, m'lady.'

'Thank you, Jane. I will come at once.'

'And I,' said Sir Aylmer with a weary snort, 'had better go and welcome this blasted Reginald, I suppose.'

'You won't forget about Hermione?'

'No, I won't forget about Hermione,' said Sir Aylmer moodily. He did not waver in his view that his daughter's future husband was bound to be a deleterious slab of damnation like all other young men nowadays, but if Hermione desired it he was prepared to coo to him like a turtle dove; or as nearly like a turtle dove as was within the scope of one whose vocal delivery was always rather reminiscent of a bad-tempered toastmaster.

He made his way to the drawing room, and finding it empty was for a moment baffled. But ex-Governors are quick-thinking men, trained to deal with emergencies. When an ex-Governor, seeking a Twistleton, arrives in the drawing room where that Twistleton ought to be and finds no Twistleton there, he does not stand twiddling his thumbs and wondering what to do. He inflates his lungs and shouts.

'REGINALD!' thundered Sir Aylmer.

It seemed to him, as the echoes died away, that he could hear the sound of movements in the collection room across the hall. He went thither, and poked his head in.

It was as he had suspected. Something, presumably of a Twistletonian nature, was standing there. He crossed the threshold, and these two representatives of the older and the younger generation were enabled to see each other steadily and see each other whole.

On both sides the reaction to the scrutiny was unfavourable. Pongo, gazing apprehensively at the rugged face with its top dressing of moustache, was thinking that this Bostock, so far from being the kindly Dickens character of his dreams, was without exception the hardest old gumboil he had ever encountered in a career by no means free from gumboils of varying hardness: while Sir Aylmer, drinking Pongo in from his lemon-coloured hair to his clocked socks and suede shoes, was feeling how right he had been in anticipating that his future son-in-law would be a pot of cyanide and a deleterious young slab of damnation. He could see at a glance that he was both.

However, he had come there grimly resolved to coo like a turtle dove, so he cooed.

'Oh, there you are. Reginald Twistleton?'

'That's right. Twistleton, Reginald.'

'H'ar yer?' roared Sir Aylmer like a lion which has just received an ounce of small shot in the rear quarters while slaking its thirst at a water hole, though, if questioned, he would have insisted that he was still cooing. 'Glad to see yer, Reginald. My wife will be down in a moment. What you doing in here?'

'I was having a look at these – er – objects.'

'My collection of African curios. It's priceless.'

'Really? How priceless!'

'You won't find many collections like that. Took me ten years to get it together. You interested in African curios?'

'Oh, rather. I love 'em.'

The right note had been struck. A sort of writhing movement behind his moustache showed that Sir Aylmer was smiling, and in another moment who knows what beautiful friendship might not have begun to blossom. Unfortunately, however, before the burgeoning process could set in, Sir Aylmer's eye fell on the remains of the whatnot and the smile vanished from his face like breath off a razor blade, to be replaced by a scowl of such malignity that Pongo had the illusion that his interior organs were being scooped out with a spade or trowel.

'Gorbl . . .!' he cried, apparently calling on some tribal god. 'How the . . . What the . . . Did *you* do that?'

'Er, yes,' said Pongo, standing on one leg. 'Frightfully sorry.'

Sir Aylmer, not without some justice, asked what was the use of being sorry, and Pongo, following his reasoning, said Yes, he saw what he meant, supplementing the words with a nervous giggle.

Many people do not like nervous giggles. Sir Aylmer was one of them. On several occasions in the old days he had had to mention this to his aides-de-camp. Not even the thought of his daughter Hermione could restrain him from bestowing on Pongo a second scowl, compared with which its predecessor had been full of loving kindness. He lowered himself to the ground, and, crouched on all fours over the remains like Marius among the ruins of Carthage, began to mutter beneath his breath about young fools and clumsy idiots. Pongo could not catch his remarks in their entirety, but he heard enough to give him the general idea.

He gulped pallidly. A sticky moisture had begun to bedew his brow, as if he had entered the hot room of some Turkish bath of the soul. Governesses in his childhood and school-masters in his riper years had sometimes spoken slightingly of his IQ, but he was intelligent enough to realise that on this visit of his, where it was so vital for him to make a smash hit with Hermione's parents, he had got off to a poor start.

It was as Sir Aylmer rose and began to say that the whatnot had been the very gem and pearl of his collection and that he wouldn't have parted with it for a hundred pounds, no, not if the intending purchaser had gone on his bended knees to add emphasis to the offer, that there was a whirring sound without, indicating that some solid body was passing down the hall at a high rate of mph. The next moment, Lady Bostock entered, moving tempestuously.

From Lady Bostock's aspect only Sherlock Holmes, perhaps, would have been able to deduce that she had just heard from the vicar over the telephone that the curate was down with measles, but even Doctor Watson could have seen that her soul had in some way been badly jolted. So moved was she that, though a polished hostess, she paid no attention to Pongo, who was now standing on the other leg.

'Aylmer!'

'Well?'

'Aylmer . . . The vicar . . .'

'WELL?'

'The vicar says Mr Brotherhood has got measles. He wants us to go and see him at once.'

'Who the devil's Mr Brotherhood?'

'The curate. You know Mr Brotherhood, the curate. That nice young man with the pimples. He has gone and got measles, and I was relying on him to judge the babies.'

'What babies?'

'The bonny babies. At the fete.'

A word about this fete. It was the high spot of Ashenden Oakshott's social year, when all that was bravest and fairest in the village assembled in the Manor grounds and made various kinds of whoopee. Races were run, country dances danced, bonny babies judged in order of merit in the big tent and tea and buns consumed in almost incredible quantities. Picture a blend of the Derby and a garden party at Buckingham Palace, add Belshazzar's Feast, and you have the Ashenden Oakshott Fete.

One can readily appreciate, therefore, Lady Bostock's concern at the disaster which had occurred. A lady of the manor, with an important fete coming along and the curate in bed with measles, is in the distressing position of an impresario whose star fails him a couple of days before the big production or a general whose crack regiment gets lumbago on the eve of battle.

'It's terrible. Dreadful. I can't think who I can get to take his place.'

Sir Aylmer, who believed in having a thorough understanding about these things at the earliest possible moment, said he was dashed if he was going to do it, and Lady Bostock said No, no, dear, she wouldn't dream of asking him.

'But I must find somebody.' Lady Bostock's eye, rolling in a fine frenzy from heaven to earth, from earth to heaven, picked on Pongo, now back on the leg he had started with, and she stared at him dazedly, like one seeing unpleasant things in a dream. 'Are you Reginald?' she said distractedly.

The emotional scene, following upon his chat with Sir Aylmer about whatnots, had left Pongo in a condition of such mental turmoil that for an instant he was not quite sure. Reginald? Was he Reginald? Was Reginald a likely thing for anyone to be? . . . Why, yes, of course. The woman was perfectly correct.

'Yes, I'm Reginald.'

'How nice to meet you at last,' wailed Lady Bostock like a soul in torment.

It is never easy offhand to find the ideal reply to such an observation. Discarding 'Yes!' as too complacent and 'What ho!' as too familiar, and not being fortunate enough to think of 'I've been looking forward so much to meeting *you*,' Pongo contented himself with another of his nervous giggles.

A sudden light came into Lady Bostock's haggard eyes.

'Have you ever judged bonny babies, Reginald?'

'Me?' said Pongo, reeling.

Before he could speak further, an angel, in the very effective disguise of Sir Aylmer, intervened to save him from the ghastly peril which had so suddenly risen to confront him.

'You don't want Reginald,' he said, and Pongo, who a moment earlier would have scoffed at the suggestion that it would ever be possible for him to want to leap at his host and kiss him on both cheeks, was conscious of a powerful urge in that direction. 'I'll tell you who gets the job.'

After uttering the words 'I'm dashed if I'm going to do it' and receiving his wife's reassuring reply, Sir Aylmer had fallen into a silence, as if musing or pondering, and it was plain now that the brain work on which he had been engaged had borne fruit. His manner had become animated, and in his eye, which, resting upon Pongo, had been dull and brooding, there was a triumphant gleam.

It was a gleam which might have puzzled an untravelled beholder, but anybody who had ever seen a Corsican feudist suddenly presented with the opportunity of wreaking a sinister vengeance on a family foe would have recognised it immediately. It was that strange, almost unearthly light which comes into the eyes of wronged uncles when they see a chance of getting a bit of their own back from erring nephews.

'I'll tell you who gets the job,' he repeated. 'William.'

'William?'

'William,' said Sir Aylmer, rolling the word round his tongue like vintage port.

Lady Bostock stared.

'But William . . . Surely, dear . . . The very last person . . .'

'William.'

'But he would hate it.'

'William.'

41

'You know how terribly shy he is.'

'William. I don't want any argument, Emily. It's no good you standing there blinding and stiffing. William judges the bonny babies. I insist. Perhaps now he'll be sorry he skulked in trains and went on toots with old Ickenham.'

Lady Bostock sighed. But a habit of obsequiousness which had started at the altar rails was too strong for her.

'Very well, dear.'

'Good. Tell him when you see him. Meanwhile, you say, the vicar wants us to go down to the vicarage and confer with him. Right. I'll drive you in the car. Come along.'

He darted through the French windows, followed by Lady Bostock, and after a few moments occupied in mopping his forehead with the handkerchief which so perfectly matched his tie and socks, Pongo followed them.

He felt he needed air. A similar sensation had often come to sensitive native chiefs at the conclusion of an interview with Sir Aylmer Bostock on the subject of unpaid hut taxes.

Sunshine and the pure Hampshire breezes playing about his temples soon did wonders in the way of restoring him to the normal. Presently, feeling almost himself again, he returned to the house, and, as always happened with those who had once seen Sir Aylmer's collection of African curios, there came over him a morbid urge to take another look at these weird exhibits, to ascertain whether they really looked as frightful as they had appeared at first sight. He passed through the French window into the collection room, and a pink policeman, who had been bicycling dreamily up the drive, uttered a sharp 'Ho!' and accelerated his pace, his eyes hard and his jaw protruding belligerently.

The policeman's name was Harold Potter. He represented

the awful majesty of the Law in Ashenden Oakshott. His pinkness was due to the warmth of the weather, and he was dreamy because he had been musing on Elsie Bean, the Manor housemaid, to whom he was affianced.

It was in order to enjoy a chat with Elsie Bean that he had come here, and until he turned the corner and was in view of the house his thoughts had been all of love. But at the sight of furtive forms slinking in through French windows Potter, the Romeo, became in a flash Potter, the sleepless guardian of the peace. His substantial feet pressed on the pedals like those of a racing cyclist.

It looked to Harold Potter like a fair cop.

And so it came about that Pongo, his opinion of the intelligence of African natives now even lower than before, was disturbed in his contemplation of their fatuous handiwork by the sound of emotional breathing in his rear. He spun round, to find himself gazing into the steely eyes of a large policeman with a ginger moustache.

'Ho!' he cried, startled.

'Ho!' said Constable Potter, like an echo in the Swiss mountains.

3

It would be idle to pretend that the situation was not one of some embarrassment. It belonged to the type which would have enchanted Lord Ickenham, who enjoyed nothing better than these little variations in the calm monotone of life, but it brought Pongo out from head to foot in a sort of prickly heat.

Unlike most of his lighthearted companions of the Drones Club, who rather made pets of policemen, tipping them when in funds and stealing their helmets on Boat-Race Night, Pongo had always had a horror of the Force. That sombreness of his on the day at the dog races, for which Lord Ickenham had reproached him, had been occasioned by the fact that a member of that Force, who might have been this one's twin brother, had been attached to his coat collar and advising him to come quietly.

He smiled a weak smile.

'Oh, hullo,' he said.

'Hullo,' replied Constable Potter coldly. 'What's all this?'

'What's all what?'

'What are you doing on these enclosed premises?'

'I've been invited here for a brief visit.'

'Ho!'

It seemed to Pongo that he was not making headway. The situation, sticky at the outset, appeared to be growing progressively stickier. He was relieved, accordingly, when a third party arrived to break up the *tête-à-tête*.

This was a small, sturdy girl of resolute appearance with blue eyes and a turned-up nose, clad in the uniform of a housemaid. She regarded with interest the picture in still life before her.

'Hullo,' she said. 'Where did you spring from, Harold? And who's this?'

'Chap I've apprehended on enclosed premises,' said Constable Potter briefly.

Pongo, who had been dabbing at his forehead, waved his handkerchief in passionate protest against this too professional view.

'What's all this rot about enclosed premises?' he demanded with spirit. 'I resent the way, officer, you keep chewing the fat about enclosed premises. Why shouldn't I be on enclosed premises, when specially invited? Here, you, what's your name, my dear old housemaid –'

'Miss Bean, my fiancée,' said Constable Potter, frigidly doing the honours.

'Oh, really? Heartiest congratulations. Pip-pip, Miss Bean.'

'Toodle-oo.'

'I hope you'll be very, very happy. Well, what I was going to say was that you will be able to bear me out that I'm a guest at this joint. I've just arrived in my car to spend a few days. I'm the celebrated Twistleton, the bird who's engaged to Miss Bostock. You must know all about me. No doubt the place has been ringing with my name.'

'Miss Hermione is engaged to a gentleman named Twistleton.'

'Exactly.'

'And Jane heard them saying at dinner that he was expected here, Harold. I believe this is him.'

'Well spoken, young Bean,' said Pongo with enthusiasm. He had taken an immediate liking to this clear-reasoning girl. 'Of course I'm him. Look,' said Pongo, turning back the pocket of his coat. 'Read this definite statement by one of the most reputable tailors in London. "R. G. Twistleton." There you are, in black and white.'

'It could be somebody else's coat that you'd bought second-hand,' argued Constable Potter, fighting in the last ditch.

Pongo gave him a look.

'Don't say such things even in jest, officer. Rather,' he said with a sudden flash of inspiration, 'ring up the vicar and ask for Sir Aylmer, who is in conference with him on the subject of bonny babies, and put it squarely up to the latter – Sir Aylmer, I mean, not the bonny babies – whether he didn't leave me here only a few moments ago after a pleasant and invigorating chat.'

'You mean you've met Sir Aylmer?'

'Of course I've met Sir Aylmer. We're just like that.'

Constable Potter seemed reluctantly convinced.

'Well, I suppose it's all right, then. I beg your pardon, sir.'

'Quite all right, officer.'

'Then I'll be saying good afternoon, sir. How about a pot of tea in the kitchen, Elsie?'

Elsie Bean elevated her small nose.

'You can go to the kitchen, if you like. Not me. Your sister's there, calling on Cook.'

'Ho!' Constable Potter stood for a moment in thought. The conflicting claims of tea and a loved one's society were plainly warring within him. One is sorry to report that the former prevailed. 'Well, I think I'll mooch along and have a cup,' he said, and mooched, as foreshadowed.

Elsie Bean looked after his retreating blue back with a frown.

'You and your sister!' she said.

The note of acerbity in her voice was so manifest that Pongo could not help but be intrigued. Here, he told himself, or he was very much mistaken, was a housemaid with a secret sorrow. He stopped mopping his forehead and cocked an inquiring eye at Elsie Bean.

'Don't you like his sister?'

'No, I don't.'

'Well, if there's any sort of family resemblance, I can fully comprehend,' said Pongo. With Constable Potter's departure Ashenden Manor seemed to him to have become a sweeter, better place. 'Why don't you like his sister? What's the matter with her?'

Elsie Bean was a friendly little soul who, though repeatedly encouraged to do so by her employers, had never succeeded in achieving that demure aloofness which is the hallmark of the well-trained maid. Too often in her dealings with the ruling classes, in circumstances where a distant 'Yes, sir,' or 'No, madam,' would have been more suitable, you would find her becoming expansive and conversational. And on the present occasion she regarded herself as a hostess.

'I'll tell you what's the matter with her. She goes on at him about how he mustn't leave the Force. It's "Don't you do it, Harold," and "Don't you let Elsie talk you into acting against your true interests," all the time. I haven't any patience.'

Pongo concentrated tensely.

'Let me see if I've got this straight,' he said. 'You want him to turn in his boots and truncheon? To cease, in a word, to be a copper?'

'R.'

'But his sister doesn't. Yes, I get the set-up. Why do you want him to turn in his boots and truncheon?' asked Pongo. A man who has been reading for the Bar for some years gets into the way of putting the pertinent question.

Elsie Bean seemed surprised that such a question should have been considered necessary.

'Well, wouldn't you? If you was a girl, would you like to be married to a policeman? Feeling your old man was hated by all. If I went home to Bottleton East and told my family I was going to get spliced to a copper, they'd have a fit. A nice thing for my brother Bert to hear, when he comes out in September.'

Pongo nodded intelligently. Until now, having supposed his companion to be a local product, he had failed to grasp the nub, but her last words made everything clear. He could quite see how a London girl, especially a child of the notoriously rather vivacious quarter of Bottleton East, might shrink from linking her lot with that of a professional tapper on shoulders and grasper of coat collars. In addition to this brother Bert – at the moment, it appeared, unhappily no longer with us – there were no doubt a number of Uncle Herbs and Cousin Georges in her entourage who, were she to commit such a *mésalliance,* would consider, and rightly, that she had inflicted a blot on the Bean escutcheon.

'I see what you mean,' he said. 'But what could he do if he resigned his portfolio? Not easy to find jobs nowadays.'

'I want him to buy a pub. He's got three hundred pounds. He won a football pool last winter.'

'The lucky stiff.'

'But he's scared of that sister of his, and I can't persuade him. "Now, listen, Harold," I keep saying, but he just hums and haws and chews his moustache. Oh, well,' said Elsie philosophically, 'I suppose it'll all come out in the wash. What's that mess on the floor?'

'It's what's left of a sort of gadget I happened to drop.'

'Does he know about it?'

'Oh, yes. The topic came up.'

'I wonder he didn't chew your head off.'

'He did look for a moment as if he were toying with some such idea. Rather a hard nut, what?'

'He's an overbearing dishpot,' said Elsie Bean.

Pongo wandered out into the hall. He had about as much as he required of the collection of African curios for the time being, and he wanted to pace up and down and ponder. He had already formed a reasonably accurate estimate of Sir Aylmer Bostock's character, but it was interesting to find it confirmed by the woman who knew.

An overbearing dishpot? The words had a disagreeable sound. His attitude towards overbearing dishpots resembled that of his companion's circle in Bottleton East towards officers of the Law. He disliked and feared them. It began to look to him as if union with Hermione Bostock, good though it might be in itself, carried with it certain disadvantages which wanted thinking over.

'And Lady Bostock?' he said. 'She flitted only briefly through my life, but she struck me as being slightly less of a man-eater.'

'Yes, she's better than what he is,' agreed Elsie Bean. 'But the one I like is Mr William.'

'Who would he be?'

'Their nephew. Mr Oakshott.'

'Oh, ah, yes. I was forgetting. I know him, or used to. Got a pink face, hasn't he?'

'Well, I'd call it more of a tomato ketchup colour. Owing to the heat of the sun in them parts. He's just come back from Brazil. He was telling me about Brazil this morning,' said Elsie, who had lost no time in buttonholing the returned wanderer and exchanging ideas with him. 'The natives there shoot birds with poisoned darts.'

'Poisoned darts?'

'R. Through blowpipes.'

Pongo was courteous, but he could not let this pass. Though it was some time since he had boned up on his Brazil, memories of *The Boy Explorers Up the Amazon* still lingered in his mind.

'Not poisoned darts.'

'That's what Mr William told me.'

'He was pulling your leg. They keep those for their wives' relations. Use your intelligence, my dear old housemaid. When a Brazilian native shoots a bird, he does it with a purpose. He intends to employ that bird subsequently in broiled or fricassee form. Obviously, then, if he soaked it with a poisoned dart, he would be defeating his own ends, because no sooner had he bitten into the liver wing than he would kick the bucket in awful agonies. And Brazilian natives, while they may be asses, are not silly asses. If you really want to know how they shoot birds, I will tell you. They fashion a rude sling – thus,' said Pongo, taking out his handkerchief and unfolding it. 'They then look about them for a handy projectile, as it might be this paperweight, and stuff it into the rude sling. This done, they whirl the contraption round their heads and . . . Oh, my God! Where did that one go?'

It had not been his intention to give a practical demonstration. He had planned to stop short of the actual discharge of the projectile, merely indicating its effects verbally. But artistic enthusiasm had carried him too far. A rending crash, and something white in the shadows at the end of the hall was lying in fragments.

'Coo!' said Elsie Bean, awed. 'You aren't half breaking up the home, are you? You'll catch it when His Nibs gets back.'

For the third time since he had entered this house of terror, Pongo's brow grew warm and damp. With that get-together of theirs over the broken whatnot still green in his memory, it seemed to him only too sickeningly certain that he would catch it when His Nibs got back.

'What was it?' he quavered, rightly speaking of the object in the past tense.

'It's a sort of sawn-off statue like, that he had presented to him when he give up being Governor of that dog's island out in Africa that he used to be Governor of. A bust, Cook says it's called. He thinks the world of it. The other morning he happened to come along while I was giving it a bit of a dusting, and you ought to have heard him go on, just because I kind of rocked it a little. "Be careful, girl! Be careful, girl! Mind what you're doing, my good girl!" Coo!'

Pongo's brow grew damper. A stylist would now have described it as beaded. And simultaneously he found himself chilled to the bone. He was a human replica of one of those peculiar puddings which lure the diner on into supposing that he is biting into a hot *soufflé* and then suddenly turn right around and become ice-cream in the middle.

Matters were even worse, he perceived, than he had feared. This was not one of those minor breakages which get passed off with a light apology on the one side and a jolly laugh on the other. It was as if Sir Aylmer Bostock had had a favourite child on whom he doted and he, Pongo, had socked that child on the occiput and laid it out good and proper. And coming right on top of the whatnot misadventure, too! What would be the effect on his temperamental host of this second and possibly even more wrath-provoking outrage?

'Golly!' he moaned, sagging at the knees. 'This is a nice bit of box fruit. Advise me, young Bean. What do I do for the best, do you think?'

It may be that Bottleton East produces an exceptionally quick-witted type of girl, or perhaps all women are like that. At any rate, Elsie Bean, with scarcely a pause for thought, provided the solution hot off the griddle.

'Well, look,' she said. 'It's kind of dark in that corner, so maybe he won't miss his old bust for a bit. He's short-sighted, I know, and he won't wear specs because he thinks they'd make him look silly. Jane heard them talking about it at dinner. If I was you, I'd hop into that car of yours and drive lickerty-split to London and get another bust. And then you drive back and stick it up. Ten to one he won't notice nothing.'

For an instant Pongo's numbed brain was incapable of following her reasoning. Then the mists cleared, and he saw that it was red-hot stuff. This girl had found the way.

Drive lickerty-split to London? No need to do that. He could procure the substitute a dashed sight nearer than London. At Ickenham Hall, to be precise. His mind shot back to last night's dinner table . . . Uncle Fred jerking a thumb at an object in the corner of the room and saying it was a bust which Sally had brought down and left in his charge, and himself – how ironical it seemed now – giving the thing a brief and uninterested glance. It wouldn't be an uninterested glance he would be giving it when he saw it again.

His spirits soared. Ickenham Hall was only a dozen miles away, and he had an owner-driver's touching faith in the ability of his Buffy-Porson to do a dozen miles, if pushed, in about three minutes and a quarter. He could be there and back and have the understudy on its pedestal long before his host had finished conferring with the vicar.

He beamed upon Elsie Bean.

'That's the set-up. I'll go and get the car.'

'I would.'

'You, meanwhile, might be putting in a bit of earnest brush-and-pan work.'

'Right ho!'

'Fine. Great. Capital. Splendid,' said Pongo, and raced for the stables.

Elsie Bean, her errand of mercy concluded, was standing on the front steps when he drove up. He was conscious, as he saw her, of a twinge of remorse, for it had just come to him that he had churlishly omitted to chuck her so much as a word of thanks for her splendid resourcefulness.

'I say,' he said, 'I forgot to mention it in the swirl and rush of recent events, but I'm most frightfully obliged to you for the very sporting way you've rallied round and saved me from the fate that is worse than death – viz.,' explained Pongo, 'getting glared at by that goggle-eyed old Jack the Ripper with the lip fungus.'

Elsie Bean said she was only too pleased, to be sure, and he took her hand in his and pressed it.

'But for you I should have been in the soup and going down for the third time. I owe you more than words can tell.'

He was still pressing her hand, and from that to kissing her in a grateful and brotherly manner was but a short step. He took it, and Bill Oakshott, coming round the corner after one of the long walks with which he was endeavouring these days to allay the pangs of frustrated love, was able to observe the courteous gesture from start to finish.

Pongo sprang into the car with a lissom bound, waved his hand and drove off, and Bill stared after him, stunned. Pongo belonged to the type of man which changes very little in appearance with the passage of the years, and he recognised him immediately.

Still, to make sure . . .

'Wasn't that Mr Twistleton?' he inquired of Elsie Bean.

'Yes, sir,' said Elsie composedly. She had no inkling of the turmoil in his soul, and would have been astounded to learn that anyone was taking exception to that kiss. In Bottleton East everybody kisses everybody else as a matter of course, like the early Christians. 'He says you were wrong about the natives, Mr William.'

'The what?'

'Those natives in Brazil. They don't shoot birds with poisoned darts, only their wives' relations. They use rude slings.'

With an effort that shook his powerful frame to its foundations Bill Oakshott contrived to keep from saying something ruder about Brazilian natives than any sling fashioned by them.

There was no room in his thoughts for Brazilian natives. All the available space was occupied by Pongo.

So this, he was saying to himself, was the man to whom Hermione had entrusted her happiness; a libertine who, once the Don Juan of his dancing class, now went about kissing housemaids on doorsteps. How right, how unerringly right, old Ickenham had been. Can the leopard change his spots, he had speculated. This leopard didn't even seem to want to.

'Gosh!' thought Bill, aghast at the stark horror of the thing.

A minor point presented itself.

'Where's he off to?' he asked, puzzled.

'London, sir.'

'London?'

'Yes, sir.'

'But he's only just arrived.'

'Yes, sir.'

'Did he say why he was going to London?'

Elsie Bean was a good accomplice, cautious, reliable, on the alert against verbal slips.

'No, sir. He just said, "Coo! I think I'll go to London," and popped off.'

Bill Oakshott drew a deep breath. It seemed to him that in the years since he had seen him last, his old friend, never very strong in the head, must have become absolutely *non compos*. Do balanced men drive to country houses and immediately upon arrival say, 'Coo! I think I'll go to London,' and drive off again? They certainly do not.

His heart, as he filled his pipe, was heavy. Sane libertines, he was thinking, are bad enough, but loony libertines are the limit.

IV

It was at a quarter to eight that evening that Lord Ickenham, after a pleasant journey to London in his car and a bath and change at his club, arrived in Budge Street, Chelsea, to pick up Sally Painter and take her to dinner.

Budge Street, Chelsea, in the heart of London's artistic quarter, is, like so many streets in the hearts of artistic quarters, dark, dirty, dingy and depressing. Its residents would appear to be great readers and very fond of fruit, for tattered newspapers can always be found fluttering about its sidewalks and old banana skins, cores of apples, plum stones and squashed strawberries lying in large quantities in its gutters. Its cats are stringy, hard-boiled cats, who look as if they were contemplating, or had just finished perpetrating, a series of murders of the more brutal type.

It was a bit of luck, accordingly, for this dishevelled thoroughfare to be toned up by Lord Ickenham's ornamental presence. With his well-cut clothes and distinguished deportment he lent to the scene a suggestion of the enclosure at Ascot on Cup Day.

And he had not been there long, strolling up and down, when Budge Street had another slice of good fortune. Round the corner from the King's Road there came hurrying a small, alert girl in beige, whose arrival intensified the Ascot note. Nobody, not even Pongo at the very height of that unfortunate discussion about the tint of his liver, had ever attempted to deny that Sally Painter was pretty: and even if she had not been, there was a jauntiness in her carriage which would have gone far to create that illusion.

To Lord Ickenham she seemed like some spirit of the summer day. Watching her as she paused to tickle a passing cat and noting how under the treatment the cat became in an instant a better, more idealistic cat, his heart went out to her.

'Hoy!' he cried paternally, and she came running up, floating into his arms like a columbine.

'I hope I haven't kept you waiting, Uncle Fred. I had to see a man about a bust.'

'Not at all,' said Lord Ickenham. Odd, he was thinking, how everybody seemed to be seeing men about busts today. It was only a few hours since Pongo had come charging into his study, clamouring for one. 'Always see men about busts. It is the secret of a happy and successful life.'

Sally linked her arm in his, and gave it a squeeze.

'It's lovely seeing you again, angel.'

'I am always well worth looking at.'

'How wonderful of you to come. And how brave! How did you manage to sneak away?'

'What extraordinary verbs you employ, child.'

'Well, didn't Aunt Jane say she would scalp you with a blunt knife next time you were AWOL?'

'In her playful way she did say something of the sort. Odd, that craving of hers to keep me vegetating in the country. But your honorary Aunt Jane is at the moment on her way to the West Indies. This has eased the situation a good deal. I thought it a good opportunity of broadening my mind.'

'Or playing hooky.'

'That is another way of putting it, of course. Well, let's find a taxi and go and get some dinner. There's one,' said Lord Ickenham, as they turned the corner. 'Hop in. Barribault's,' he said to the driver, and Sally closed her eyes in a sort of ecstasy. A girl who as a rule dined sparingly in Soho, she found enchantment in the mere name of London's premier restaurant.

'Barribault's? We're not dressed.'

'Grill room. Ev. dress not oblig.'

'But do I look smart enough?'

'My dear, you look like Helen of Troy after a good facial.'

Sally leaned back against the cushions.

'Barribault's!' she murmured.

'We Earls step high,' Lord Ickenham assured her. 'The best is none too good for us.'

'It must be great being an Oil.'

'It's terrific. I often lie awake at night, aching with pity for all the poor devils who aren't.'

'Though I suppose you know you're an anachronistic parasite on the body of the State? Or so Otis says. He's just become a Communist.'

'He has, has he? Well, you can tell him from me that if he starts any nonsense of trying to hang me from a lamp post, I shall speak very sharply to him. Doesn't he like Earls?'

'Not much. He thinks they're bloodsuckers.'

'What an ass that boy is, to be sure. Where's the harm in sucking blood? We need it, to keep us rosy. And it isn't as if I hadn't had to work for my little bit of gore. People see me now the dickens of a fellow with five Christian names and a coronet hanging on a peg in the hats and coats cupboard under the stairs, and they forget that I started at the bottom of the ladder. For years I was a younger son, a mere Honourable.'

'Why have you never told me this?'

'I hadn't the heart to. A worm of an Hon. In Debrett, yes, but only in small print.'

'You're making me cry.'

'I can't help that. Do you know how they treat Hons, Sally? Like dogs. They have to go into dinner behind the Vice Chancellor of the County Palatinate of Lancaster.'

'Well, it's all over now, darling.'

'The only bit of sunshine in their lives is the privilege of being allowed to stand at the bar of the House of Lords during debates. And I couldn't even do that, my time being earmarked for the cows I was punching in Arizona.'

'I didn't know you had ever punched cows.'

'As a young man, hundreds. I had a beautiful punch in those days, straight and true, like the kick of a mule, and never travelling more than six inches. I also jerked soda, did a bit of newspaper work, which was when I met your father, and had a shot at prospecting in the Mojave Desert. But was I happy? No. Because always at the back of my mind, like some corroding acid, was the thought that I had to go into dinner behind the Vice Chancellor of the County Palatinate of Lancaster. In the end, by pluck and perseverance, I raised myself from the depths and became what I am today. I'd like to see any Vice Chancellor of the County Palatinate of Lancaster try to squash in ahead of me now.'

'It's like something out of Horatio Alger.'

'Very like. But I'm boring you. I'm afraid we fellows who have made good have a tendency to go rambling on about our early struggles. Tell me of yourself. How are you doing these days, Sally?'

'Well, I still go into dinner behind fashion editresses, but aside from that I'm making out pretty satisfactorily.'

'Trade good?'

'Not so bad.'

The cab drew up at the ornate portal of Barribault's Hotel,

and they made their way to the grill room. As they took their seats, Sally was sniffing luxuriously.

'Heaven!' she said.

'Hungry?'

'I'm always hungry.'

Lord Ickenham looked at her a little anxiously.

'You're sure you're not hard up, Sally?'

'Not a bit. Busts are quite brisk. It's odd, when you think how hideous most people are, that so many of them should want to hand their faces down to posterity.'

'You wouldn't deceive me?'

'No, honestly. I'm opulent.'

'Then why did you send me that SOS? What is the very urgent matter you wanted to see me about, with the "very" underlined?'

Sally was silent for a moment, but only because she was eating caviare. It did not often come her way.

'Oh, that? It's about Otis.'

'My God!'

'Well, it is. I'm sorry.'

'Otis again! A thing I've noticed all my life is that the nicest girls always have the ghastliest brothers. It seems to be a law of nature. Well, what's the trouble this time, and what do you want me to do?'

'I'll explain about the trouble later. What I want you to do is to ask Pongo to do something for me.'

'Pongo?'

'I can't very well approach him direct,' said Sally.

There was a sudden flatness in her voice which did not escape Lord Ickenham's quick ear. He leaned across and petted her hand.

'A shame about you and Pongo, Sally.'

'Yes.'

There was a silence. Lord Ickenham stole a glance across the table. Sally was gazing into the middle distance, her eyes, or so it seemed to him, suspiciously bright and with a disposition to moisture which disquieted him. It is rarely that an uncle is able to understand how a nephew of his can possibly cast a fatal spell and, fond as he was of Pongo, Lord Ickenham could not see him as a breaker of hearts. Yet it appeared plain that his loss had left a large gap in this girl's life. Her air was the air of one who was pining for Pongo, and it was a relief when the waiter, arriving with *truite bleue,* broke a tension which had begun to be uncomfortable.

'Tell me about Otis,' he said.

Sally smiled a rather twisted smile.

'You needn't be tactful, Uncle Fred. I don't mind talking about Pongo. At least . . . No, of course I don't. Have you seen him lately?'

'He left me this afternoon. He turned up yesterday and spent the night.'

'How was he looking?'

'Oh, very well.'

'Did he speak about me?'

'Yes. And when I cursed him for being ass enough to part brass rags with you, he told me the inside story.'

'About my wanting him to smuggle Alice Vansittart's jewels into America?'

'Yes.'

'I was a fool to get mad. And it was all so unnecessary, as it turned out.'

'The Vansittart decided on reflection to pay duty?'

'No. But I thought of a much better way of slipping the

stuff through. I'm not going to tell even you what it was, but it's a peach of a way. It can't fail. Alice is crazy about it.'

She spoke with a girlish animation which encouraged Lord Ickenham to hope that her heart was, after all, not irretrievably broken. That bright, moist look had gone from her eyes, leaving in its place a gleam not unlike that of which Pongo had so disapproved, when he had seen it in the eyes of his Uncle Fred.

'She is, is she?'

'When I told her, she clapped her hands in glee.'

'You realise, of course, that it is very wrong to deceive the United States Customs authorities?'

'Yes, it makes me miserable. Poor darlings.'

'Still, there it is. So you and Pongo need not have split up at all.'

'No.'

'It was silly of him to take your breaking the engagement so seriously. My dear wife broke ours six times, and each time I came up smiling.'

'I ought to have remembered that Pongo does take things seriously.'

'Yes. A saintly character, but muttonheaded.'

'And now he's gone and got engaged to Hermione, only daughter of Sir Aylmer Bostock and Lady Bostock, of Ashenden Manor, Ashenden Oakshott, Hants. Oh, well. Do you know her, Uncle Fred?'

'No. I've seen her photograph.'

'So have I. It was in the *Tatler*. She's very good-looking.'

'If you admire that type of looks.'

'Pongo seems to.'

'Yes. For the moment you might describe him as being under the ether. But there will be a bitter awakening.'

'You can't know that just from seeing her photograph.'

'Yes, I can. She'll give him the devil.'

'Oh, poor angel.'

There was another silence.

'Well, what is it you want me to ask him to do for you?' said Lord Ickenham. 'I may mention that I'm pretty sure he will do it, whatever it is. He's still damned fond of you, Sally.'

'Oh, no.'

'He is, I tell you. He confessed as much, in so many words.'

A dazzling smile flashed out on Sally's face. The waiter, who was bringing chicken *en casserole*, caught it head on and nearly dropped the dish.

'Did he?'

'And don't forget that he still retained enough of the old affection to send you a customer in the shape of Sir Aylmer Bostock.'

'Was it Pongo who got me that job? How like him,' said Sally softly. 'I love him for that. Though unfortunately it was through my doing that bust that poor Otis's trouble came about.'

'How did that happen?'

'Well, to begin at the beginning, I did the bust.'

'Quite.'

'And during the process, of course, my sitter and I talked of this and that.'

'Was his conversation entertaining?'

'Not very. He was rather inclined to compare my efforts to their disadvantage with those of a sculptor who did a bust of him when he retired.'

'The one that stands – or stood – in the hall at Ashenden?'

'Yes. However did you know?'

'Wait, my child. I shall shortly be telling you a story of my own. Go on. He conversed with you, but you did not find him very entertaining.'

'No. But he said one thing that gripped my attention, and that was that he had written his Reminiscences and had decided after some thought to pay for their publication. He spoke like a man who had had disappointments. So I said to myself, "Ha! A job for Otis." '

'I begin to see. Otis took it on and made a mess of it?'

'Yes. In a negligent moment he slipped in some plates which should have appeared in a book on Modern Art which he was doing. Sir Aylmer didn't like any of them much, but the one he disliked particularly was the nude female with "Myself in the Early Twenties" under it. The first thing I knew about it was when he sent the bust back. Lady Bostock brought it round to my studio with a stiff note. And now he's bringing an action for enormous damages. If it comes off, it will smash Otis's poor little publishing firm. It's all rather unfortunate.'

'Most. But characteristic of Otis.'

'Poor lamb, he's dreamy.'

'Poor fish, he's a nightmare. I suppose you put up money for his publishing firm?'

'A certain amount.'

'Oh, heavens. Well, I'm sorry to say it, my dear, but if what you tell me is correct, any jury will give Bostock Otis's head on a charger.'

'I know. If the thing ever comes into court. That's why I need Pongo's help. I want him to use his influence with Sir Aylmer to get him to withdraw the suit. He might persuade him to settle for some smallish amount which wouldn't ruin Otis.'

'That would be the happy ending, of course. But is Pongo *persona grata* with him?'

63

'Surely?'

'I wonder. It all depends on how he has come out with that bust. Strange that Otis's future as a publisher, which I don't care a damn about, and your little bit of money, which I do, should depend on Pongo's ability to sneak a clay bust into Ashenden Manor and get away with it. Odd. Bizarre, you might say. Life can be very complicated at times.'

'What do you mean? What bust?'

'That is the story I am about to relate. Have you had enough to eat? Then let's go and have our coffee in the lounge. Yes,' said Lord Ickenham, when they had seated themselves in two of the luxurious armchairs which Barribault's Hotel provides for its patrons, 'very complicated indeed. I told you Pongo came to my place last night.'

'Yes.'

'Today, after lunch, he started out for Ashenden, to fascinate the old folks. I waved him a tender farewell, and thought that that was the last I should see of him for at least a week. I was wrong. He was back again in under two hours. Deeply agitated. More like a cat on hot bricks than anything human.'

'But why?'

'Because, in endeavouring to demonstrate to the Ashenden Manor housemaid how Brazilian natives shoot birds with rude slings, he had happened to break that bust in the hall, of which you were speaking just now.'

'Oh, golly.'

'Hullo! You agitated, too?'

'Of course I'm agitated. Don't you see, Uncle Fred? Sir Aylmer adores that bust. He'll be furious with Pongo –'

'Thus rendering Pongo in no position to plead for Otis? Yes, that seems to follow. But calm yourself. All may yet be well. His motive in coming to me was to borrow another bust to put on the bereaved pedestal, in the hope that the substitution would not be noticed.'

'That was bright.'

'Yes, much too bright for Pongo. It must have been the housemaid who suggested it. He isn't what I would call a quick-witted chap. I remember so well his confusion of mind when they were asking him his name that day at the dog races. He had got as far as "Tw –" when I was fortunately able to lean across and whisper to him that he was Edwin Smith of 11, Nasturtium Road, East Dulwich.'

'And what were you?'

'George Robinson, of number fourteen in the same thoroughfare. Yes, I think we may safely attribute to the housemaid any swift intelligence that was displayed on this occasion. Well, I gave him a bust and he drove off with it. We have no means of knowing as yet, of course, if the simple ruse has proved effective, but I think we may feel reasonably optimistic. He tells me it is darkish in the corner of the hall where the original used to stand, and I don't suppose Mugsy is in the habit of scrutinising it too carefully. Just a casual glance in passing, and he toddles off to the garden to enjoy the sunshine.'

'Why do you call him Mugsy?'

'We always used to at school.'

'Were you and Sir Aylmer at school together?'

'For years.'

'Then couldn't you plead with him?'

'No, I could not. I was telling his nephew, whom I met in the train yesterday, that I once gave young Mugsy Bostock six with a fives bat, and no doubt the incident still rankles. Pongo is the one who must plead.'

'If everything has gone well.'

'I feel convinced that it has. He says Mugsy is short-sighted and won't wear spectacles, and he described the housemaid as staunch and true and not at all the sort to squeal to the big four.'

'You're a great comfort, Uncle Fred.'

'I try to be, my dear. Sweetness and light, that is my slogan.'

'It was lucky you happened to have a bust handy.'

'Extraordinarily fortunate. For one reason and another Ickenham Hall has never been very well provided with them. Statues, yes. If you came to me with a hurry call for a nude Venus, I could fill the order without any trouble whatsoever. My grandfather specialised in them. "Home isn't home," he used to say, running a thoughtful hand through his whiskers, "without plenty of nude Venuses." The result being that in certain parts of the grounds you have the illusion of having wandered into a Turkish bath on ladies' night. But busts, no. We Ickenhams have somehow never gone in for busts. So if it hadn't been for you providentially leaving one in my care—'

It is not easy to rise in a single bound from a Barribault armchair, but Sally had done so. Her face was pale, and she was staring with wide, horrified eyes.

'Uncle Fred! You didn't give him that one?'

'Yes. Why, what's wrong?'

Sally dropped back into her chair.

'It had Alice's jewels in it,' she said in a toneless whisper.

'What!'

'Yes. I slipped them in at the top of the plaster, and Alice was going to call for the bust next week and take it to America. That was the "way" I was telling you I thought of.'

'Well, dash my wig and buttons!' said Lord Ickenham.

There followed a pregnant silence. Having dashed his wig and buttons, Lord Ickenham, though nobody could have called him an unresourceful man, seemed at a loss. He scratched his chin, he twirled his moustache, he drummed with his fingers on the side of his chair, but without obtaining anything in the nature of an inspiration.

Finally he rose.

'Well, it's no good saying I'm sorry, my dear. Nor is there much to be gained by pointing out that I meant well. What you want is a policy, not remorseful bleatings. I think I'll take a turn up and down outside. The fresh air may assist the flow of thought. And the flow of thought would certainly seem to need all the assistance it can get.'

He went out through the revolving door, his head bowed, his hands clasped behind his back. When he returned some minutes later, it was with a message of hope. His face had cleared and he was his old bright self again.

'It's all right, my child. This little difficulty can be very simply adjusted. It just needed concentration. You did tell me Mugsy had returned that bust you did of him? You have it at the studio?'

'Yes.'

'Then all is well. We will go down to Ashenden tomorrow in the car, taking it with us, and I will substitute it for the one now in residence.'

'But –'

'Don't say "But".'

'How –?'

'And don't say "How". It's the sort of thing the boys in the back room used to say to Columbus when he told them he was going to discover America, and look how silly he made them feel. I'll find a way. Don't bother your head about the trifling details, leave them to me. You go home and pack a few necessaries and get a good night's rest, while I remain and iron out the one or two points I haven't got quite straight yet. More

67

coffee? No? Then off you go. Bless my soul,' said Lord Ickenham with boyish relish, as he escorted her to the door, 'what a providential thing that this should have happened. Something on these lines was just what I was needing, to stimulate me and bring back the flush of youth. I feel as I did when Pongo and I started out last spring for Blandings Castle in the roles of Sir Roderick Glossop, the brain specialist, and his nephew Basil. Did he ever tell you about that?'

'No.'

'Odd. I should have thought it would have been one of his dearest memories. You shall have the whole story tomorrow on the journey down. Well, good night, my dear,' said Lord Ickenham, assisting Sally into her taxi. 'Sleep well, and don't worry. You can trust me to look after everything. This is the sort of situation that brings out the best in me. And when you get the best in Frederick Altamont Cornwallis, fifth Earl of good old Ickenham, you've got something.'

PART TWO

V

I

It was the custom of Lady Bostock, when the weather was fine, to sit in a garden chair on the terrace of Ashenden Manor after luncheon, knitting socks for the deserving poor. A believer, like Lord Ickenham, in spreading sweetness and light, she considered, possibly correctly, that there is nothing that brings the sunshine into grey lives like a sock or two.

On the day following the events which have just been recorded the weather was extremely fine. Soft white clouds floated across a sky of the purest blue, the lake shone like molten silver, and from the adjacent flower-beds came the murmur of bees and the fragrant scent of lavender and mignonette. It was an afternoon to raise the spirits, lighten the heart and set a woman counting her blessings one by one.

Nor did Lady Bostock omit to do this. She recognised these blessings as considerable. It was pleasant to be home again, though she had never really enjoyed life in the country, preferring Cheltenham with its gay society. Mrs Gooch, the cook, had dished up an inspired lunch. And ever since the assignment of judging the bonny babies at the fête had been handed to his nephew William, Sir Aylmer had been in a mood which could almost be called rollicking, a consummation always devoutly to be wished by a wife whose life work it was to keep him in a good temper. She could hear him singing in his study now. Something about his wealth being a burly spear and brand and a right good shield of hides untanned which on his arm he buckled – or, to be absolutely accurate, ber-huckled.

So far, so good. And yet, despite the fineness of the day, the virtuosity of Mrs Gooch and the joviality of her husband, Lady Bostock's heart was heavy. In these days in which we live, when existence has become a thing of infinite complexity and fate, if it slips us a bit of goose with one hand, is pretty sure to give us the sleeve across the windpipe with the other, it is rarely that we find a human being who is unmixedly happy. Always the bitter will be blended with the sweet, and in this *mélange* one can be reasonably certain that it is the former that will predominate.

A severe indictment of our modern civilisation, but it can't say it didn't ask for it.

As Lady Bostock sat there, doing two plain, two purl, or whatever it is that women do when knitting socks, a sigh escaped her from time to time. She was thinking of Sally Painter.

Budge Street, Chelsea, brief though her visit there had been, had made a deep impression on this sensitive woman. She had merely driven up in a cab, rung the bell of Sally's studio, handed her parcel to the charwoman and driven swiftly off again, but she had seen enough to recognise Budge Street for the sort of place she had read about in novels, where impoverished artists eke out a miserable existence, supported only by hope. How thankful, she thought, impoverished Miss Painter must have been to get the commission to model that bust of Aylmer, and what anguish must have been hers on having it thrown back on her hands.

She had mentioned this to Sir Aylmer as they were returning from their conference with the vicar, and had been snubbed with a good deal of brusqueness. And now, though she was too loyal a wife to criticise her husband even in thought, she could not check a fleeting regret that he was always so splendidly firm.

Was there nothing, she asked herself, as she remembered the admirable luncheon which she had recently consumed and pictured Sally gnawing a dry crust and washing it down with a cup of water, was there nothing that she could do? Useless, of course, to make another attempt to persuade Aylmer to change his mind, but suppose she were to send the girl a secret cheque . . .

At this point her musing was interrupted and her despondency increased by the arrival of Bill Oakshott, who came heavily along the terrace smoking a sombre pipe. She eyed him with a sad pity. Ever since she had given him the bad news, the sight of him had made her feel like a soft-hearted Oriental executioner who, acting on orders from the front office, has had to do unpleasant things to an Odalisque with a bow string. It seemed to her sometimes that she would never be able to forget the look of horror and despair which had leaped into his crimson face. Traces of it still lingered on those haggard features.

'Hullo, Aunt Emily,' he said in sepulchral tones. 'Knitting a sock?'

'Yes, dear. A sock.'

'Oh?' said Bill, still speaking like a voice from the tomb. 'A sock? Fine.'

He stood there, staring before him with unseeing eyes, and she touched his hand gently.

'I wouldn't worry about it too much, dear.'

'I don't see how one could,' said Bill. 'How many of these frightful babies will there be?'

'There were forty-three last year.'

'Forty-three!'

'Be brave, William. If Mr Brotherhood could do it, you can.'

The flaw in this reasoning was so obvious that Bill was able to detect it at once.

'Curates are different. They train them specially to judge bonny babies. At the theological colleges. Start them off with ventriloquists' dummies, I shouldn't wonder. Forty-three, did you say? And probably dozens more this time. These blighters breed like rabbits. Gosh, I wish I was back in Brazil.'

'Oh, William.'

'I do. What a country! Nothing but flies and ticks and alligators and snakes and scorpions and tarantulas and a sort of leech that drops on you from trees and sucks your blood. Not a baby to be seen for miles. Listen, Aunt Emily, can't I get someone else to take this ghastly job on?'

'But who?'

'Yes, that's the snag, of course,' said Bill morosely. 'Mugs fat-headed enough to let themselves be talked into judging forty-three bonny babies, all dribbling out of the side of the mouth, must be pretty scarce, pretty scarce. Well, I think I'll be pushing along, Aunt Emily. It seems to help a little if I keep moving.'

He plodded off, listlessly puffing smoke, leaving behind him an aunt with an aching heart. And it was perhaps because Lady Bostock was now so near the nadir of depression that she thought she might as well make a complete job of it. So she began to think of Pongo.

It frequently happens that prospective sons-in-law come as a rather painful shock to their prospective mothers-in-law, and the case of Lady Bostock had provided no exception to the rule. Immediately on seeing Pongo she had found herself completely at a loss to understand why her daughter should have chosen him as a mate. From the very start she had felt herself to be in the presence of one whose soul was not attuned to hers. At moments, indeed, only her perfect breeding had restrained her from beating him over the head with the sock which she was knitting for the deserving poor.

Analysing his repellent personality, she came to the conclusion that while she disliked his nervous giggle, his lemon-coloured hair and the way he had of drooping his lower jaw and letting his eyes get glassy, the thing about him that particularly exasperated her was his extraordinary jumpiness.

Of this she had witnessed a manifestation only an hour or so ago, as they were leaving the dining room after lunch. As they started to cross the hall, Aylmer had moved in the direction of that bust of his, as if to give it a flick with his handkerchief, as he sometimes did, and Reginald had bounded in his tracks with a soft, animal yelp, recovering his composure only when Aylmer, abandoning the idea of flicking, had moved on again.

A strange young man. Was he half – or even a quarter – witted? Or was his mind, if he had a mind, burdened by some guilty secret?

Speculations like these, indulged in on a warm day after a rather heavy lunch, are apt to induce drowsiness. Her eyelids began to flutter. Somewhere out of sight a lawnmower was purring hypnotically. The west wind played soothingly on her face.

Lady Bostock slept.

But not for long. Her eyes had scarcely closed when the word 'EMILY', spoken at the extreme limit of a good man's lungs, jerked her from her slumber as if a charge of trinitrotoluol had been exploded beneath her chair.

Sir Aylmer was leaning out of the study window.

'EMILY!'

'Yes, dear? Yes, dear?'

'Come here,' roared Sir Aylmer, like a bo'sun addressing an able-bodied seaman across the deck in the middle of a hurricane. 'Wantcher.'

2

As Lady Bostock made her way to the study, her heart was racing painfully. There had been that in her husband's manner which caused her to fear unnamed disasters, and her first glance at him as she crossed the threshold told her that her apprehensions had been well founded.

His face was purple, and his moustache, always a barometer of the emotions, was dancing about beneath his laboured breath. She had not beheld such activity in it since the night years ago when the youngest and most nervously giggling of the aides-de-camp, twiddling the nut-crackers during the dessert course at dinner at Government House, had snapped the stem of one of his favourite set of wineglasses.

He was not alone. Standing at a respectful distance in one of the corners, as if he knew his place better than to thrust himself forward, was Constable Harold Potter, looking, as policemen do at such moments, as if he had been stuffed by a good taxidermist. She stared from one to the other, bewildered.

'Aylmer! What is it?'

Sir Aylmer Bostock was not a man who beat about bushes. When he had disturbing news to impart, he imparted it.

'Emily,' he said, quivering in every hair, 'there's a damned plot afoot.'

'A what?'

'A PLOT. An infernal outrage against the public weal. You know Potter?'

Lady Bostock knew Potter.

'How do you do, Potter?' she said.

'How do you do, m'lady?' said Constable Potter, coming unstuffed for an instant in order to play his part in the courteous exchanges and then immediately getting stuffed again.

'Potter,' said Sir Aylmer, 'has just come to me with a strange story. Potter!'

'Sir?'

'Tell her ladyship your strange story.'

'Yes, sir.'

'It's about Reginald,' said Sir Aylmer, to whet the interest of the audience. 'Or, rather,' he added, exploding his bombshell, 'the fellow who's posing as Reginald.'

Lady Bostock's eyes were already bulging to almost their maximum extent, but at these words they managed to protrude a little further.

'Posing?'

'Yes.'

'What do you mean?'

'What I say. I can't put it any plainer. The chap who's come here pretending to be Reginald Twistleton is an impostor. He isn't Reginald Twistleton at all. I had my suspicions of him all along. I didn't like his eye. Sly. Shifty. And that sinister giggle of his. What I'd call a criminal type. Potter!'

'Sir?'

'Get on with your strange story.'

'Yes, sir.'

Constable Potter stepped forward, his helmet balanced against his right hip. A glazed look had come into his eyes. It was the look which they always assumed when he was giving evidence in court. His gaze was directed some two feet above Sir Aylmer's head, so that his remarks seemed to be addressed to a bodiless spirit hovering over the scene and taking notes in an invisible notebook.

'On the sixteenth inst.—'

'Yesterday.'

'Yesterday,' proceeded Constable Potter, accepting the emendation. 'On the sixteenth inst., which was yesterday, I was proceeding up the drive of Ashenden Manor on my bicycle, when my attention was drawn to a suspicious figure entering the premises through a window.'

'The window of my collection room.'

'The window of Sir Aylmer Bostock's collection room. I immediately proceeded to follow the man and question him. In reply to my inquiries he made the statement that his name was Twistleton and that he was established as a guest at this residence.'

'Well, so he is,' said Lady Bostock, speaking a little dazedly.

Sir Aylmer waved an imperious hand.

'Wait, wait, wait, wait, WAIT. Mark the sequel.'

He paused, and stood puffing at his moustache. Lady Bostock, who had sunk into a chair, picked up a copy of the parish magazine and began to fan herself with it.

'We're coming to the part where he turns out not to be Twistleton,' said Sir Aylmer, allowing his moustache to subside like an angry sea after a storm. 'Carry on, Potter.'

Constable Potter, who had momentarily removed the glazed look from his eyes, put it back again. Raising his chin, which he had lowered in order to rest the neck muscles, he once more addressed the bodiless spirit.

'Having taken the man's statement, I proceeded to put searching questions to him. These appearing to establish his bona fides, I withdrew, leaving him in the company of Bean, a housemaid, whose evidence had assisted me in establishing the conclusion that his bona fides had been' – Constable Potter paused, searching for the telling verb – 'established,' he said. 'But—'

'Here comes the sequel.'

'But I was not wholly satisfied, and I'll tell you why,' said Constable Potter, suddenly abandoning the official manner and becoming chatty. 'The moment I saw this chap, I had a sort of feeling that his face was kind of familiar, but I couldn't place him. You know how it is. And, what's more, I could have taken my oath that last time we'd met his name hadn't been Twistleton—'

'Or anything like it,' said Sir Aylmer, adroitly snatching the conversational ball from the speaker and proceeding to carry it himself. 'I must start by telling you . . . ARE YOU ASLEEP, EMILY?'

'No, dear. No, dear,' cried Lady Bostock, who had been rash enough to close her eyes for an instant in order to relieve a shooting pain across the forehead.

'I must start by telling you that before Potter came to Ashenden Oakshott he used to be a member of the London police force, and this afternoon, as he was smoking a pipe after his lunch—'

'Cigarette, sir,' interpolated the officer respectfully. He knew the importance of exactitude on these occasions. 'A gasper.'

'—It suddenly flashed on him,' went on Sir Aylmer, having given him a dangerous look, 'that where he had seen this fellow before was at some dog races down Shepherd's Bush way, when he had arrested him, together with an accomplice, and hauled him off in custody.'

'Aylmer!'

'You may well say "Aylmer!" It seems that Potter keeps a scrap album containing newspaper clippings having to do with cases with which he has been connected, and he looked up this scrap album and found that the chap's name, so far from being Twistleton, is Edwin Smith, of 11, Nasturtium Road, East Dulwich. Edwin Smith,' repeated Sir Aylmer, somehow contriving by his intonation to make it seem a name to shudder at. 'Now do you believe me when I say he's an impostor?'

Women, having no moustaches, are handicapped at moments like this. Lady Bostock had begun to pant like a spent horse, but it was not the same thing. She could not hope to rival her husband's impressiveness.

'But what is he doing here?'

'Potter's view is that he is the advance man of a gang of burglars. I think he's right. These fellows always try to simplify matters for themselves by insinuating an accomplice into the house to pave the way for them. When the time is ripe, the bounder opens a window and the other bounders creep in. And if you want to know what this gang is after at Ashenden Manor, it sticks out a mile. My collection of African curios. Where did Potter find this chap? In my collection room. Where did I find him? Again in my collection room. My collection fascinates him. He can't keep away from it. You agree, Potter?'

Constable Potter, though not too well pleased at the way in which he had been degraded from the position of star witness to that of a mere Yes-man, was forced to admit that he agreed.

Lady Bostock was still panting softly.

'But it seems so extraordinary.'

'Why? Its value is enormous.'

'I mean, that he should take such a risk.'

'These fellows are used to taking risks. Eh, Potter?'

'Yes, sir.'

'Doing it all the time, aren't they?'

'Yes, sir.'

'Dangerous devils, what?'

'Yes, sir,' said Constable Potter, now apparently resigned to his demotion.

'But he must have known that Reginald was expected here. How could he tell that he was not going to run into him?'

'My dear Emily, don't be childish. The gang's first step would, of course, be to make away with Reginald.'

'Make away with him? How?'

'Good Lord, how do chaps make away with chaps? Don't you ever read detective stories?'

Constable Potter saw his chance, and took it.

'They telephone 'em, m'lady, telling them to come to ruined mills, and then lock 'em up in the cellar. Or they—'

'—Slip drugs in their drink and carry them off on yachts,' said Sir Aylmer, once more seizing the ball. 'There are a hundred methods. If we looked into it, I expect we should find that the real Reginald is at this moment lying bound and gagged on a pallet bed in Limehouse. Eh, Potter?'

'Yes, sir.'

'Or in the hold of a tramp steamer bound for South America?'

'Yes, sir.'

'I shouldn't wonder if they weren't sticking lighted matches between his toes to make him write them cheques,' said Sir Aylmer dispassionately. 'Well, all right, Potter, that's all. We won't keep you. Would you like a glass of beer?'

'Yes, sir,' said Constable Potter, this time with real enthusiasm.

'Go and get one in the kitchen. And now,' said Sir Aylmer, as the door closed, 'to business.'

'Where are you going?'

'To confront this impostor and kick him out, of course.'

'But, Aylmer.'

'Now what?'

'Suppose there is some mistake.'

'How can there be any mistake?'

'But suppose there is. Suppose this young man is really Reginald, and you turn him out of the house, we should never hear the last of it from Hermione.'

3

Something of the gallant fire which was animating him seemed to pass out of Sir Aylmer Bostock. He blinked, like some knight of King Arthur's court, who, galloping to perform a deed of derring-do, has had the misfortune to collide with a tree. Though keeping up a brave front, he, like his wife, had always quailed before Hermione. Native chiefs, accustomed to leap like fawns at a waggle of his moustache, would have marvelled at this weakness in one who had always seemed to them impervious to human emotions, but it existed.

' 'M, yes,' he said thoughtfully. 'Yes, I see what you mean.'

'She would be furious.'

'That's true.'

'I really don't know what to think myself,' said Lady Bostock distractedly. 'Potter's story did seem very convincing, but it is just possible that he is mistaken in supposing that this man who has come here as Reginald is really Edwin Smith.'

'I'd bet a million on it.'

'Yes, dear, I know. And I must say I have noticed something curiously furtive about the young man, as if he had a guilty secret. But –'

An idea occurred to Sir Aylmer.

'Didn't Hermione give some sort of description of this young poop of hers in that letter she wrote you saying she was engaged?'

'Why, of course. I had forgotten. It's in my desk. I'll go and get it.'

'Well?' said Sir Aylmer a few moments later.

Lady Bostock was skimming through the document.

'She says he is tall and slender, with large, lustrous eyes.'

'There you are! This chap hasn't got lustrous eyes.'

'Wouldn't you say his eyes were lustrous?'

'Certainly not. Like a couple of damned poached eggs. What else?'

'He is very amusing.'

'You see!'

'Oh!'

'What?'

'She says William used to know him as a boy.'

'She does? Then William's evidence will clinch the thing. Where is he? WILLIAM! WILLIAM!! WILLIAM!!!'

It is rarely that this sort of thing does not produce results. Bill Oakshott, who was still on the terrace, smoking his pipe and pondering over his numerous misfortunes, came clattering up the stairs as if pulled at the end of a string.

The fear – or hope – that his uncle was being murdered left him as he entered the room, but not his bewilderment at the summons.

'Hullo?' he said gropingly.

'Oh, there you are,' said Sir Aylmer, who was still bellowing out of the window. 'William, this fellow who calls himself Reginald Twistleton, how about him?'

'How about him?'

'Exactly. How about him?'

'How do you mean, how about him?'

'Good God, boy, can't you understand plain English? I mean, how about him?'

Lady Bostock explained.

'We are terribly upset, William. Your uncle thinks that the man who came yesterday is not Reginald, but an impostor pretending to be Reginald.'

'What on earth gives him that idea?'

'Never mind what on earth gives me that idea,' said Sir Aylmer, nettled. 'You knew Reginald Twistleton as a boy?'

'Yes.'

'Good. That's established,' said Sir Aylmer, borrowing from Constable Potter's non-copyright material. 'Now, then. When you saw him yesterday, did you recognise him?'

'Of course.'

'Don't say "Of course" in that airy way. When had you seen him last?'

'About twelve years ago.'

'Then how can you be sure you recognised him?'

'Well, he looked about the same. Grown a bit, of course.'

'Have you discussed boyhood days with him?'

'No.'

'Have you asked him a single question, the response to which would prove that he had known you as a boy?'

'Why, no.'

'There you are, then.'

'But he answers to the name of Pongo.'

Sir Aylmer snorted.

'Of course he answers to the name of Pongo. Do you suppose that an impostor, when addressed as Pongo by somebody claiming to be an old friend of the man he was impersonating, would not have the elementary intelligence to dissemble? Your evidence is completely valueless.'

'Sorry.'

'No good being sorry. Well, I shall have to look into the thing for myself. I shall take the car and go over to Ickenham Hall. The real Reginald is Ickenham's nephew, so the old lunatic will presumably have a photograph of him somewhere on the premises. A glance at that will settle the matter.'

'What a splendid idea, Aylmer!'

'Yes,' said Sir Aylmer, who thought well of it himself. 'Just occurred to me.'

He shot from the room as if propelled from a rude sling in the hands of a Brazilian native, and hurried down the stairs. In the hall he was obliged to check his progress for an instant in order to glare at Pongo, who like a murderer returning to the scene of his crime, had come thither to gaze at the substitute bust and ask himself for the hundredth time what were its chances of getting by.

'Ha!' said Sir Aylmer.

'Oh, hullo,' said Pongo, smiling weakly.

Sir Aylmer eyed him with that blend of horror and loathing with which honest men eye those who call themselves Twistleton when they are really Edwin Smith of 11, Nasturtium Road, East Dulwich, especially when these latter smile like minor gangsters caught in the act of committing some felony. It seemed to him that if ever he had seen furtive guilt limned on a human face, he had seen it now.

'Ha!' he said again, and went off to get his car.

A few minutes after he had steered it out into the road, tooting fiercely, for he was a noisy driver, another car, coming from the opposite direction, drew up outside the gate.

At its wheel was Lord Ickenham, and beside him Sally.

VI

I

Lord Ickenham cast an alert eye up the curving drive, and gave his moustache a carefree twiddle. His air was that of a man who has arrived at some joyous tryst. A restful night and a good lunch had brought his always resilient nature to a fine pitch of buoyancy and optimism. There is an expression in common use which might have been invented to describe the enterprising peer at moments such as this; the expression 'boomps-a-daisy'. You could look askance at his methods, you could shake your head at him in disapproval and click your tongue in reproof, but you could not deny that he was boomps-a-daisy.

'This might be the place, don't you think?' he said.

'It is.'

'You speak confidently.'

'Well, I've been here before. When I was doing the bust.'

'Didn't Mugsy come to the studio?'

'Of course not. Great men like him don't come to the studios of poor working girls.'

Lord Ickenham took her point.

'True,' he said. 'I can't get used to the idea of young Mugsy Bostock being a big pot. To me he remains permanently a pie-faced stripling bending over a chair while I assure him that what is about to occur is going to hurt me more than it does him. A black lie, of course. I enjoyed it. One of the hardest things in life is to realise that people grow up. Nothing, for instance, can convince me that I am not a sprightly young fellow of twenty-five, and, as for Pongo, the idea of him being old enough to contemplate marriage fills me with a perpetual astonishment. To me, he still wears sailor suits.'

'He must have looked sweet in a sailor suit.'

'No, he didn't. He looked foul. Like a ballet girl in a nautical musical comedy. But enough of this idle chatter. The time has come,' said Lord Ickenham, 'to discuss strategy and tactics.'

He spoke with the gay lilt in his voice which had so often in the past struck a chill into the heart of his nephew.

'Strategy and tactics,' he repeated. 'Here is the house. We have the bust. All that is needed is to effect an entry into the former, carrying the latter. This, accordingly, I shall now proceed to do. You spoke?'

'No, I only sort of gurgled. I was going to say "How?" but I mustn't, must I, because of Columbus and the boys in the back room.'

Lord Ickenham seemed amazed.

'My dear girl, you are surely not worrying yourself about the simple mechanics of the thing? There are a thousand ways, all child's play to one of my gifts. If I droop my moustache, thus, do I look like a man come to inspect the drains?'

'No.'

'If I turn it up at the ends, so, do I suggest the representative of a journal of rural interest, anxious to obtain Mugsy's views on the mangel-wurzel situation?'

'Not a bit.'

'Then I must try something else. I wonder if Mugsy has a parrot.'

'I know he hasn't. Why?'

88

'Didn't Pongo ever tell you of our afternoon at The Cedars, Mafeking Road, Mitching Hill?'

'No. What was The Cedars, Mafeking Road, Mitching Hill?'

'A suburban villa, heavily fortified and supposed to be impregnable. But I got in with absurd ease. One moment, I was outside its barred gates, lashed by an April shower; the next, in the sitting room, toasting my toes at the gas fire. I told the maid I had come from the bird shop to clip the parrot's claws and slipped Pongo in with the statement that he was Mr Walkinshaw, my assistant, who applied the anaesthetic. I'm surprised he never mentioned it. I don't like the way he seems to have kept things from you. An unhealthy spirit. Yes, I think I may say with all due modesty that I am at my best when impersonating officials from bird shops who have called to prune the parrot, and I am sorry to hear you say that Mugsy has not got one. Not that I'm surprised. Only the gentler, kindlier type of man keeps a parrot and makes of it a constant friend. Ah, well, no doubt I shall be able to effect an entry somehow.'

'And what do you do then?'

'That's the easy part. I have the bust under my coat, I engage Mugsy in conversation, and at a selected moment I suddenly say, "Look behind you!" He looks behind him, and while his back is turned I switch the busts and come away. So let's go.'

'Wait,' said Sally.

'Is this a time for waiting? The Ickenhams have never waited.'

'Well, they're going to start now. I've a much better plan.'

'Better than mine?' said Lord Ickenham incredulously.

'Better in every way,' said Sally firmly. 'Saner and simpler.'

Lord Ickenham shrugged his shoulders.

'Well, let's hear it. I'll bet I'm not going to like it.'

'You don't have to like it. You are going to stay in the car—'

'Absurd.'

'—While I take that bust to the house.'

'Ridiculous. I knew it was going to be rotten.'

'I shall try, of course, to put the deal through unobserved. But if I am observed, I shall have my story ready, which is more than you would have done.'

'I would have had twenty stories ready, each better than the last.'

'Each crazier than the last. Mine will be a good one, carrying conviction in every syllable. I shall say I came to see Sir Aylmer—'

'I wish you would call him Mugsy. It's friendlier.'

'I won't call him Mugsy. I shall say I came to see Sir Aylmer, bringing the bust with me, in the hope that I could persuade him to relent and accept it after all.'

'Loathsome.'

'I may even cry a little.'

'Revolting. Where's your pride?'

'The worst that can happen is that he will show me to the door and dismiss me with a cold gesture.'

'And then,' said Lord Ickenham, brightening, 'we will start all over again, this time putting the affair in older and wiser hands than yours. Well, all right. On that understanding I don't mind you trying your way. I don't like it. It's tame. It degrades me to the position of a super supporting a star, and you get all the fun. Still, carry on, if you must. I shall stay here and sulk.'

He lit a cigar, and watched her as she walked up the drive. At the point where it curved out of sight, she turned and waved her hand, and he waved back, filled with a not unmanly emotion. Good old Sally, he was feeling. What a girl!

Lord Ickenham was a man with many friends in the United

States where he had spent twenty years of his life, and of all these friends the one of whom he had been fondest was the late George Painter, that amiable and impecunious artist with whom he had shared so many of the joys and sorrows of an agreeably chequered youth. He had loved George, and he loved his daughter Sally.

Sally was just the sort of girl that appealed to him most, the sort America seems to turn out in thousands, gay, grave, and adventurous, enjoying life with an almost Ickenhamian relish and resolutely refusing to allow its little difficulties to daunt her spirit.

How admirably, for instance, after the first shock, she had reacted to that unquestionably nasty wallop he had handed her in the lobby of Barribault's Hotel. No tears, no wringing of the hands, no profitless reproaches and recriminations. In the best and deepest sense of the words, a pippin of a girl. And why Pongo had let her go, simply from some finnicky objection to being disembowelled by New York port officials, baffled Lord Ickenham. It was one of the things that make a man who is getting on in years despair of the younger generation.

Time marched on. He looked at his watch. About now, he felt, she would be nearing the front door; about now, doing the quick glide through the hall and the rapid substitution of bust for bust. It would not be long before he saw her again, no doubt threading her way cautiously through the bushes that fringed the drive. He kept a keen eye riveted on those, but when she did appear she was walking in full view, and the first thing that attracted his attention was the fact that her hands were empty. At some point in her progress to and from the house, it would seem, she and her precious burden had parted company.

He could make nothing of this. His eyebrows rose in a silent query. Her face, he saw, was grave. It wore a strained look.

As she reached the car, however, her normal gaiety of disposition seemed to assert itself. She broke into a gurgling laugh, and his eyebrows rose again.

'We are amused?'

'Well, it was funny,' said Sally. 'I can't help laughing, though the absolutely rock-bottom worst has happened, Uncle Fred. We really are up against it now. You'll never guess.'

'I shan't try. Tell me.'

Sally leaned against the side of the car. Her face had become grave once more.

'I must have a cigarette first.'

'Nerves vibrating?'

'I'm shattered.'

She smoked in silence for a moment.

'Ready?'

'Waiting.'

'Very well, then, here it comes. When I got to the house, I found the front door open, which seemed to me about as big a piece of luck as I could want—'

'Always mistrust too much luck at the outset of any enterprise,' said Lord Ickenham judicially. 'It's simply part of Fate's con game. But I mustn't interrupt you. Go on.'

'I looked carefully over both shoulders. Nobody seemed to be about. I listened. I couldn't hear anybody in the hall. Everything was silent. So I sneaked in.'

'Quite.'

'And tiptoed across the hall.'

'You couldn't have done better.'

'And put the bust . . . Shall I call it Bust A, to distinguish it from Bust B?'

'By all means.'

'You've got them clear? Bust A was the one I was toting, and Bust B the one with poor Alice's jewels in it.'

'Exactly.'

Sally drew at her cigarette. Her manner was absent, as if she were reliving an episode which had affected her deeply. She came to herself with something of the air of a sleeper awakening.

'Where was I?'

'Tiptoeing across the hall.'

'Yes, of course. Sorry to be so goofy.'

'Quite all right, my child.'

'I tiptoed across the hall and shifted Bust B from its stand and put Bust A in its place and gathered up Bust B and started to come away . . . fairly quickly. No sense in hanging around, I mean.'

'None whatever. Never outstay your welcome.'

'And just as I got to the door of the room where Sir Aylmer keeps his collection of African curios, out came Lady Bostock from the drawing room.'

'Dramatic.'

'I'll say it was dramatic. The memory of that moment is going to haunt me for the rest of my life. I don't suppose I shall sleep again for months and months and months.'

'We all sleep too much.'

'She said, "Who's that?"'

'And you, I suppose, said, "Me," meaning that it was you.'

'I hadn't time to say anything, because she suddenly leaped forward with a sort of pitying cluck—'

'A what?'

'A cluck. Of pity. Like a nice hen. She really is a good sort, Uncle Fred. I had never realised it before. When I was down

93

here, doing the bust, she always seemed stiff and distant. But it was just her manner. She has a heart of gold.'

'A neat phrase, that. I must remember it. In what way did she exhibit this golden heart?'

'Why, by swooping down on me and grabbing the bust and saying in a hoarse whisper that she knew exactly why I had brought it and that she was terribly sorry for me and had begged Sir Aylmer to change his mind, but he wouldn't, so she would keep the bust and send me a cheque secretly and everything would be all right. And then she went into the collection room and locked it up in a cupboard, hurriedly, like a murderer concealing the body. And then she hustled me out. She didn't actually say, "Fly!" but it amounted to that. And it all happened so quickly that there wasn't a thing I could do.'

'And there the bust is?'

'Yes. Locked up in a cupboard in Sir Aylmer's collection room with all Alice's jewels in it. Tie that for a disaster, Uncle Fred.'

All through the narrative, Lord Ickenham had been reviving like a watered flower. His air, as it reached its culminating point, was that of one hearing tidings of great joy.

'Disaster?' he said exuberantly. 'What do you mean, disaster? This is the most admirable thing that could have happened. I now have something I can get my teeth into. It is no longer a question merely of effecting an entry into the house, but of getting myself established there. And if there is one thing I enjoy more than another, it is getting established in other people's houses. It brings the roses to my cheeks and tones up my whole system. Here is the immediate procedure, as I see it. You will drive on to Ickenham, which will serve us as a base, and I will take my suitcase and put up at the local inn and weave my subtle schemes. Expect sensational results shortly.'

'You are really going to establish yourself at the house?'

'I am.'

'And I still mustn't say, "How?"'

'You certainly must not. You just leave everything to me, confident that I shall act for the best, as always. But you look grave, my child. I hope not from any lack of faith in my vision and enterprise?'

'I was thinking of Pongo. What will he do, when you suddenly appear?'

'I should imagine he will get the start of his young life and skip like the high hills. And an excellent thing, too. Pongo is a chap who wants taking out of himself.'

The car drove off, and Lord Ickenham hoisted his suitcase and set off for the village. He was just wishing that he had thought of asking Sally to drop him at the inn, for it was a heavy suitcase, when something large and tomato-coloured loomed up before him, and he recognised Bill Oakshott.

2

In Bill Oakshott's demeanour, as he approached, there was the suggestion of a somnambulist who, in addition to having blisters on both feet, is wrestling with an unpleasant nightmare. The scene through which he had recently passed, following so swiftly upon his election as judge of the Bonny Babies contest, had shaken to its foundations a system already weakened by the knowledge that Hermione Bostock loved another, and that other a libertine who kissed housemaids on doorsteps. In response to Lord Ickenham's whoop of welcome he stared dully, like a dying halibut.

'Oh, hullo, Lord Ickenham,' he said.

'Well, well, well!' cried the fifth Earl buoyantly. The hour or two which he had spent with this massive youth had left him with a strong appreciation of his sterling worth, and he was delighted to see him again. 'Well, well well, well, well! Bill Oakshott in person. Well met by moonlight, proud Oakshott.'

'Eh?'

'Adaptation of Shakespearian quotation. But let it go. It is not of the slightest importance. And how is every little thing with you, Bill Oakshott? Fine?'

'Well, to be absolutely accurate,' said Bill, 'no.'

Lord Ickenham raised his eyebrows.

'Not fine?'

'No. Bloody awful.'

'My dear chap, you surprise and shock me. I should have thought you would have been so glad to get back from a ghastly country like Brazil that life would have been roses, roses all the way. What's wrong?'

With his affairs in such disorder, Bill was in need of all the sympathy he could get. He decided to withhold nothing from this cordial and well-disposed old buster. It would not have taken much to make him sob on Lord Ickenham's chest.

'Well, to start with,' he said, touching on the most recent of the spiritual brickbats which had assailed his soul, 'my uncle's gone off his onion.'

Lord Ickenham pursed his lips.

'Nuts?'

'Completely nuts.'

'Indeed? That must jar you a good deal. Nothing spoils the quiet home atmosphere more than a goofy uncle on the premises. When did this tragedy occur?'

'Just now.'

'It came on suddenly?'

'Like a flash.'

'What caused it?'

'Pongo.'

Lord Ickenham seemed at a loss.

'You aren't telling me that a single day of Pongo has been enough to set a host sticking straws in his hair? If it had been two weeks . . . What were the symptoms?'

'Well, he gibbered a good bit, and now he's driven over to your place to get a photograph of Pongo.'

'Why?'

'To find out what he looks like.'

'Can't he see what he looks like?'

'He doesn't believe Pongo is Pongo.'

'But doesn't Pongo admit it?'

'He thinks he's an impostor.'

'Why?'

'I don't know. I tell you he's potty. I was out on the terrace and I heard him yelling for me, and I went to the study, and he said, hadn't I known Pongo when he was a kid? And I said, yes. And he said, how did I know after all these years that this was the same chap and he was absolutely convinced that Pongo wasn't Pongo, and the only way to settle it was to drive to your place and get a photograph of him.'

Lord Ickenham shook his head.

'A fruitless quest. A man like myself, refined, sensitive, with a love for the rare and the beautiful, does not surround himself with photographs of Pongo. I could do him a nude Venus, if he would like one. Yes, it certainly looks as though you were right, Bill Oakshott, and that Mugsy's brain had come unstuck; the result, no doubt, of some sunstroke in the days when he was the curse of Africa. I'm not surprised that you are worried. The only thing I can suggest is that you give him plenty of aspirins, humour him in conversation and keep him away from razors, dinner knives and other sharp instruments. But apart from this everything is pretty smooth?'

Bill Oakshott laughed one of those hollow, mirthless laughs.

'Is it! If that was all I had to worry me, I should be singing like a lark.'

Lord Ickenham eyed him with concern. In his look, disappointment that he would not be able to hear his young friend singing like a lark was blended with distress at the news that he had further reasons for gloom.

'Don't tell me there is more? What else has happened, my ill-starred youth?'

Bill quivered, and for a moment could not speak.

'I saw Pongo kiss the housemaid,' he said in a low throaty voice.

Lord Ickenham was perplexed.

'But why shouldn't he?'

'Why shouldn't he? Dash it, he's engaged to my cousin Hermione.'

Lord Ickenham's face cleared.

'I see. Ah, yes, I understand. Her happiness is a matter of concern to you, and you do not like to think that she may be linking her lot with that of a Casanova. My dear chap, don't give the matter another thought. He does that sort of thing automatically. Where you or I would light a cigarette and throw off an epigram, Pongo kisses the housemaid. It means nothing. A purely unconscious reflex action.'

'H'm,' said Bill.

'I assure you,' said Lord Ickenham. 'You'll find it in all the case books. They have a scientific name for it. Housemaid-itis? No. No, it's gone. But that ends your catalogue of woe?

Apart from your uncle's strange seizure and this mannerism of Pongo's, you have nothing on your mind?'

'Haven't I!'

'You have? Is this the head upon which all the sorrows of the world have come? What is the next item?'

'Babies!'

'I beg your pardon?'

'Bonny babies.'

Lord Ickenham groped cautiously for his meaning.

'You are about to become a father?'

'I'm about to become a blasted judge.'

'You speak in riddles, Bill Oakshott. What do you mean, a judge?'

'At the fete.'

'What fete?' said Lord Ickenham. 'You are forgetting that I am a stranger in these parts. Tell me the whole story in your own words.'

He listened with interest while Bill did so, and the latter had no lack of sympathy to complain of when he had finished revealing the facts in connection with Sir Aylmer Bostock's hideous vengeance.

'Too bad, too bad,' said Lord Ickenham. 'But we might have foreseen something of the sort. As I warned you, these ex-Governors are tough eggs. They strike like lightning. So you are for it?'

'Unless I can find someone else to take on the job.' A sudden thought flushed Bill's brow. 'I say, will you do it?'

Lord Ickenham shook his head.

'Were the conditions right,' he said, 'I would spring to the task, for I can imagine no more delightful experience than judging a gaggle of bonny babies at a rural fete. But the conditions are not right. Mugsy would not accept my nomination.

Between him and myself there is, alas, an unfortunate and I fear insurmountable barrier. As I told you on the train it is only the other day that he was curving his person into the posture best adapted for the receipt of six of the juiciest with a fives bat, and I was the motivating force behind the fives bat.'

'But, dash it, he'll have forgotten that.'

'Already?'

'Wasn't it forty years ago?'

'Forty-two. But you grievously underestimate the suppleness of my wrist at the age of eighteen, if you suppose that anyone to whom I administered six with a fives bat would forget it in forty-two years.'

'Well, if he hasn't forgotten it, what does it matter? You'll just have a good laugh together over the whole thing.'

'I disagree with you, Bill Oakshott. Why after your recent experience of his dark malignity you should suppose young Mugsy to be a sort of vat or container for the milk of human kindness, I cannot imagine. You must know perfectly well that in the warped soul of Mugsy Bostock there is no room for sweetness and light. Come now, be honest. Does he not chew broken glass and conduct human sacrifices at the time of the full moon? Of course he does. And yet you cling to this weak pretence that, with the old wounds still throbbing, he will forget and forgive.'

'We could try him.'

'Useless. He would merely scowl darkly and turn me from his door – or your door, didn't you tell me it was? And suppose he did not? Suppose he welcomed me? What then? It would mean starting an association which would last the rest of our lives. He would always be popping over to my place, and I would be expected to pop over here. Wife would meet wife, presents would be exchanged at Christmas, it would be appalling. Even to oblige you, my dear fellow, I could not contemplate such a thing. Did you say, "Oh, hell!"?'

'Yes.'

'I thought you did, and it wrung my heart.'

There was a silence. Bill stared moodily at a passing beetle.

'Then I'm sunk.'

'But why? Have you no friends?'

'I've lost touch with them all, being away. The only one I could lay my hands on is Plank.'

'Who is Plank? Ah, yes, I remember. The head of the expedition you went on.'

'That's right. Major Brabazon-Plank.'

'*Brabazon*-Plank? You interest me strangely. I was at school with a fellow named Brabazon-Plank. He still owes me two bob. Is your Brabazon-Plank a pear-shaped chap, rather narrow in the shoulders and very broad in the beam?'

'Yes.'

'Practically all backside?'

'Yes.'

'Then it must be the same fellow. Bimbo we used to call him. Extraordinary what a mine of my old schoolmates you are turning out to be. You don't seem able to mention a name without it proving that of someone with whom in one way or another I used once to pluck the gowans fine. And you think you could contact Bimbo?'

'I have his address in London. We came back on the boat together. But it wouldn't be any use contacting him. If anyone suggested that he should judge bonny babies, he would run like a rabbit. He has a horror of them.'

'Indeed? The well-known baby fixation. See the case books.'

'All the way home on the boat he was moaning that when he got to England he would have to go and see his sisters, and he didn't know how he was going to face it, because all of them were knee-deep in babies which he would be expected to kiss. No, Plank's no good.'

'Then really,' said Lord Ickenham, 'it looks as if you would have to fall back on me.'

Bill, who had been staring dully at the beetle, transferred his gaze to his companion. It was a wide-eyed, gaping gaze, speaking eloquently of a mind imperfectly adjusted to the intellectual pressure of the conversation.

'Eh?'

'I say that you will be compelled, for want of anything better, to avail yourself of my poor services. Invite me to your home, and in return for this hospitality I will judge these bonny babies.'

Bill continued to gape.

'But you said you wouldn't.'

'Surely not?'

'Yes, you did. Just now.'

Lord Ickenham's perplexity vanished.

'Ah, I see where the confusion of thought has arisen,' he said. 'You misunderstood me. I merely meant that, for the reasons which I explained to you, it was impossible for that fine old English aristocrat, Frederick Altamont Cornwallis, Earl of Ickenham, to come barging in on an establishment of which Mugsy Bostock formed a part. What I am proposing now is that I shall throw a modest veil over my glittering identity.'

'Eh?'

'You do keep saying "Eh?" don't you? It is surely quite simple. I am most anxious to visit Ashenden Manor, of which I hear excellent reports, and I suggest that I do so incognito.'

'Under another name, do you mean?'

'Exactly. What a treat it is to deal with an intelligence like yours, Bill Oakshott. Under, as you put it so luminously, another name. As a matter of fact, I never feel comfortable going to stay at houses under my own name. It doesn't seem sporting.'

Bill Oakshott's was not a mind readily receptive of new ideas. As he stared at Lord Ickenham, his resemblance to a fish on a slab was more striking than ever.

'You'll call yourself something else?' he said, for he was a man who liked to approach these things from every angle.

'Precisely.'

'But—'

'I never like that word "But".'

'You couldn't get away with it.'

Lord Ickenham laughed lightly.

'My dear fellow, at The Cedars, Mafeking Road, in the suburb of Mitching Hill last spring I impersonated in a single afternoon and with complete success not only an official from the bird shop, come to clip the claws of the parrot, but Mr Roddis, lessee of The Cedars, and a Mr J. G. Bulstrode, a resident of the same neighbourhood. It has been a lasting grief to me that I was given no opportunity of impersonating the parrot, which I am convinced I should have done on broad, artistic lines. Have no anxiety about my not being able to get away with it. Introduce me into the house, and I will guarantee to do the rest.'

The clearness with which he had expounded his scheme had enabled Bill to grasp it, but he was looking nervous and unhappy, like a man who has grasped the tail of a tiger.

'It's too risky. Suppose my uncle found out.'

'Are you afraid of Mugsy?'

'Yes.'

'More than of the bonny babies?'

Bill quivered. In every limb and feature he betrayed his consciousness of standing at a young man's crossroads.

'But what's the procedure? You mean you just blow in, calling yourself Jones or Robinson?'

'Not Robinson. I have had occasion in the past to call myself Robinson, but it would not do now. You overlook the fact that the judge of a contest of this importance must be a man who counts. He must have authority and presence. I suggest that I come as Major Brabazon-Plank. It would give me genuine pleasure to impersonate old Bimbo, and I can think of no one more suitable. The whole thing is so plausible. You run into your old chief Plank, who happens to be passing by on a motor tour, and what more natural than that you should insist on him stopping off for a day or two at your home? And, having stopped off, what more natural than that he, learning of this very important and attractive job, a job which will render him the cynosure of all eyes and is in addition right up his street, he being passionately fond of babies, should insist on having it assigned to him? And the crowning beauty of the scheme is that I don't see how Mugsy can do anything about it. We've got him cold. It isn't as if Plank were just an ordinary man. Plank is a hell of a celebrity, and his wishes have to be deferred to. If you ask me, Bill Oakshott, if you care to have my unbiased opinion of the set-up, I think the thing's in the bag.'

Into Bill's fishlike eyes a gleam of enthusiasm had crept. His air was that of a red-faced young man who has been convinced by the voice of reason. He still feared the shape of things to come, should he fall in with his benefactor's suggestion, but he feared still more the shape of things to come, should he not.

Stamped indelibly on his mental retina was the memory of last year's fete, when he had watched the Rev. Aubrey Brotherhood preparing to embark on his duties in the big tent. Intrepid curate though he was, a man who could dominate the rowdiest Mothers' Meeting, the Rev. Aubrey had paled visibly at the task confronting him. Forty-three village matrons, holding in their arms in the hope of catching the judge's eye forty-three babies of almost the maximum repulsiveness . . .

'Right!' he cried with sudden resolution. 'Fine. Let's go.'

'Yes, let's,' said Lord Ickenham. 'You can carry the suitcase.'

They walked down the road. Bill, who had begun to think things over again, was a little silent and thoughtful, but Lord Ickenham was all gaiety and animation. He talked well and easily of this and that, and from time to time pointed out objects of interest by the wayside. They had just reached the Manor gates, when the uproar of an approaching car caused Bill to turn his head: and, having turned it, he paled beneath his tan and tottered slightly.

'Oh, golly, here comes my uncle. I say, do you think we really ought—'

'Tush, Bill Oakshott,' said Lord Ickenham, prompt in the hour of peril to stimulate and encourage. 'This is weakness. Stiffen the sinews, summon up the blood. Let us stand our ground firmly, and give him a huge hello.'

3

Sir Aylmer Bostock had spent four minutes at Ickenham Hall, all on the front doorstep, and of these four minutes there had not been one which he had not disliked. Sometimes in our wanderings about the world we meet men of whom it is said that they have passed through the furnace. Of Sir Aylmer it would be more correct to say that he had passed through the frigidaire.

If you call at a country house where you are not known and try to get the butler to let you come in and search the premises for photographs of his employer's nephew, you will generally find this butler chilly in his manner, and Coggs, the major-domo of Ickenham Hall, had been rather chillier than the average. He was a large, stout, moon-faced man with an eye like that of a codfish, and throughout the proceedings he had kept his eye glued on Sir Aylmer's, as if peering into his soul. And anyone who has ever had his soul peered into by a codfish will testify how extremely unpleasant such an ordeal is.

The message in that eye had been only too easy to read. Coggs had not actually accused Sir Aylmer of being after the spoons, but the charge might just as well have been clothed in words. In a voice of ice he had said, no, sir, I fear I cannot accede to your request, sir, and had then terminated the interview by backing a step and shutting the door firmly in the visitor's face. And when we say firmly, we mean with a bang which nearly jarred the latter's moustache loose from its foundations.

All this sort of thing is very galling to a proud and arrogant man, accustomed for years to having his lightest word treated as law, and it was consequently in no sunny mood that Sir Aylmer heard Lord Ickenham's huge hello. He was still snorting and muttering to himself, and a native chief who had encountered him in this dangerous mental condition would have called on his protecting ju-ju for quick service and climbed a tree.

Lord Ickenham was made of sterner stuff. He stepped out into the road and gave the huge hello, as planned.

'Hello, there, Mugsy,' he carolled. 'A very hearty pip-pip to you, my bright and bounding Bostock.'

It was probably astonishment at being addressed by a name which he supposed that he had lived down years ago, rather than the fact that the speaker was blocking the way, that caused Sir Aylmer to apply the brakes. He brought the car to a halt and leaned forward, glaring through the windscreen. Close scrutiny of Lord Ickenham afforded no clue to the latter's identity. All that Sir Aylmer was able to say with certainty was that this must be some old schoolfellow of his, and he wished he had had the moral courage to drive on and run over him.

It was too late to do this now, for Lord Ickenham had advanced and was standing with a friendly foot on the running board. With an equally friendly hand he slapped Sir Aylmer on the back, and his smile was just as friendly as his hand and foot. Sir Aylmer might not be glad to see this figure from the past, but the figure from the past was plainly glad to see Sir Aylmer.

'Mugsy,' he said with kindly reproach, 'I believe you've forgotten me.'

Sir Aylmer said he had. He contrived to convey in his manner the suggestion that he would willingly do so again.

'Too bad,' said Lord Ickenham. 'How evanescent are youth's gossamer friendships. Well, to put you out of your suspense, for I see that you are all keyed up, I'm Plank.'

'Plank?'

'Major Brabazon-Plank, Uncle Aylmer,' said Bill, emboldened by the suavity with which his accomplice was conducting these delicate *pourparlers*. 'Major Plank ran that expedition I went on to Brazil.'

Lord Ickenham was obliged to demur.

'Don't let him mislead you, Mugsy. In a strictly technical sense I suppose you might say I ran that expedition. Officially, no doubt, I was its head. But the real big noise was Bill Oakshott here. He was the life and soul of the party, giving up his water ration to the sick and ailing, conducting himself with cool aplomb among the alligators and encouraging with word and gesture the weaker brethren who got depressed because they couldn't dress for dinner. Chilled Steel Oakshott, we used to call him. You should be proud of such a nephew.'

Sir Aylmer appeared not to have heard these eulogies. He was still wrestling with what might be called the Plank angle of the situation.

'Plank?' he said. 'You can't be Plank.'

'Why not?'

'The Plank who was at school with me?'

'That very Plank.'

'But he was a fellow with an enormous trouser seat.'

'Ah, I see what is on your mind. Yes, yes. As a boy, quite true, I was bountifully endowed with billowy curves in the part you have indicated. But since those days I have been using Slimmo, the sovereign remedy for obesity. The results you see before you. You ought to try it yourself, Mugsy. You've put on weight.'

Sir Aylmer grunted. There was dissatisfaction in his grunt. Plainly, he was unwilling to relinquish his memories of a callipygous Plank.

'Well, I'm damned if I would have recognised you.'

'Nor I you, had not Bill Oakshott given me the office. We've both altered quite a bit. I don't think you had a white moustache at school, did you? And there's no ink on your collar.'

'You're really Plank?'

'None other.'

'And what are you doing here?'

'I'm on a motor tour.'

'Oh, are you?' said Sir Aylmer, brightening. 'Then you'll be wanting to get along. Goodbye, Plank.'

Lord Ickenham smiled a gentle, reassuring smile.

'That sad word will not be required here, Mugsy. Prepare to receive tidings of great joy. I'm coming to stay.'

'What!'

'I had intended to hurry on, but when Bill Oakshott became pressing, I could not refuse. Especially when he told me of this fete which is breaking loose shortly and promised that if I consented to be his guest at Ashenden Manor I might judge the Bonny Babies contest. That decided me. I would go fifty miles to judge bonny babies. Sixty,' said Lord Ickenham. 'Or make it a hundred.'

Sir Aylmer started like a tiger that sees its Indian villager being snatched away from it. His face, already mauve, became an imperial purple.

'You're not going to judge the bonny babies!'

'Yes, I am.'

'No, you're not.'

Lord Ickenham was a genial man, but he could be firm.

'I don't want any lip from you, young Mugsy,' he said sternly. 'Let me give you a word of warning. I see by the papers that you are about to stand for Parliament. Well, don't forget that I could swing the voting against you pretty considerably, if I wanted to, by letting an idealistic electorate in on some of the shady secrets of your boyhood. You won't like it, Mugsy, when questions about your boyhood are thundered at you from the body of the hall while you are outlining your views on the Tariff problem. Do I judge those bonny babies?'

Sir Aylmer sat brooding in silence, his Adam's apple moving up and down as if he were swallowing something hard and jagged. The stoutest man will quail at the prospect of having the veil torn from his past, unless that past is one of exceptional purity. He scowled, but scowling brought no solace. He chewed his moustache, but gained no comfort thereby.

'Very well,' he said at length, speaking as if the words were being pulled out of him with a dentist's forceps. His eye, swivelling round, rested for an instant on Bill's, and the young man leaped convulsively. 'Oh, very well.'

'Good,' said Lord Ickenham, his cheery self once more. 'That's settled. And now you shall take me home and show me the model dairy.'

'What model dairy?'

'Haven't you a model dairy? The stables, then.'

'I don't keep horses.'

'Odd. I was always led to believe that hosts at English country houses were divided into two classes: those who, when helpless guests were in their power, showed them the stables and those who showed them the model dairy. There was also, I understood, a minor subdivision which showed them the begonias, but that is a technicality into which we need not go. No model dairy, you say? No horses? Then perhaps I had better be going to the inn, where I have one or two things to do. These seen to, I will present myself at the house, and the revels can commence. And as you are doubtless anxious to hurry on and get my room – one with a southern exposure, if possible – swept and garnished, I won't detain you. You coming with me, Bill Oakshott?'

'I think I'll stay here and smoke a pipe.'

'Just as you please. We shall all meet then, at Philippi, and very jolly it will be, too.'

It was with a light and elastic step that Lord Ickenham made his way to the Bull's Head in Ashenden Oakshott's High Street. He was well satisfied with the progress of affairs. Something attempted, something done had, in his opinion, earned the spot of beer to which he had been looking forward for some considerable time, for this spreading of sweetness and light is thirsty work. After putting through a telephone call to his home and speaking to Sally, he sat down to a tankard, and was savouring its amber contents with quiet relish, when the door of the saloon bar burst open with a good deal of violence and Bill Oakshott entered.

That Bill was not at his serenest and most tranquil was indicated at once to Lord Ickenham's experienced eye by his appearance and deportment. His hair was ruffled, as if he had been passing a fevered hand through it, and that glazed look was back in his eyes. He was a young man who, when things went awry, always endeavoured, after the fashion of the modern young man, to preserve the easy repose of manner of a Red Indian at the stake, but it was plain that whatever had occurred to upset him now was of a magnitude which rendered impossible such an exhibition of stoicism.

'Ah, Bill Oakshott,' said Lord Ickenham affably. 'You could not have arrived at a more opportune moment. You find me enjoying a well-earned gargle, like Caesar in his tent the day he overcame the Nervii. I stress the adjective "well-earned", for I think you will admit that in the recent exchanges I put it across the Nervii properly. Have you ever seen an ex-Governor so baffled? I haven't, and I doubt if anyone has. But you seem disturbed about something, and I would recommend some of this excellent beer. It will strengthen you and help you to look for the silver lining.'

He went to the counter, remained there a while in conversation with the stout blonde behind it, and returned bearing a foaming tankard.

'Nice girl,' he said paternally. 'I've been telling her about Brazil. Quaff that, Bill Oakshott, and having quaffed spill what is on your mind.'

Bill, who had been sitting with his head clasped in his hands, took a deep draught.

'It's about this business of your coming to the house as Plank.'

'Ah yes?'

'You can't go on with it.'

Lord Ickenham raised his eyebrows.

'Can't? A strange word to use to the last of a proud family. Did my ancestors say "Can't" on the stricken fields of the Middle Ages, when told off to go and fight the Paynim? As a matter of fact,' said Lord Ickenham confidentially, 'I believe lots of them did, as you can verify by turning up Richard Coeur de Lion's dispatches, so perhaps it is a pity that I asked the question. Why do you say I can't go on with it?'

'Because you jolly well can't. Shall I tell you what's happened?'

'Do. I'm all agog.'

Bill finished his tankard, and seemed to draw from it strength to continue.

'After you went away,' he said tonelessly, 'Uncle Aylmer drove off in the car, leaving me stuck there with the suitcase.'

'A low trick.'

'I yelled to him to stop and take the damned thing, because it weighed a ton and I didn't want to have to lug it all the way up the drive, but he wouldn't. And I was just starting off with it, when Potter came along on his bike.'

'Who is Potter?'

'The policeman.'

'Ah yes. Pongo spoke of him, I remember. A zealous officer.'

'So I said, "Oh, Potter" and he said, "Sir?" and I said, "You in a hurry?" and he said, "No, sir," and I said, "Then I wish you'd take this suitcase up to the house." And he said. "Certainly, sir," and hoisted it aboard his bike.'

'I like your dialogue,' said Lord Ickenham critically. 'It's crisp and good. Do you ever write?'

'No.'

'You should. You'd make a packet. But I'm interrupting you.'

'You are a bit.'

'It shall not occur again. You had got to where Potter said, "Certainly, sir." Then what?'

'I said, "It belongs to Major Brabazon-Plank. He's coming to stay." And Potter said . . . Could I have another beer?'

'Had he already had some beer?'

'I mean, could I have, now? I think it might pull me together.'

Lord Ickenham repeated his trip to the counter.

'You were saying,' he said, having returned with the life-giving fluid, 'that you told Potter that the suitcase belonged to Major Brabazon-Plank. In response to which?'

Bill drank deeply, gasped a little and spoke with a sort of frozen calm.

'In response to which he said, his bally face lighting up joyfully, "Major Brabazon-Plank? Did you say Major Brabazon-Plank? Coo, I know him well. He comes from my old village. Played cricket with him, I have – ah, hundreds of times. If conveni-ent, Mr William, I'll step up and shake him by the hand after I've had my tea." So now what?'

Lord Ickenham remained for a moment in thought.

'You're kidding me, Bill Oakshott. Nobody but a practised writer could have told that story so superbly. Beneath your magic touch Potter seems to live and breathe. You publish your stuff secretly under another name. I believe you're one, if not more, of the Sitwells. But we can go into that later. "So now what?" you say. Yes, I agree that the problem is one that presents certain features of interest, but all problems can be solved with a little earnest thought. How did you articulate when you spoke the words "Brabazon-Plank"? Distinctly?'

'Yes.'

'You didn't mumble?'

'No.'

'So you couldn't say that what you had really said was "Smith" or "Knatchbull-Huguessen"?'

'No.'

Lord Ickenham reflected.

'Well, then, what we must do is tell him that I am your Plank's brother.'

'Do you think you could get away with that?'

'There are no limits to what I can get away with when I am functioning properly. We might go and call upon him now. Where does he live?'

'Just round the corner.'

'Then finish up your beer and let's be off.'

Except for the royal arms over the door and a notice saying 'Police Station', there was nothing about the residence of Constable Potter to suggest there here was the dreadful headquarters of Law and Justice. Like so many police stations in English villages, it was a cheerful little cottage with a thatched roof and a nice little garden, the latter at the moment occupied by Mr Potter's nephew Basil, aged nine months, who was taking a nap in his perambulator. Lord Ickenham, reaching the garden gate, cocked an inquiring eye at this vehicle.

'Is Potter a married man?'

'No. That's his sister's baby. She lives with him. Her husband's a steward on one of the South American boats. He's away most of the time. Of course, he comes back sometimes.'

'Yes, one guesses that.'

Through an open window there came the sound of a female voice, high and penetrating. It was touching on the subject of socks. How, it was asking, did the invisible person it was addressing contrive to get so many and such large holes in his all the time? The voice itself attributed the phenomenon to carelessness and a wilful lack of consideration for those who had to work their fingers to the bone, darning them. Lord Ickenham consulted Bill with a raised eyebrow.

'Would that be the lady speaking now?'

'Yes.'

'To Potter?'

'I suppose so.'

'She seems to be giving him beans.'

'Yes. He's scared stiff of her, so Elsie tells me.'

'Elsie?'

'The housemaid.'

'Ah, yes, the one Pongo . . . I forget what I was going to say.'

'I know what you were going to say.'

'Well, well, we need not go into that now. Let us saunter in, and let our first move be to examine this bonny baby more closely. It will all be practice for the great day.'

VII

I

Inside the cottage, in the cosy little kitchen, Constable Potter, guardian of Ashenden Oakshott's peace, at his ease in his shirt sleeves, was enjoying high tea.

The word 'enjoying' is perhaps ill chosen, for he was partaking of the meal under the eye of his sister, Mrs Bella Stubbs, who, if not his best friend, had always been his severest critic. She had already told him not to put his elbows on the table, not to gollop his food like that and not to help himself to butter with his herringy knife, and at the moment when Bill and Lord Ickenham arrived had begun, as has been shown, to touch on the subject of his socks, one of which she held in her hand for purposes of demonstration.

Constable Potter was twenty-eight years old, his sister thirty-three. The simplest of mathematical calculations, therefore, will show that when he was seven she had been twelve, and a strong-willed sister of twelve can establish over a brother of seven a moral ascendancy which lasts a lifetime. In those formative years which mean so much, Harold Potter had been dragged about by the hand, slapped, scolded and told by the future mother of George Basil Percival Stubbs not to do practically everything he wanted to do. She had even – crowning indignity – blown his nose.

These things leave their mark. It was the opinion of Elsie Bean, repeatedly expressed, that her Harold was a cowardy custard; and in the main, one feels, the verdict of history will be that Elsie was right. It is unpleasant to think of an officer of the Law cowering in his chair when a woman puts a finger through a hole in one of his socks and waggles it, but it cannot be disputed that while watching Mrs Stubbs do this Constable Potter had come very near to cowering.

To ease the strain, he bent forward to help himself to butter, being careful this time to use the knife allotted to that purpose, and the movement enabled him to see through the window the corner of the garden where George Basil Percival was taking his siesta.

' 'Ullo,' he said, glad to change the subject. 'There's somebody on the lawn.'

'Never mind about the lawn. I'm talking about this sock.'

'It's a tall gentleman.'

'Look at it. Like a sieve.'

'A tall gentleman with a grey moustache. He's poking your Basil in the stomach.'

He had said the one thing calculated to divert his companion's thoughts from the sock topic. A devoted mother, Mrs Stubbs held the strongest possible views on the enormity of gentlemen, whether tall or short, coming into the garden and poking her offspring in the stomach at a moment when his well-being demanded uninterrupted repose.

'Then go and send him away!'

'Right ho.'

Constable Potter was full to the brim. He had eaten three kippered herrings, four boiled eggs and half a loaf of bread, and his impulse would have been to lean back in his chair like a gorged python and give his gastric juices a chance to fulfil themselves. But, apart from the fact that his sister Bella's word was law, curiosity overcame the urge to digest. Scrutinising

Lord Ickenham through the window, he had a sort of feeling that he had seen him before. He wanted to get a closer view of this mysterious stranger.

In the garden, when he reached it, Lord Ickenham, wearying of his attentions to Basil's stomach, had begun to tickle the child under the chin. Bill, who was not very fond of babies and in any case preferred them to look less like Edward G. Robinson, had moved aside as if anxious to disassociate himself from the whole unpleasant affair, and was thus the first to see the newcomer.

'Oh, hullo, Potter,' he said. 'We thought we'd look in.'

'I was anxious,' said Lord Ickenham, 'to make the acquaintance of one of whom I had heard so much.'

Constable Potter seemed a little dazed by these civilities.

'Ho!' he said. 'I didn't catch the name, sir.'

'Plank. Brabazon-Plank.'

There was a loud hiccough. It was Constable Potter registering astonishment; and more than astonishment, suspicion. There were few men, in Ashenden Oakshott at any rate, more gifted with the ability to recognise funny business when they were confronted with it, and here, it seemed to Harold Potter, was funny business in excelsis. He fixed on Lord Ickenham the stern and accusing gaze which he would have directed at a dog caught in the act of appearing in public without a collar.

'Brabazon-Plank?'

'Brabazon-Plank.'

'You're not the Major Brabazon-Plank I used to play cricket with at Lower Shagley in Dorsetshire.'

'His brother.'

'I didn't know he had a brother.'

'He kept things from you, did he? Too bad. Yes, I am his elder brother. Bill Oakshott was telling me you knew him.'

'He said you was him.'

'Surely not?'

'Yus, he did.' Constable Potter's gaze grew sterner. He was resolved to probe this thing to the bottom. 'He give me your suitcase to take to the house, and he said, "This here belongs to Major Brabazon-Plank."'

Lord Ickenham laughed amusedly.

'Just a slip of the tongue, such as so often occurs. He meant Brabazon-Plank, *major*. As opposed to my brother, who, being younger than me, is, of course, Brabazon-Plank, *minor*. I can understand you being confused,' said Lord Ickenham with a commiserating glance at the officer, into whose face had crept the boiled look of one who finds the conversation becoming too abstruse. Three kippers, four eggs and half a loaf of bread, while nourishing the body, take the keen edge off the mental powers. 'And what renders it all the more complex is that as I myself am a mining engineer by profession, anyone who wants to get straight on the Brabazon-Plank situation has got to keep steadily before him the fact that the minor is a major and the major a miner. I have known strong men to break down on realising this. So you know my minor, the major, do you? Most interesting. It's a small world, I often say. Well, when I say "often", perhaps once a fortnight. Why are you looking like a stuck pig, Bill Oakshott?'

Bill came with a start out of what appeared to be a sort of trance. Pongo, who had had so many opportunities of observing his Uncle Fred in action, could have told him that a trancelike condition was almost always the result of being associated with this good old man when he was going nicely.

'Was I?'

'Yes.'

'Sorry.'

'Don't mention it. Ah, whom have we here?'

Mrs Stubbs had made her appearance, coming towards them with a suggestion in her manner of a lioness hastening to the aid of an imperilled cub. Annoyed by her brother's tardiness in getting rid of these intruders, she had decided to take the matter in hand herself.

'Oh, hullo, Mrs Stubbs,' said Bill. 'We were just giving your baby the once over.'

Lord Ickenham started.

'Your baby? Is this remarkably fine infant yours, madam?'

His bearing was so courteous, his manner so reverent that Mrs Stubbs, who had come in like a lioness, began to envisage the possibility of going out like a lamb.

'Yes, sir,' she said, and went so far as to curtsy. She was not a woman who often curtsied, but there was something about this distinguished-looking elderly gentleman that seemed to call for the tribute. 'It's my little Basil.'

'A sweet name. And a sweet child. A starter I hope?'

'Sir?'

'You have entered him for the Bonny Baby contest at the fete?'

'Oh, yes, sir.'

'Good. Excellent. It would have been madness to hide his light under a bushel. Have you studied this outstanding infant closely, Bill Oakshott? If not, do so now,' said Lord Ickenham, 'for you will never have a better chance of observing a classic yearling. What hocks! What pasterns! And what lungs!' he continued, as George Basil Percival, waking, like Abou ben Adhem, from a deep dream of peace, split the welkin with a sudden howl. 'I always mark heavily for lungs. I should explain, madam, that I am to have the honour of acting as judge at the contest to which I have referred.'

'You are, sir?'

'I am, indeed. Is your husband at home? No? A pity. I would have advised him to pick up a bit of easy money by putting his shirt on this child for the Bonny Baby stakes. Have you a shirt, Mr Potter? Ah, I see you have. Well, slap it on the stable's entry and fear nothing. I have at present, of course, no acquaintance with local form, but I cannot imagine that there will be another competitor of such supreme quality as to nose him out. I see myself at the close of the proceedings raising Basil's hand in the air with the words "The winnah!" Well, Mrs Stubbs,' said Lord Ickenham, with a polished bow in the direction of his hostess and a kindly 'Kitchy-kitchy' to the coming champ, who was staring at him with what a more sensitive man would have considered offensive curiosity, 'we must be pushing along. We have much to do. Goodbye, Mrs Stubbs. Goodbye, baby. Goodbye, off——'

He paused, the word unspoken. Constable Potter had suddenly turned and was making for the cottage at a high rate of speed, and Lord Ickenham stared after him a little blankly.

'Gone without a cry!' he said. 'I suppose he forgot something.'

'His manners,' said Mrs Stubbs tartly. 'The idea!'

'Ah, well,' said Lord Ickenham, always inclined to take the tolerant view, 'what are manners, if the heart be of gold? Goodbye again, Mrs Stubbs. Goodbye, baby. As I say, we must be moving. May I repeat what a privilege it has been to get together with this superb child in what I may term his training quarters and urge you once more, with all the emphasis at my disposal, to put the family shirt on him for the big event. There could be no sounder investment. Goodbye,' said Lord Ickenham, 'goodbye, goodbye,' and took his departure, scattering sweetness and light in all directions.

Out in the road he paused to light a cigar.

'How absurdly simple these things are,' he said, 'when you have someone with elephantiasis of the brain, like myself, directing the operations. A few well-chosen words, and we baffle the constable just as we baffled Mugsy. Odd that he should have left us so abruptly. But perhaps he went in to spray his temples with *eau de Cologne*. I got the impression that he was cracking under the strain a little when I was dishing out that major and minor stuff.'

'How did you come to think of that?'

'Genius,' said Lord Ickenham modestly. 'Pure genius.'

'I wonder if he swallowed it.'

'I think so. I hope so.'

'You laid it on a bit thick about that ruddy baby.'

'Kind words are never wasted, Bill Oakshott. And now for Ashenden Manor, I think, don't you, and the warm English welcome.'

Bill seemed uncertain.

'Do you know, I believe I could do with some more beer.'

'You feel faint?'

'I do, rather.'

'All right, then, you push on to the pub. I must try to find Pongo. Would he be in the house?'

'No, I saw him going out.'

'Then I will scour the countryside for him. It is vital,' said Lord Ickenham, 'that I put him abreast of the position of affairs before he has an opportunity of spilling the beans. We don't want him charging in when I am chatting with Mugsy and calling me "Uncle Fred". Before we settle down to the quiet home evening to which I am looking forward so much, he must be informed that he is losing an uncle but gaining a Brazilian explorer. So for the moment, bung ho. Where was it

I told Mugsy that we would all meet? Ah, yes, at Philippi. See you there, then, when you have drunk your fill.'

2

In times of spiritual disturbance there is nothing like a brisk mystery thriller for taking the mind off its anxieties. Pongo's first move after parting from Sir Aylmer Bostock had been to go to his room and get his copy of *Murder in the Fog*; his second to seek some quiet spot outside the grounds, where there would be no danger of meeting the ex-Governor on his return, and soothe himself with a good read. He found such a spot at the side of the road not far from the Manor gates, and soon became absorbed.

The treatment proved almost immediately effective. That interview with Sir Aylmer in the hall had filled him with numbing fears and rendered him all of a twitter, but now he found his quivering ganglia getting back to mid-season form: and, unlike the heroine of the tale in which he was immersed, who had just got trapped in the underground den of one of those Faceless Fiends who cause so much annoyance, he was feeling quite tranquil, when a shadow fell on the page, a well-remembered voice spoke his name, and he looked up to see his Uncle Fred standing before him.

If there is one occasion more than another when joy might be expected to be unconfined and happiness to reign supreme, it is surely, one would say, when a nephew in the course of a country ramble encounters an uncle who in his time has often dandled him on his knee. At such a moment one would anticipate the quick indrawing of the breath, the raising of the eyes thankfully to heaven and the meeting of hand and hand in a fervent clasp.

It is unpleasant, therefore, to have to record that in Pongo's bosom, as he beheld Lord Ickenham, joy was not the predominating emotion. He could scarcely, indeed, have appeared more disconcerted if the Faceless Fiend from the volume in his hand had popped from its pages to confront him.

'Uncle Fred!' he ejaculated. The burned child fears the fire, and bitter experience had taught Pongo Twistleton to view with concern the presence in his midst of Ickenham's fifth Earl. One recalls the words, quoted in a previous chapter, of the thoughtful crumpet. 'Good Lord, Uncle Fred, what on earth are you doing here?'

Lord Ickenham, unlike Sir Aylmer Bostock, was a man who believed in breaking things gently. With a tale to unfold whose lightest word would harrow up his nephew's soul and make his two eyes, like stars, start from their spheres, he decided to hold it in for the time being and to work round gradually and by easy stages to what Pongo would have called the nub. With a gentle smile on his handsome face, he lowered himself to the ground and gave his moustache a twirl.

'Just pottering to and fro, my boy, just pottering to and fro. This road is open for being pottered in at this hour, I believe.'

'But I left you at Ickenham.'

'The parting was agony.'

'You told me you were going to London.'

'So I did.'

'You never said a word about coming here.'

'No, but you know how it is. Things happen. One's plans become modified.'

A passing ant paused to investigate Pongo's wrist. He flung it from him, and the ant, alighting on its head some yards to the sou'-sou'-east, went off to warn other ants to watch out for earthquakes.

'I might have known it,' he cried passionately. 'You're going to start something.'

'No, no.'

'Then what's up?'

Lord Ickenham considered the question.

'I don't know that I would go so far as to say that anything was actually *up*. The word is too strong. Certain complications have arisen, it is true, but nothing that cannot be adjusted by a couple of cool, calm men of the world who keep their heads. Let me begin at the beginning. I went to London and gave Sally dinner, and in the course of the meal she revealed why it was that she had wanted to see me so urgently. It seems that her brother Otis is in trouble again. She asked me to tell you all about it and endeavour to enlist your aid.'

As the story of Otis Painter and Sir Aylmer Bostock's Reminiscences unfolded itself, relief poured over Pongo in a healing wave. He blamed himself for having so readily fallen a prey to the agitation which the unexpected appearance of his Uncle Fred was so apt to occasion in him. Up to this point he had been standing. He now sat down with the air of a man who is at his ease. He even laughed, a thing which he was seldom able to do when in conference with his uncle.

'Rather funny,' he said.

'The matter is not without its humorous aspect,' Lord Ickenham agreed. 'But we must not forget that if the action goes through, Sally stands to lose a lot of money.'

'That's true. So she wants me to plead with the old boy and get him to settle the thing out of court. Well, I'll do what I can.'

'You speak doubtfully. Doesn't he love you like a son?'

'I wouldn't say absolutely like a son. You see, I broke one of his African curios.'

'You do break things, don't you? And this has rankled?'

'I fancy it has to some extent. When I met him in the hall just now, he gave me a nasty look and a couple of distinctly unpleasant "Ha!"'s. The slant I got was that he had been thinking me over and come to the conclusion that I was a bit of a louse. Still, he may come round.'

'Of course he will. You must persevere.'

'Oh, rather.'

'That's the spirit. Keep after him, exerting all your charm. Remember what it means to Sally.'

'Right ho. And is that really all you wanted to see me about?'

'I think so. Except . . . Now what else was it I wanted to see you about? . . . Ah, yes, I remember. That bust of Sally's. The one you borrowed from my place.'

'Oh, the old busto? Yes, of course. Well, everything went according to plan. I sneaked it in all right. A testing experience, though. If you knew what I went through, beetling across the hall with the thing in my possession, expecting every moment to feel old Bostock's hot breath on the back of my neck!'

'I can readily imagine it. I wonder,' said Lord Ickenham, 'if you know how these busts are made? Sally has been explaining it to me. It is a most interesting process. You first model the clay. Then you slap on it a coat of liquid plaster.'

'Oh, yes?'

'After that you wait a little while until the plaster becomes fairly hard, when you divide it into two neat halves and throw away the clay. You then fill the mould with plaster.'

'Very jolly, if you like that sort of thing,' said Pongo tolerantly. 'How was Sally looking?'

'At first, radiant. Later, somewhat perturbed.'

'About Otis, you mean?'

'About Otis – and other things. But let me finish telling you about the way busts are made. You fill the mould with plaster, leaving a small empty space at the top. This,' said Lord Ickenham, feeling that he had now broken the thing sufficiently gently, 'you utilise as a repository for any jewels that any friend of yours may wish to smuggle into the United States.'

'What!' Pongo shot up in a whirl of arms and legs. Another ant, which climbed on to his wrist in a rather sceptical spirit, took as impressive a toss as its predecessor had done, and might have been observed some moments later rubbing its head and telling a circle of friends that old George had been right when he had spoken of seismic disturbances. 'You don't mean –?'

'Yes. Inadvertently, intending no harm, we appear to have got away with the bust in which Sally had cached her friend Alice Vansittart's bit of stuff. The idea came to her, apparently, shortly after you had refused to help her out. It seems a pity now that you were not more amenable. Of course, as Hamlet very sensibly remarked, there's nothing either good or bad but thinking makes it so; still, a rather sticky situation has unquestionably been precipitated. The Vansittart sails for New York next week.'

'Oh, my gosh!'

'You see the drama of the thing? I thought you would. Well, there it is. You will agree with me, I think, that we are in honour bound to return these trinkets. Can't go snitching a poor girl's little bit of jewellery. Not done. Not cricket.'

Pongo nodded. Nobody could teach him anything about *noblesse oblige*. He shrank from repeating the dreadful performance to which he had forced himself on his arrival at the house, but he quite saw that it had to be done.

'That's right,' he said. 'I'll have to nip over to Ickenham and get another bust. Will Coggs be able to dig me out one?'

'No,' said Lord Ickenham. 'And if he could, it would not be

any good. Another complication has occurred, which I must now relate to you. You remember the bust Sally did of Sir Aylmer, the one that was to have been presented to the village club, poor devils. Piqued at the result of this Otis business, he returned it to her, and I brought her down here this afternoon in my car and she crept into the house and substituted it for the one with Miss Vansittart's jewels in it. And just as she was getting away with the latter, Lady Bostock intercepted her, took it away from her and locked it up in a cupboard in the room where the African curios are. And there it now is. So—'

Pongo interrupted, speaking quickly and forcefully. There are limits to what *noblesse* obliges.

'I know what you're going to say,' he cried. 'You want me to sneak down in the middle of the night and break open the cupboard and pinch it. Well, I'm jolly well not going to do it.'

'No, no,' said Lord Ickenham. 'Calm yourself, my dear boy. I would not dream of burdening you with such a responsibility. I will do the pinching.'

'You?'

'In person.'

'But you can't get into the house.'

'I wish people wouldn't tell me I can't do things. It is all going to be perfectly simple. My young friend, Bill Oakshott, has invited me to stay at Ashenden Manor. He wants me to judge the Bonny Babies contest at a fete they are having here shortly. Why his choice fell upon me, one cannot say. I suppose he knew I was good. These things get about.'

Pongo gazed up at the reeling sky and sent his haggard eyes roaming over a countryside that had broken into a sort of Ouled Nail muscle dance. His face was drawn, and his limbs twitched. Lord Ickenham, watching him, received the impression that he did not like the idea of his, Lord Ickenham's, approaching visit to Ashenden Manor.

'You're coming to the house?' he gasped.

'I go into residence this evening. And, by the way,' said Lord Ickenham, 'another small point. I nearly forgot to mention it. My name during my visit will be Brabazon-Plank. Major Brabazon-Plank, the well-known Brazilian explorer. Don't forget it, will you.'

From between Pongo's hands, which he had clasped on either side of his head, as if to prevent it dividing itself into two neat halves like a plaster bust, there proceeded a low moaning sound. Lord Ickenham regarded him sympathetically and, in an endeavour to relieve the situation of some of its tenseness, began to chant in a pleasant baritone an old song hit of his youth. And he was interested some moments later to find that this, starting as a solo, seemed suddenly to have turned into a duet. Glancing over his shoulder, he perceived the reason. Constable Potter was riding up on his bicycle, shouting 'Hoy!'

3

Lord Ickenham was always the soul of courtesy. You had only to shout 'Hoy!' at him from a bicycle to have him drop everything and give you his immediate attention.

'Ah, officer,' he said. 'You crave an audience?'

Constable Potter dismounted, and stood for a space bent over the handlebars, puffing. His sharp ride, taken at a moment when he was loaded down above the Plimsoll mark with eggs, bread, tea and kippered herrings, had left him short of breath. Lord Ickenham, in his considerate way, begged him to take his time.

Presently the puffing ceased, and Harold Potter spoke.

'Ho!' he said.

'Ho to you,' replied Lord Ickenham civilly. 'Have a cigar?'

With an austere gesture Constable Potter declined the cigar. A conscientious policeman does not accept gifts at the hands of the dregs of the criminal world, and such he now knew this man before him to be.

Ever since that odd episode in the garden, the reader of this record, the chronicler is aware, has been in a fever of impatience to learn what it was that sent this splendid upholder of law and order shooting into his cottage with such curious abruptness. This can now be revealed. The social lapse which had caused Mrs Bella Stubbs to purse her lips and comment acidly on his lack of manners had been occasioned by the fact that he had got the goods on Lord Ickenham. He had remembered where he had seen him before, and he had hurried indoors to consult his scrap album and ascertain his name. Having ascertained his name, he had mounted his bicycle and ridden off to confront and denounce him.

He fixed Lord Ickenham with a gimlet-like eye.

'Brabazon-Plank!' he said.

'Why,' asked Lord Ickenham, 'do you say "Brabazon-Plank" in that strange tone, as if it were some kind of expletive?'

'Ho!'

'Now we're back where we started. This is where we came in.'

Constable Potter decided that the time had come to explode his bombshell. On his face was that hard, keen look which comes into the faces of policemen when they intend to do their duty pitilessly and crush a criminal like a snake beneath the heel. It was the look which Constable Potter's face wore when he was waiting beneath a tree to apprehend a small boy who was up in its branches stealing apples, the merciless expression that turned it to flint when he called at a house to serve a summons on somebody for moving pigs without a permit.

'Brabazon-Plank, eh? You call yourself Brabazon-Plank, do you? Ho! You look to me more like George Robinson of 14, Nasturtium Road, East Dulwich.'

Lord Ickenham stared. He removed the cigar from his mouth and stared again.

'Don't tell me you're the cop who pinched me that day at the dog races!'

'Yus, I am.'

A bubbling cry like that of some strong swimmer in his agony proceeded from Pongo's lips. He glared wildly at the helmeted figure of doom. Lord Ickenham, in sharp contradistinction, merely beamed, like one of a pair of lovers who have met at journey's end.

'Well, I'll be dashed,' he said cordially. 'What a really remarkable thing. Fancy running into you again like this. I'd never have known you. You've grown a moustache since then, or something. My dear fellow, this is delightful. What are you doing in these parts?'

There was no answering cordiality in Harold Potter's manner as he intensified the gimlet quality of his gaze. He was taut and alert, as became an officer who, after a jog-trot existence of Saturday drunks and failures to abate smoky chimneys, finds himself faced for the first time with crime on a colossal scale.

For that this was the real big stuff he had no doubt whatsoever. All the evidence went, as he himself would have said, to establish it. On the previous afternoon that shambling miscreant, Edwin Smith, had insinuated himself into Ashenden Manor under the alias of Twistleton. This evening along came his sinister associate, George Robinson, under the alias of Brabazon-Plank. And here they were together by the roadside, plotting. If you could not call this the Muster of the Vultures, it would be interesting, Harold Potter felt, to know what set of circumstances did qualify for that description.

'What are *you* doing in these parts, is more like it,' he retorted. 'You and your pal Edwin Smith there.'

'So you've recognised him, too? You have an extraordinary memory for faces. Like the royal family. What are we doing in these parts, you ask? Just paying a country-house visit.'

'Oh, yes?'

'I assure you.'

'You think you are,' corrected Constable Potter. 'But a fat lot of country-house visiting you're going to do.'

Lord Ickenham raised his eyebrows.

'Pongo.'

'Guk?'

'I think the gentleman intends to unmask us.'

'Guk.'

'Do you intend to unmask us, Mr Potter?'

'Yus.'

'I wouldn't.'

'Ho!'

There was infinite kindliness in Lord Ickenham's voice as he went on to explain himself. You could see that he felt the deepest sympathy for Constable Potter.

'No, honestly I wouldn't. Consider what will happen. I shall be ejected—'

'You're right, you'll be ejected!'

'—And my place as judge of the Bonny Babies contest taken by another judge, less prejudiced in favour of your sister's little Basil. The child will finish among the also-rans, and in this event will not your sister make inquiries? And having made them and ascertained that it was through your agency that I was disqualified, will she not have a word or two to say to you on the subject? Think it over, my dear chap, and I fancy you will agree with me that the conditions for unmasking are none too good.'

It sometimes happens to a policeman that he is sharply censured by a bench of magistrates. When this occurs, he feels as if he had been kicked in the stomach by a mule and the world becomes black. The effect of these words on Constable Potter was to give him the illusion that he had been censured by half a dozen benches of magistrates, all speaking at once. His jaw drooped like a lily, and in a low voice, instinct with emotion, he uttered the word 'Coo!'

'You may well say "Coo!" ' agreed Lord Ickenham. 'I know Mrs Stubbs only slightly, of course, but she struck me as a woman of high spirit, the last person to mince her words to the man instrumental in robbing her child of the coveted trophy. Potter, I would think twice.'

Constable Potter only needed to think once. For a long instant there was a silence, one of those heavy silences which seem to be made of glue. Then, still without speaking, he mounted his bicycle and rode off.

Lord Ickenham was a fighter who could always be generous to a beaten foe.

'Amazingly fine stuff there is in our policemen,' he said. 'You crush them to earth, and they rise again. You think you've baffled them, and up they pop, their helmets still in the ring. However, this time I fancy the trick has been done. There, in my opinion, pedalled a policeman whose lips are sealed.'

Pongo, always prone to the gloomy view, demurred.

'How do you know? He was heading for the house. He's probably gone off to tell old Bostock the whole story.'

133

'You say that because you do not know his sister. No, no. Sealed lips, my dear Pongo, sealed lips. You have now nothing whatever to worry about.'

Pongo uttered a mirthless laugh of a quality which would have extorted the admiration of Bill Oakshott, a specialist in that line.

'Nothing to worry about? Ha! With you coming to stay with Hermione's people under a – what's the word –'

'Pseudonym?'

'Pseudonym. And planning to prowl about busting open cupboards!'

'Don't let that trivial matter give you the slightest anxiety, my dear boy. I shall attend to that tonight, and then we can all settle down and enjoy ourselves.'

'Tonight?'

'Yes. I phoned Sally from the inn, and everything is arranged. She will drive over in my car and be waiting in the garden outside the collection room at one ack emma. I shall secure the bust and hand it to her, and she will drive off with it. As simple as that.'

'Simple!'

'What can go wrong?'

'A million things. Suppose you're caught.'

'I am never caught. They know me in the Underworld as The Shadow. I wish I could cure you of this extraordinary tendency of yours always to look on the dark side.'

'Well, what other sides are there?' said Pongo.

4

The dinner hour was approaching. In her room, Lady Bostock had finished dressing and was regarding herself in the mirror, wishing, not for the first time, that she looked less like a horse. It was not that she had anything specific against horses; she just wished she did not look like one.

Footsteps sounded outside the door. Sir Aylmer entered. There was a heavy frown on his face, and it was plain that something had occurred to disturb his always easily disturbed equanimity.

'Emily!'

'Yes, dear?'

'I've just been talking to Potter.'

'Yes, dear?'

'Damn fool!'

'Why, dear?'

Sir Aylmer picked up a hairbrush, and swished it. There was a wealth of irritation in the movement.

'Do you remember,' he asked, 'the time I played Dick Dead-eye in Pinafore at that amateur performance in aid of the Lower Barnatoland Widows and Orphans?'

'Yes, dear. You were splendid.'

'Do you remember the scene where Dick Deadeye goes to the captain to warn him his daughter is going to elope, and won't come out with anything definite?'

'Yes, dear. You were wonderful in that scene.'

'Well, Potter was like that. Mystic.'

'Mystic?'

'It's the only word. Kept hinting that I must be on my guard, but wouldn't say why. I tried to pin him down, but it was no use. It was as if his lips had been sealed. All I could get out of him was that he thought danger threatened us, probably to-night. What are you wriggling like that for?'

Lady Bostock had not wriggled, she had shuddered.

'Danger?' she faltered. 'What did he mean?'

'How the dickens should I know what he meant, when every time he started to say anything he stopped as if somebody had clapped a hand over his mouth? I believe the man's half-witted. But he did go so far as to advise me to be on the alert, and said that he was going to lurk in the garden and watch the house carefully.'

'Aylmer!'

'I wish you wouldn't bellow "Aylmer" like that. You've made me bite my tongue.'

'But, Aylmer—'

'Thinking it over, I have come to the conclusion that he must have found out something further about this impostor who calls himself Twistleton, but why he couldn't say so is more than I can imagine. Well, if this so-called Twistleton is planning to make any sort of move tonight, I shall be ready for him.'

'Ready?'

'Ready.'

'What are you going to do?'

'Never mind,' said Sir Aylmer, rather inconsistently for one who had reproached Constable Potter for being mystic. 'My plans are all perfected. I shall be ready.'

PART THREE

VIII

The quiet home evening to which Lord Ickenham had so looked forward had drawn to a close. Curfews had tolled the knell of parting day, lowing herds wound slowly o'er the lea. Now slept the crimson petal and the white, and in the silent garden of Ashenden Manor nothing stirred save shy creatures of the night such as owls, mice, rats, gnats, bats and Constable Potter. Down in the village the clock on the church tower, which a quarter of an hour ago had struck twelve, chimed a single chime, informing Pongo, pacing the floor of his bedroom overlooking the terrace, that in just forty-five minutes the balloon was due to go up.

As Pongo paced the floor, from time to time quivering all over like a Brazilian explorer with a touch of malaria, he was still in faultless evening dress, for the idea of going to bed on this night of fear had not even occurred to him. A young man visiting the parents of the girl he loves, and knowing that at one sharp an uncle of the maximum eccentricity will be starting to burgle the house, does not hop between the sheets at eleven-fifteen and sink into a dreamless sleep. He stays up and shudders. Pongo had made one or two attempts to divert his thoughts by reading *Murder in the Fog,* but without success. There are moments when even the most faceless of fiends cannot hope to grip.

In a past the contemplation of which sometimes affected

him as if he had bitten into a bad oyster, Pongo Twistleton had frequently been called upon to tremble like an aspen when an unwilling participant in the activities of his Uncle Fred, but seldom had he done it more wholeheartedly than now. He was feeling rather as the heroine of *Murder in the Fog* was wont to do when she got trapped in underground dens, the illusion that his nerves were sticking two inches out of his body and curling at the ends being extraordinarily vivid. And it is probable that mental distress would have unstrung him completely, but for the fact that in addition to suffering agony of the soul he was also in the process of dying of thirst, and this seemed to act on the counter-irritation principle.

The thirst of which he was dying was one of those lively young thirsts which seem to start at the soles of the feet and get worse all the way up. Growing in intensity ever since his arrival at the house, it had reached its peak at eleven o'clock tonight, when Jane, the parlourmaid, had brought the bedtime decanter and syphon into the drawing room. He was no weakling, but having to sit there watching his host, his uncle and Bill Oakshott getting theirs like so many stags at eve – he himself, in deference to his known prejudice against alcoholic liquor, having been served with barley water – had tested his iron control almost beyond endurance.

For some minutes he continued to pace the floor, cursing the mad impulse which had led him to tell Hermione that he never touched the stuff and sketching out in his mind the series of long, cool ones with which, if he ever got out of here alive, he would correct this thirst of his. And then, as he reached the end of the carpet and was about to turn and pace back again, he stopped abruptly with one foot in the air, looking so like *The Soul's Awakening* that a seasoned art critic would have been deceived. Two chimes had just sounded from the church tower, and it was as if they had been the voice of a kindly friend whispering in his ear.

'Aren't you,' they seemed to say, 'overlooking the fact that that decanter is still in the drawing room? One merely throws this out as a suggestion.' And he saw that here was the solution of what had appeared to be an impasse. His guardian angel, for he presumed it was his guardian angel, had pointed out the way. Hats off to the good old guardian angel, was Pongo's attitude.

A minute later he was in the corridor. Three minutes later he was in the drawing room. Three and a quarter minutes later he was pouring with trembling fingers what promised to be the snifter of a lifetime. And four minutes later, reclining in an armchair with his feet on a small table, he had begun to experience that joy, than which there is none purer, which comes to the unwilling abstainer who has at last succeeded in assembling the materials, when from immediately behind him a voice spoke.

All the voice actually said was 'Coo!' but it was enough. Indeed, in the circumstances, a mere clearing of the throat would have been sufficient. His knotted and combined locks parted, each particular hair standing on end like quills upon the fretful porcupine: his heart broke from its moorings and crashed with a dull thud against his front teeth: and with a wordless cry he shot toward the ceiling.

It was only some moments later, after he had hit the ceiling twice and was starting to descend to terra firma, that the mists cleared from his eyes and he was able to perceive that the intruder was not, as he had supposed, Sir Aylmer Bostock, but Elsie Bean, his old playmate of the rude sling days. She was standing by the door with a hand to her heart, panting a little, as housemaids will when they enter drawing rooms at twenty minutes to one in the morning and find them occupied by the ruling classes.

The relief was stupendous. Pongo's equanimity returned, and with it a warm gush of the milk of human kindness. To a man who had been anticipating an embarrassing interview with Sir Aylmer Bostock in his dressing gown Elsie Bean was like something the doctor had ordered. He had no objection whatever to Elsie Bean joining him, quite the reverse. A chat with one of the finest minds in Bottleton East was just what he was in the mood for. He beamed on the girl, and having released his tongue, which had got entangled with his uvula, spoke in a genial and welcoming voice.

'What ho, Bean.'

'What ho, sir.'

'It's you, is it?'

'Yes, sir.'

'You gave me a start.'

'You gave *me* a start, sir.'

'Making two starts in all,' said Pongo, who had taken mathematics at school. 'You must forgive me for seeming a little perturbed for a moment. I thought you were mine host. Thank God you weren't. Do you remember in your inimitable way describing him as an overbearing dishpot? You were right. A dishpot he is, and a dishpot he always will be, and to hell with all dishpots is my view. Well, come along in, young Bean, and tell me your news. How's the Harold situation developing? Any change on the Potter front?'

Elsie Bean's face clouded. She tossed her head, plainly stirred.

'Harold's a mess,' she said, with the frankness which comes naturally to those reared in the bracing air of Bottleton East. 'He's an obstinate, pig-headed, fat-headed, flat-footed copper. I've no patience.'

'He still refuses to send in his papers?'

'R.'

A pang of pity shot through Pongo. Nothing that he had seen of Constable Potter had tended to build up in his mind the picture of a sort of demon lover for whom women might excusably go wailing through the woods, but he knew that his little friend was deeply attached to this uniformed perisher and his heart bled for her. He was broad-minded enough to be able to appreciate that if you are enamoured of a fat-headed copper and obstacles crop up in the way of your union with him, you mourn just as much as if he were Gregory Peck or Clark Gable.

'He came round tonight after supper, and we talked for an hour and a half, but nothing I could say would move him.'

'No dice, eh? Too bad.'

'It's that sister of his. She won't let him call his soul his own. I don't know what's to come of it, I'm sure.'

A pearly tear appeared at the corner of Elsie Bean's eye, and she sniffed in an overwrought way. Pongo patted her head. It was the least a man of sensibility could do.

'I wouldn't despair,' he said. 'These things seem sticky at the moment, but they generally iron out straight in the end. Give him time, and you'll find he'll be guided by the voice of love.'

Elsie Bean, having sniffed again, became calmer. There was good stuff in this girl.

'What would guide him a lot better,' she said, 'would be being bopped on the nose.'

'Bopped on the nose?'

'R.'

Of the broad, general principle of bopping Constable Potter on the nose Pongo was, of course, a warm adherent. It was a thing that he felt should be done early and often. But he was unable to see how it could pay dividends in the present circumstances.

'I don't quite follow.'

'That would knock some sense into him. Harold's nervous.'

'Nervous?' said Pongo incredulously. He had detected no such basic weakness in the flatty under advisement. A man of iron, he would have said.

'That's why he got himself shifted to the country from London, where he used to be. He found it too hot being a rozzer in London. He had some unpleasant experiences with blokes giving him shiners when he was pinching them, and it shook him. He come here for peace and quiet. So if he found it was too hot being a rozzer here as well, he wouldn't want to be a rozzer anywhere. He'd give his month's notice, and we'd all be happy.'

Pongo saw her point. He could scarcely have done otherwise, for it had been admirably put.

'True,' he said. 'You speak sooth, Bean.'

'If only someone would bop him on the nose, he wouldn't hesitate, not for a moment. *You* wouldn't bop him on the nose, would you?'

'No, I would not bop him on the nose.'

'Or squash in his helmet when he wasn't looking?'

Pongo was sorry for the idealistic girl, but he felt it due to himself to discourage this line of thought from the outset.

'A man like Harold is always looking,' he said. 'No, I wish you luck, young Bean, and I shall follow your future career with considerable interest, but don't count on me for anything more than heartfelt sympathy. Still, I fully concur in your view that what you require is an up-and-coming ally, who will drive home to Harold the risks of the profession, thus causing him to see the light, and I strongly recommend featuring your brother Bert in the part. It's a pity he doesn't come out till September. What's he in for?'

'Resisting of the police in the execution of their duty. He sloshed a slop on the napper with a blunt instrument.'

'There you are, then. The People's Choice. Tails up, my dear old housemaid. Provided, of course, that his sojourn in the coop has not weakened Bert as a force, you should be hearing the warbling of the blue bird by early October at the latest. Meanwhile, switching lightly to another topic, what on earth are you doing here at this time of night?'

'I came to get some whisky.'

All the host in Pongo sprang to life. He blushed for his remissness.

'I'm frightfully sorry,' he said, reaching for the decanter. 'Ought to have offered you a spot ages ago. Can't imagine what I was thinking of.'

'For Harold,' Elsie Bean explained. 'He's lurking in the garden. He chucked a stone at my window, and when I popped my head out he asked me in a hoarse whisper to bring him a drop of something. And I remembered Jane always took the whisky in here last thing before bed. Lurking in the garden!' she proceeded with bitterness. 'What's he lurking in gardens for? Doing some sort of copper's job, I suppose. If he'd give up being a copper, he could stay in bed like other folks. I've no patience.'

She sniffed, and Pongo, fearing another pearly tear, hastened to apply first aid.

'There, there,' he said. 'You mustn't let it get you down. Right will prevail. Have a cigarette?'

'Thanks.'

'Turkish this side, Virginian that,' said Pongo.

He had taken one himself a few moments before, and he

proceeded now to light hers from his own. And it was while their faces were in the close juxtaposition necessitated by this process that Bill Oakshott entered the room.

Whether one is justified in describing Bill Oakshott and Pongo Twistleton as great minds is perhaps a question open to debate. But they had exhibited tonight the quality which is supposed to be characteristic of great minds, that of thinking alike. Pongo, yearning for a snootful, had suddenly remembered the decanter in the drawing room, and so had Bill.

Ever since his meeting that afternoon with Lord Ickenham, Bill Oakshott's emotions had been rather similar to those which he would have experienced, had he in the course of a country walk discovered that his coat tails had become attached to the rear end of the Scotch express en route from London to Edinburgh. Like most of those who found themselves associated with the effervescent peer when he was off the chain and starting to go places, he was conscious of a feeling of breathlessness, shot through with a lively apprehension as to what was coming next. This had induced sleeplessness. Sleeplessness had induced thirst. And with thirst had come the recollection of the decanter in the drawing room.

With Bill, as with Pongo, to think was to act, and only in a minor detail of technique had their procedure differed. Pongo, not knowing whether the bally things creaked or not, had descended the stairs mincingly, like Agag, while Bill, more familiar with the terrain, had taken them three at a time, like a buffalo making for a water hole. He arrived, accordingly, somewhat touched in the wind, and the affectionate scene that met his eyes as he crossed the threshold took away what remained of his breath completely. Elsie Bean, entering the room, had said, 'Coo!' Bill for the moment was unable to utter at all. He merely stood and goggled, shocked to the core.

The theory which Lord Ickenham had advanced in extenuation of Pongo's recent kissing of this girl whose nose he was now so nearly touching with his own had not satisfied Bill Oakshott. It might have been, as the kindly peer had said, a mere mannerism, but Bill thought not. The impression he had received on the previous afternoon had been of a licentious clubman operating on all twelve cylinders, and that was the impression he received now. And at the thought that it was in the hands of an all-in Lothario like this that Hermione Bostock had placed her life's happiness his sensitive soul quivered like a jelly. The outlook, to Bill's mind, was bad.

Pongo was the first to break an awkward silence.

'Oh, hullo,' he said.

'Oh, hullo, sir,' said Elsie Bean.

'Oh, hullo,' said Bill.

His manner, as he spoke, was distrait. He was trying to decide whether the fact of Pongo not being, as he had at one time supposed, off his onion improved the general aspect of affairs or merely rendered it darker and sadder. It was plain now that Elsie Bean had been mistaken on the previous day when she had asserted that the other had said, 'Coo! I think I'll go to London,' and had driven thither. He had merely, it appeared, taken a short spin somewhere in his Buffy-Porson, which was quite a reasonable thing to do on a fine afternoon. But was this good or bad? Bill had said in his haste that loony libertines are worse than sane ones, but now he was not so sure. It might be a close thing, but were you not entitled to shudder even more strongly at a libertine who was responsible for his actions than at one who was not?

On one point, however, his mind was clear. It was his intention, as soon as they were alone together, to buttonhole this squire of dames and talk to him like an elder brother – as, for instance, one could imagine Brabazon-Plank *major* talking to Brabazon-Plank *minor*.

The opportunity of doing this came earlier than those familiar with Elsie Bean and her regrettable tendency to be a mixer would have anticipated. It is true that all her instincts urged the gregarious little soul to stick around and get the conversation going, but though sometimes failing to see eye to eye with Emily Post she was not without a certain rudimentary regard for the proprieties, and her social sense told her that this would not be the done thing. When a housemaid in curling pins and a kimono finds herself in a drawing room at one in the morning with her employer and a male guest, she should as soon as possible make a decorous exit. This is in Chapter One of all the etiquette books.

So with a courteous 'Well, good night, all,' she now withdrew. And it was not very long after the door had closed that Pongo, who had become conscious of a feeling of uneasiness, as if he were sitting in a draught, was able to perceive what it was that was causing this. He was being looked at askance.

The rather delicate enterprise of looking askance at an old boyhood friend is one that different men embark on in different ways. Bill's method – for while he was solid on the point that it was about time that a fearless critic came along and pointed out to Pongo some of the aspects in which his behaviour deviated from the ideal, he found it difficult to overcome his natural shyness – was to turn bright vermilion and allow his eyes to protrude like a snail's. He also cleared his throat three times.

Finally he spoke.

'Pongo.'

'Hullo?'

Bill cleared his throat again.

'Pongo.'

'On the spot.'

Bill took a turn up and down the room. It was not easy to think of a good opening sentence, and when you are talking like an elder brother to libertines the opening sentence is extremely important, if not vital. He cleared his throat once more.

'Pongo.'

'Still here, old man.'

Bill cleared his throat for the fifth time, and having replied rather testily in the negative to Pongo's query as to whether he had swallowed a gnat or something, resumed his pacing. This brought his shin into collision with a small chair which was lurking in the shadows, and the sharp agony enabled him to overcome his diffidence.

'Pongo,' he said, and his voice was crisp and firm, 'I haven't mentioned it before, because the subject didn't seem to come up somehow, but when I returned from Brazil the day before yesterday, I was told that you were engaged to my cousin Hermione.'

'That's right.'

'Congratulations.'

'Thanks.'

'I hope you will be very happy.'

'You betcher.'

'And I hope – here's the nub – that you will make *her* happy.'

'Oh, rather.'

'Well, will you? You say you will, but I'm dashed if I see how it's going to be done, if you spend your time hobnobbing with housemaids.'

'Eh?'

'You heard.'

'Hobnobbing with housemaids?'

'Hobnobbing with housemaids.'

The charge was one which few men would have been able to hear unmoved. Its effect on Pongo was to make him mix himself another whisky and soda. Grasping this, like King Arthur brandishing his sword Excalibur, he confronted his accuser intrepidly and began a spirited speech for the defence.

It was inaccurate, he pointed out, to say that he spent his whole time hobnobbing with housemaids. Indeed, he doubted if he could justly be said to hobnob with them at all. It all depended on what you meant by the expression. To offer a housemaid a cigarette is not hobbing. Nor, when you light it for her, does that constitute nobbing. If you happen – by the merest chance – to be in a drawing room at one in the morning with a housemaid, you naturally do the civil thing, behaving like a well-bred English gentleman and putting her at her ease.

You chat. You pass the time of day. You offer her a gasper. And when she has got her hooks on it, you light it for her. That, at least, was Pongo's creed, and he believed it would have been the creed of Sir Galahad and the Chevalier Bayard, if he had got the name correctly, neither of whom had to the best of his knowledge ever been called hobnobbers. He concluded by saying that it was a pity that some people, whose identity he did not specify, had minds like sinks and, by the most fortunate of chances remembering a good one at just the right moment, added that to the pure all things were pure.

It was a powerful harangue, and it is not surprising that for an instant Bill Oakshott seemed to falter before it, like some sturdy oak swayed by the storm. But by dint of thinking of the righteousness of his cause and clearing his throat again, he recovered the quiet strength which had marked his manner at the outset.

'All that,' he said coldly, 'would go a lot stronger with me, if I hadn't seen you kissing Elsie Bean yesterday.'

Pongo stared.

'Kissing Elsie Bean?'

'Kissing Elsie Bean.'

'I never kissed Elsie Bean.'

'Yes, you did kiss Elsie Bean. On the front steps.'

Pongo clapped a hand to his forehead.

'Good Lord, yes, so I did. Yes, you're perfectly right. I did, didn't I? It all comes back to me. But only like a brother.'

'Like a brother, my foot.'

'Like a brother,' insisted Pongo, as if he had spent his whole life watching brothers kiss housemaids. 'And if you knew the circumstances—'

Bill raised a hand. He was in no mood to listen to any tale of diseased motives. He drew a step nearer and stared bleakly at Pongo, as if the latter had been an alligator of the Brazilian swamps whom he was endeavouring to quell with the power of the human eye.

'Twistleton!'

'I wish you wouldn't call me Twistleton.'

'I will call you Twistleton, blast you. And this is what I want to say to you, Twistleton, by way of a friendly warning which you will do well to bear in mind, if you don't want your head pulled off at the roots and your insides ripped from your body—'

'My dear chap!'

'—With my naked hands. Cut it out.'

'Cut what out?'

'You know what. This Don Juan stuff. This butterfly stuff. This way you've got of flitting from flower to flower and sipping. Lay off it, Twistleton. Give it a miss. Curb that impulse. Kiss fewer housemaids. Try to remember that you are engaged to be married to a sweet girl who loves and trusts you.'

'But—'

Pongo, about to speak, paused. Bill had raised his hand again.

The gesture of raising the hand is one which is generally more effective in costume dramas, where it always suffices to quell the fiercest crowd, than in real life: and what made it so potent now was probably the size of the hand. To Pongo's excited imagination it seemed as large as a ham, and he could not overlook the fact that it was in perfect proportion with the rest of his companion's huge body; a body which even the most casual eye would have recognised as being composed mostly of rippling muscle. Taking all this into consideration, he decided to remain silent, and Bill proceeded.

'I suppose you're wondering what business it is of mine?'

'No, no. Any time you're passing—'

'Well, I'll tell you,' said Bill, departing from a lifetime's habit of reticence. 'I've loved Hermione myself for years and years.'

'No, really?'

'Yes. Years and years and years. I've never mentioned it to her.'

'No?'

'No. So she knows nothing about it.'

'Quite. She wouldn't, would she?'

'And loving her like this I feel that it is my job to watch over her like a—'

'Governess?'

'Not governess. Elder brother. To watch over her like an elder brother and protect her and see that no smooth bird comes along and treats her as the plaything of an idle hour.'

This surprised Pongo. The idea of anyone treating Hermione Bostock as the plaything of an idle hour was new to him.

'But –' he began again, and once more Bill raised his hand, bigger and better than ever. In a dreamlike way, Pongo found himself wondering what size he took in gloves.

'As the plaything of an idle hour,' repeated Bill. 'I don't object to her marrying another man—'

'Broad-minded.'

'At least, I do – it's agony – but what I mean is, it's up to her, and if she feels like marrying another man, right ho! So long as it makes her happy. All I want is her happiness.'

'Very creditable.'

'But get this, Twistleton,' continued Bill, and Pongo, meeting his eye, was reminded of that of the headmaster of his private school, with whom some fifteen years previously he had had a painful interview arising from his practice of bringing white mice into the classroom. 'This is what I want to drive into your nut. If I found that that other man was playing fast and loose with her, two-timing her, Twistleton, breaking her gentle heart by going and whooping it up round the corner, I would strangle him like a—'

He paused, snapping his fingers.

'Dog?' said Pongo, to help him out.

'No, not dog, you silly ass. Who the dickens strangles dogs? Like a foul snake.'

Pongo might have argued, had he felt like going into the thing, that the number of people who strangle foul snakes must be very limited, but he did not feel like going into the thing. In a sort of coma he watched his companion look askance at him again, stride to the table, mix himself a medium-strong whisky and soda, drain it and stride to the door. It closed, and he was alone.

And he was just beginning to lose that stunned sensation of having been beaten over the head with something hard and solid which must have come to the policeman whom Elsie Bean's brother Bert had sloshed on the napper with a blunt instrument, when from across the hall, from the direction of the room where Sir Aylmer Bostock kept his collection of African curios, there proceeded an agonised cry, followed by the sound of voices.

Pongo, crouched in his armchair like a hare in its form, his eyes revolving and his heart going into a sort of adagio dance, was unable to catch what these voices were saying, but he recognised them as those of Sir Aylmer and Lord Ickenham. The former appeared to be speaking heatedly, while the intonation of the latter was that of a man endeavouring to pour oil on troubled waters.

Presently the door of the collection room slammed, and a few moments later that of the drawing room opened, and Lord Ickenham walked in.

3

Whatever the nature of the exchanges in which he had been taking part, they had done nothing to impair Lord Ickenham's calm. His demeanour, as he entered, was the easy, unembarrassed demeanour of an English peer who has just remembered that there is a decanter of whisky in a drawing room. As always at moments when lesser men would have been plucking at their ties and shaking in every limb, this excellent old man preserved the suave imperturbability of a fish on a cake of ice. It seemed to Pongo, though it was difficult for him to hear distinctly, for his heart, in addition to giving its impersonation of Nijinsky, was now making a noise like a motorcycle, that the head of the family was humming light-heartedly.

'Ah, Pongo,' he said, making purposefully for the decanter and seeming in no way surprised to see his nephew. 'Up and about? One generally finds you not far from the whisky.' He filled his glass, and sank gracefully into a chair. 'I always think,' he said, having refreshed himself with a couple of swallows and a sip, 'that this is the best hour of the day. The soothing hush, the grateful stimulant, the pleasant conversation on whatever topic may happen to come up. Well, my boy, what's new? You seem upset about something. Nothing wrong, I hope?'

Pongo uttered a curious hissing sound like the death-rattle of a soda-water syphon. He found the question ironical.

'I don't know what you call wrong. I've just been told that I'm extremely apt to have my insides ripped out.'

'Who told you that?'

'Bill Oakshott.'

'Was he merely reading your future in the tea leaves, or do you mean that he proposed to do the ripping?'

'He proposed to do the ripping with his bare hands.'

'You amaze me. Bill Oakshott? That quiet, lovable young man.'

'Lovable be blowed. He's worse than a Faceless Fiend. He could walk straight into the Chamber of Horrors at Madame Tussaud's, and no questions asked. He also said he would pull my head off at the roots, and strangle me like a foul snake.'

'Difficult to do that, if he had pulled your head off.

Assuming, as I think we are entitled to assume, that the neck would come away with the head. But what had you been doing to Bill Oakshott to stir his passions thus?'

'He didn't like my being in here with Elsie Bean.'

'I don't think I remember who Elsie Bean is. One meets so many people.'

'The housemaid.'

'Ah, yes. The one you kiss.'

Pongo raised a tortured face heavenwards, as if he were calling for justice from above.

'I don't kiss her! At least, I may have done once – like a brother – in recognition of a signal service which she had rendered me. The way you and Bill Oakshott talk, you'd think this Bean and I spent twenty-four hours a day playing postman's knock.'

'My dear boy, don't get heated. My attitude is wholly sympathetic. I recollect now that Bill told me he had been a little disturbed by the spectacle of the embrace. He has the interests of your fiancée at heart.'

'He's in love with her.'

'Really?'

'He told me so.'

'Well, well. Poor lad. It must have been a severe jolt for him when I mentioned in the train that she was engaged to you. I feel a gentle pity for Bill Oakshott.'

'I don't. I hope he chokes.'

'The astonishing thing to my mind is that a man like Mugsy can have a daughter who seems to fascinate one and all. One would have expected Mugsy's daughter to be something on the lines of the Gorgon, with snakes instead of hair. Did you happen to hear him just now?'

'Golly, yes. What was all that?'

'Just Mugsy in one of his tantrums.'

'Did he catch you going into the collection room?'

'He was there already. Sleeping among his African curios. All wrong, it seemed to me. Either a man is an African curio, or he is not an African curio. If he is not, he ought not to curl up with them at night.' A cloud came into Lord Ickenham's handsome face, and his voice took on a disapproving note. 'You know, Pongo, there is a kind of low cunning about Mugsy which I do not like to see. Can you conceive the state of mind of a man who would have his bed moved into the collection room and sleep there with a string tied to his big toe and to the handle of the door?'

'He didn't?'

'He certainly did. It's the deceit of the thing that hurts me. Naturally I assumed, when we all wished each other good night and went our separate ways, that Mugsy was off to his bedroom like any decent householder, so I toddled down to the collection room at zero hour without a thought of unpleasantness in my mind. A nice, easy, agreeable job, I was saying to myself. I sauntered to the door, grasped the handle, turned it and gave it a sharp pull.'

'Gosh!'

'I don't know if you have ever, while walking along a dark street, happened to step on an unseen cat? I once had the experience years ago in Waverly Place, New York, and the picture seemed to rise before my eyes just now, when that awful yowl rent the air.'

'What on earth did you say?'

'Well, Mugsy did most of the saying.'

'I mean, how did you explain?'

'Oh, that? That was simple enough. I told him I was walking in my sleep.'

'Did he believe it?'

'I really don't know. The point seemed to me of no interest.'

'Well, this dishes us.'

'Nonsense. That is the pessimist in you speaking. All that has happened is that we have sustained a slight check—'

'Slight!'

'My dear Pongo, there are a thousand ways of getting around a trifling obstacle like this. Mugsy is sleeping in the collection room, is he? Very well, then we simply sit down and think out a good method of eliminating him. A knock-out drop in his bedtime whisky-and-soda would, of course, be the best method, but I happen to have come here without my knock-out drops. Idiotic of me. It is madness to come to country houses without one's bottle of Mickey Finns. One ought to pack them first thing after one's clean collars. But I'm not worrying about Mugsy. If I can't outsmart an ex-Governor, what was the use of all my early training in the United States of America? The only thing that bothers me a little is the thought of Sally, bless her heart. She is out there in the garden, watching and waiting like Mariana at the moated grange—'

Pongo uttered a stricken cry.

'And so is that blighted Potter out there in the garden, watching and waiting like Mariana at the ruddy moated grange. I'd clean forgotten Elsie Bean told me so. She came in here to get a drink for him.'

Lord Ickenham stroked his chin.

'H'm. I did not know that. He's out in the garden, eh? That may complicate matters a little. I hope—'

He broke off. Shrilling through the quiet night, the front doorbell had begun to ring, loudly and continuously, as if someone had placed a large, fat thumb on the button and was keeping it there.

Lord Ickenham looked at Pongo. Pongo looked at Lord Ickenham.

'Potter!' said Lord Ickenham.

'The rotter!' said Pongo.

IX

I

It is a characteristic of England's splendid police force at which many people have pointed with pride, or would have pointed with pride if they had happened to think of it, that its members, thanks to the rigid discipline which has moulded them since they were slips of boys, are always able to bear with philosophic fortitude the hardships and disappointments inseparable from their chosen walk in life. They can, in a word, take it as well as dish it out.

If, for example, they happen to be lurking in the garden of a country house in the small hours, when even a summer night tends to be a bit chilly, and ask their friends to bring them a drop of something to keep the cold out, and after a longish wait it becomes evident that this drop is not going to materialise, they do not wince nor cry aloud. 'Duty, stern daughter of the voice of God,' they say to themselves, and go on lurking.

It had been so with Constable Potter. In their recent Romeo and Juliet scene Elsie Bean had spoken hopefully of whisky in the drawing room, but he quite realised that obstacles might arise to prevent her connecting with it. And as the minutes went by and she did not appear, he assumed that these obstacles had arisen and with a couple of 'Coo's and a stifled oath dismissed the whole subject of whisky from his mind.

In surroundings such as those in which he was keeping his

vigil a more spiritual man might have felt the urge to try his hand at roughing out a little verse, so much was there that was romantic and inspirational in the garden of Ashenden Manor at this hour. Soft breezes sighed through the trees, bringing with them the scent of stock and tobacco plant. Owls tu-whitted, other owls tu-whooed. Add the silent grandeur of the fine old house and the shimmer of distant water reflecting the twinkling stars above, and you had a set-up well calculated to produce another policeman-poet.

But Harold Potter had never been much of a man for poetry. Even when alone with Elsie Bean in the moonlight he seldom got much further in that direction than a description of the effect which regulation boots had on his corns. What he thought of was beef sandwiches. And he was just sketching out in his mind the beef sandwich supreme which he would eat on returning to his cottage, when in the darkness before him he discerned a dim form. Like himself, it appeared to be lurking.

He pursed his lips disapprovingly. He had taken an instant dislike to this dim form.

It was not the fact that it was dim that offended him. In the garden of Ashenden Manor at one in the morning a form had got to be dim. It had no option. The point, as Constable Potter saw it, was that forms, dim or otherwise, had no business to be in the garden of Ashenden Manor at one in the morning, and he stepped forward, his blood circulating briskly. This might or might not be big stuff, but it had all the appearance of big stuff. 'Intrepid Officer Traps Nocturnal Marauder' seemed to him about the angle from which to look at the thing.

' 'Ullo,' he boomed. He should have said: 'What's all this?' which is the formula laid down for use on these occasions in *What Every Young Policeman Ought to Know*, but, as so often happens, excitement had made him blow up in his lines. ' 'Ullo. What are *you* doing here?'

The next moment any doubt which he might have entertained as to the bigness of the stuff was resolved. With a startled squeak the dim figure, which had leaped some six inches into the air on being addressed, broke into hurried flight, and with the deep bay, so like a bloodhound's, of the policeman engaged in the execution of his duty he immediately proceeded to bound after it. 'Night Chase in Darkened Garden', he was feeling as he dropped into his stride.

Into races of a cross-country nature the element of luck always enters largely. One notices this in the Grand National. Had the affair been taking place on a cinder track, few punters would have cared to invest their money on the constable, for he was built for endurance rather than speed and his quarry was showing itself exceptionally nippy on its feet. But in this more difficult going nimbleness was not everything. Some unseen obstacle tripped the dim form. It stumbled, nearly fell. Constable Potter charged up, reached out, seized something. There was a rending sound and he fell back, momentarily deprived of his balance. When he recovered it, he was alone with the owls and the stars. The dim form had disappeared, and he stood there with his hands full of what seemed to be the major part of a woman's dress.

It was at this point that he felt justified, despite the advanced hour, in going to the front door and ringing the bell. And it was not long afterwards that the door opened and he strode masterfully into the hall.

He found himself playing to a gratifyingly full house. He was, indeed, doing absolute capacity. You cannot punch front doorbells in the small hours without attracting attention, and Ashenden Manor had turned out *en masse* to greet him.

In addition to such members of his personal circle as Mrs Gooch, the cook, Elsie Bean, his betrothed, Jane, the parlourmaid, and Percy, the boy who cleaned the knives and boots, he noticed Sir Aylmer Bostock, looking like Clemenceau on one of his bad mornings, Lady Bostock, looking like a horse, and their nephew William, looking large and vermilion. There was also present, and a shudder ran through him as he saw them, the scum of the East Dulwich underworld in the person of the scoundrels George Robinson and Edwin Smith. The former was, as ever, debonair; the latter seemed agitated.

Constable Potter fondled his moustache. This was his hour, the high spot in his life when he was going to be fawned on by one and all. Or he thought it was until, just as he was about to speak, Sir Aylmer, who after the incursion of Lord Ickenham had managed to get to sleep again and had woken up cross, exploded like a bomb.

'POTTER!'

'Sir?' said the zealous officer, somewhat taken aback by his manner.

'Was it YOU making that infernal noise?'

'Sir?'

'Ringing the damned bell at this hour! Waking everybody up! Ruining my night's rest! WHAT THE DEVIL DO YOU MEAN BY IT?'

'But, sir, I've caught a marauder.'

'A what?'

'A nocturnal marauder, sir.'

'Then where is he? Don't tell me you let him get away?'

'Well, yes, sir.'

'Ass! Fool! Idiot! Imbecile!' said Sir Aylmer.

Constable Potter was wounded.

'It wasn't my fault, sir. The garments give when I clutched them.'

With the manner of Counsel putting in Exhibit A, he thrust beneath his interlocutor's eyes the flimsy fragment which he was holding, and Sir Aylmer inspected it closely.

'This is a woman's dress,' he said.

'A female's,' corrected Constable Potter, always indefatigable in his quest for exactitude. 'I observed her engaged in suspicious loitering, and when I up and apprehended her she come apart in my hands.'

At this dramatic recital of events which, even if colourlessly related, could scarcely have failed to chill the spine, there proceeded from the group of female members of the staff, huddled together for mutual support, a cry, or as Constable Potter would probably have preferred to put it, an ejaculation, consisting of the monosyllable 'OW!' Weighing the evidence, one would say that the speaker was not Elsie Bean, who would have said 'Coo!' but is more likely to have been Mrs Gooch or Jane the parlourmaid. The interruption had the unfortunate effect of attracting Sir Aylmer's attention to the group, and he started immediately to make his presence felt.

'EMILY!'

'Yes, dear?'

'What are all these women doing here?' Sir Aylmer's reddening eye passed from Mrs Gooch to Jane the parlourmaid, from Jane the parlourmaid to Elsie Bean. 'Good God! The place is full of damned women. Send 'em to bed.'

'Yes, dear.'

'Dishpot!' cried a clear young voice, this time unmistakably that of Miss Bean. She had been looking forward to spending most of the rest of the night in the hall, listening to tales of stirring events and commenting on them in her friendly way, and to get the bum's rush like this in the first five minutes was very bitter to her independent spirit. Not since the evening of her seventh birthday when, excitement having induced an attack of retching and nausea, she had been led out of the Bottleton East Theatre Royal halfway through her first pantomime, had she experienced such a sense of disappointment and frustration.

Sir Aylmer started. These were fighting words.

'Who called me a dishpot?'

'I did,' replied Elsie Bean with quiet fortitude. 'An overbearing dishpot, that's what you are, and I would like to give my month's notice.'

'*I* would like to give my month's notice,' said Mrs Gooch, struck by the happy thought.

'So would I like to give my month's notice,' said Jane the parlourmaid, falling in with the mob spirit.

Sir Aylmer clutched his dressing gown. For a moment it seemed as if it were his intention to rend it, like a minor prophet of the Old Testament.

'EMILY!'

'Yes, dear?'

'Are you or are you not going to throw these women out?'

'Yes, dear. At once, dear.'

Briskly, though with a leaden heart, for none knew better than she the difficulty of obtaining domestic help in the country, Lady Bostock shepherded the rebels through the door. Of the wage-earning members of the household only Percy, the knives and boots boy, remained, a pimpled youth with a rather supercilious manner. He had lighted a cigarette, and his whole demeanour showed his satisfaction that the women had gone and that the men could now get together and thresh the thing out in peace.

Sir Aylmer drew a deep breath like a speaker at a public meeting after the hecklers have been ejected.

'Potter.'

'Sir?'

'Tell me your story again.'

The constable told his story again, even better than before, for he had been able to think of some new words, and Sir Aylmer listened frowningly.

'Where was this woman?'

'This Mystery Woman,' corrected Constable Potter. 'In the garden, sir.'

'What part of the garden?'

'Near the window of the room where you keep your thingamajigs, sir.'

'My *what*?'

'Those objects from Africa, sir. Curios is, I believe, the name.'

'Then call them curios.'

'Yes, sir.'

'Not thingamajigs.'

'No, sir.'

'What was she doing?'

'Lying in wait, sir.'

'What for?'

'Don't know, sir.'

Percy flicked the ash off his cigarette.

'If you arst me,' he said, throwing out the suggestion for what it was worth, 'she was expecting the arrival of her accomplice. This is the work of a gang.'

He would have done better to remain in modest obscurity. Compelled by his official status to accept meekly the recriminations of landed proprietors who were also members of the bench of magistrates, Constable Potter could be very terrible when dealing with knives and boots boys, and he had been wanting some form of relief for his feeling ever since Sir Aylmer had called him an ass, a fool, an idiot and an imbecile. To advance and seize Percy by the left ear was with him the work of an instant, to lead him to the door and speed him on his way with a swift kick the work of another. A thud and a yelp, and Percy had ceased to have a seat at the conference table. Constable Potter returned to his place, his air that of a man who has carried out a pleasant task neatly and well.

Percy's head appeared round the door.

'And so would I like to give my month's notice,' he said, and withdrew once more.

Lord Ickenham, who had been a genial spectator, spoke for the first time.

'A clean sweep, Mugsy. What, all my pretty chickens at one fell swoop! Too bad. Very difficult these days to get servants in the country.'

Sir Aylmer did not reply. The same thought had come to him independently, and he was beginning to be a little dubious as to the wisdom of his forthright policy in dealing with domestics. It was Constable Potter who now came before the meeting with a few well-judged words.

'Not but what there ain't a lot in what the lad said,' he observed. He was not fond of Percy, suspecting him of being the hidden hand which had thrown half a brick at him the other day as he cycled up the drive, but he could give credit where credit was due. 'About its being a gang, what I mean. Women don't conduct burglaries on their own hook. They have pals. Established inside the house as like as not,' he added with a significant glance.

It was Pongo who spoke next, as if impelled to utterance

by a jab in the trouser seat from a gimlet or bradawl. In saying that Constable Potter's glance was significant, we omitted to state that it was at the last of the Twistletons that it had been directed, nor did we lay anything like sufficient stress on its penetrating qualities. It was silly of us to describe as merely significant something so closely resembling a death ray.

'What are you looking at *me* for?' he asked weakly.

Constable Potter, who could be as epigrammatic as the next man when he wanted to, replied that a cat may look at a king. And he was just smiling at his ready wit, when Sir Aylmer decided that the time for finesse and dissembling was past and that what was required here was direct frontal attack. All the evening he had been irked by the necessity of playing the genial host – or the fairly genial host – to this rat of the underworld, and now not even the thought of possible repercussions from his daughter Hermione could restrain him from speaking out.

'I'll tell you why he's looking at you, my man. Because he happens to be aware that you're a scoundrel and an impostor.'

'Who, me?'

'Yes, you. You thought you had fooled us, did you? Well, you hadn't. Potter!'

'Sir?'

'Tell your story about your previous meeting with this fellow.'

'Very good, sir,' said Constable Potter, quickly applying the necessary glaze to his eyes and starting to address the bodiless spirit in mid-air. 'Here's what transpired. On the . . . Cool! I've forgotten when it was, I'd have to look up my scrap album to establish the exact inst., but it was about a year ago, when I was in the C division in the metropolis and they'd put me on duty at the dog races down Shepherd's Bush way. Accused was drawn to my attention along of making himself conspicuous by conduct like as it might have been of a disorderly nature, and I apprehended him. Questioned while in custody, he stated his name was Smith.'

'Not Twistleton?'

'No, sir. Edwin Smith, of 11, Nasturtium Road, East Dulwich.'

'So what have you to say to that?' demanded Sir Aylmer.

Lord Ickenham intervened.

'My dear Mugsy, the whole thing is obviously an absurd misunderstanding. One sees so clearly what must have happened. Scooped in by the police and reluctant to stain the fine old Twistleton escutcheon by revealing his true identity, the boy gave a false name. You've done it yourself a hundred times.'

'I haven't!'

Lord Ickenham shrugged his shoulders.

'Have it your own way, Mugsy. The point is immaterial, and I would be the last man to awaken painful memories. But I can assure you that this is really Reginald Twistleton. Bill Oakshott happened to mention it only this afternoon. He was telling me that you had gone off your onion—'

'He was, was he?'

'—And when I inquired as to the symptoms, he explained that you had got this extraordinary idea that his old friend Reginald Twistleton was not his old friend Reginald Twistleton, whereas that is in reality what his old friend Reginald Twistleton is nothing else but. You will testify, Bill Oakshott, to the hundred per cent Twistletonity of this Reginald?'

'Fine. I mean, oh rather.'

'There you are, then, Mugsy.'

Sir Aylmer blew at his moustache.

'William on his own statement has not seen Reginald

Twistleton for more than twelve years. How can he possibly claim to recognise him? Ha! William!'

'Hullo?'

'I see how we can settle this matter. Ask him questions.'

'Questions?'

'About your school days.'

'Pongo and I weren't at school together. I met him in the holidays at Lord Ickenham's place.'

'That alone would seem to be a guarantee of respectability,' said Lord Ickenham. 'A very exclusive house, that, I have always understood. By the way, how did you get on there this afternoon, Mugsy?'

'Never mind,' said Sir Aylmer shortly. 'What was he doing at Lord Ickenham's?'

'He was staying there.'

Sir Aylmer reflected. An inspiration came to him.

'Was there a dog there?'

'Eh?'

'A dog.'

'Oh, you mean a dog. Yes, a—'

'Don't tell him, don't tell him. Ask him.'

Lord Ickenham nodded.

'I see what you mean, Mugsy. Very shrewd. If he was staying at Ickenham Hall, he would remember the resident dog. Boys always remember dogs. Do you remember that dog, prisoner at the bar?'

'Of course I remember the dog. It was a sheepdog.'

'Correct, Bill Oakshott?'

'Absolutely.'

'Called –?'

'Mittens.'

'Accurate, Bill Oakshott?'

'Definitely. Right on the bull's-eye. Want any more, Uncle Aylmer?'

'No,' said Sir Aylmer.

'I should hope not,' said Lord Ickenham. 'You've been making an ass of yourself, Mugsy.'

'Oh, have I?' said Sir Aylmer, stung. 'Well, let me tell you that I think the time has now come to ask you some questions.'

'Me?'

'Yes. How do I know who you are? You come here claiming to be Plank, and you don't look a bit like Plank, as I remember him—'

'But I explained about the absence of the billowy curves. Slimmo. In the small half-crown or the larger three-and-sixpence bottle. You mix it with your food, and it acts as a gentle, agreeable remedy for hypertrophy of the trouser seat, not habit-forming.'

'I don't believe you are Plank. How do I know that William did not pick up the first stranger he met and talk him into coming and judging the Bonny Baby contest, so that he could get out of it himself?'

'Ridiculous. You have only to look at that pure brow, those candid eyes—'

'There are some damned funny things going on here,' proceeded Sir Aylmer firmly, 'and I intend to get to the bottom—'

'Like Slimmo.'

'This afternoon a man I don't remember from Adam comes and insinuates himself into the house, saying he is an old schoolfellow of mine. Tonight Potter catches a woman prowling in my garden—'

'Not so much prowling, sir, as lurking.'

'SHUT UP!'

'Yes, sir.'

'Potter catches a woman prowling in my garden, obviously trying to establish communication with some man in the house. Who was that man?'

'Ah.'

'It wasn't me.'

'One hopes not, Mugsy.'

'It wasn't William. It wasn't that boy who was in here just now, the one that cleans the knives and boots—'

'How do you know? If I were you, I would watch that boy, watch him closely.'

'It was presumably not Reginald, seeing that Reginald really is Reginald. That leaves you.'

'But, Mugsy, this is absurd. You say this woman was trying to establish communication with some man in the house. Why? What possible evidence have you of that? I see her as some poor, homeless waif who wandered into your garden trying to find shelter for the night in the tool shed or the byre, whatever a byre may be—'

'Poor, homeless waif be damned. And if she was trying to find shelter in the tool shed, why didn't she go there, instead of hanging about—'

'Loitering suspiciously, sir.'

'SHUT UP! Instead of hanging about outside the window of my collection room. She was one of a gang of burglars, that's what she was, and I'm going to find out who the rest of them are. You say you're Plank. Prove it.'

Lord Ickenham beamed.

'My dear Mugsy, why didn't you say so at first? Prove it? Of course I can prove it. But is not the fact that I have been calling you Mugsy from the start in itself a proof?'

'No. You could have found out somewhere that I used to be called that at school.'

'Then let us touch on some of the things which I could not have found out except by actual daily contact with you in those far-off days. Who pinched jam sandwiches at the school shop, Mugsy? Who put the drawing pin on the French master's chair? Who got six of the best with a fives bat for bullying his juniors? And talking of bullying juniors, do you recollect one term a frail, golden-haired child arriving at the old seminary, a frail, wistful child who looked to you like something sent from heaven? You swooped on that child, Mugsy, as if you had been an Assyrian coming down like a wolf on the fold. You pulled his golden hair. You twisted his slender arm. And just as you had started twisting it, it suddenly uncoiled itself in one of the sweetest left hooks I have ever witnessed and plugged you in the eye. Ten minutes later, after we had helped you to bed, investigation revealed that the child was the previous year's public-school bantamweight champion, who had been transferred to us from his former place of education because his father thought the air in our part of the world was better for his lungs. On another occasion—'

He paused. A horrible cackling sound, like a turkey with laryngitis, had interrupted the flow of his narrative. It was Constable Potter laughing. He was not a man who laughed easily, and he had not wanted to laugh now. He had, indeed, tried not to laugh. But his sense of the humorous had been too much for him.

'Uck, uck, uck,' he gurgled, and Sir Aylmer turned on him with all the fury of a bantam-weight champion whose arm has been twisted.

'POTTER!'

'S-sir?'

'Get out! What the devil are you doing, lounging about in

here, when you ought to be finding that woman you were fool enough to let escape?'

The rebuke sobered Constable Potter. He saw that he had been remiss.

'Yes, sir.'

'What do you mean, "Yes, sir?"'

'I mean, no, sir. I mean I'll start instituting a search instanter. It oughtn't to be so hard to find her. She'll be practically in the nood, as the expression is, and that,' said Constable Potter who, when he thought at all, thought clearly, 'will render her conspicuous.'

With a courteous inclination of the head he passed through the door, stern and vigilant, and Sir Aylmer prepared to follow his example.

'I'm off to bed,' he said shortly. 'It must be two o'clock.'

'Past two,' said Lord Ickenham, consulting his watch. 'How time flies when one is agreeably occupied. Then let us all go to bed.'

He linked his arm in that of Pongo, who was breathing stertorously like a fever patient, and together they made their way up the stairs.

2

The bedroom which had been allotted to Lord Ickenham was a spacious apartment on the second floor, looking out over the park. It was thither that he conducted Pongo, bringing him to rest on the *chaise longue* which stood beside the window.

'Relax, my boy,' he said, tidying up his nephew's legs, which were showing a tendency to straggle and gently placing a cushion behind his head. 'You seem a little overwrought.

You remind me of an old New York friend of mine named Bream Rockmeteller on the occasion one Fourth of July when somebody touched off a maroon beneath his chair. That same stunned look. Odd. I should have thought that the clearing up of that Edwin Smith misunderstanding would have made you feel as if you had just had a fortnight at Bracing Bognor.'

Pongo sat up, his legs once more shooting out in all directions.

'Come, come,' said Lord Ickenham, rearranging them. 'Are you a man or an octopus? One ought to tie you up with a system of ropes.'

Pongo ignored the rebuke. His eyes were stony.

'Uncle Fred,' he said, speaking in a low, metallic voice, 'I don't know if you know it, but you're Public Scourge Number One. You scatter ruin and desolation on every side like a ruddy sower going forth sowing. Life, liberty and the pursuit of happiness aren't possible when you're around. You're like the Black Death or one of those pestilences of the Middle Ages, taking their toll of thousands.'

His vehemence seemed to occasion Lord Ickenham a mild surprise.

'But, my dear boy, what have I done?'

'All that stuff about my giving a false name at the dog races.'

'Well, I'm dashed. I was looking on that as my day's good deed. But for my timely intervention——'

'I was just going to deny the whole thing, when you butted in.'

Lord Ickenham shook his head.

'You would never have got away with it. Heaven knows that there are few more fervent apostles of the creed of stout denial than myself – I have been practising it for thirty years with your aunt – but it would not have served here. The copper's word would have been accepted, and you would have been branded in Mugsy's eyes as a burglar.'

'Well, look what I'm branded in his eyes as now. A chap who goes on toots and gets pinched at dog races. What's Hermione going to say when he tells her about it? The moment the facts are placed before her, she'll sit down and write me a stinker, calling our engagement off.'

'You think so?'

'I can see her dipping the pen.'

'Well, that'll be good. If I were you, I would give three rousing cheers and let it go at that.'

'I won't give three rousing cheers. I worship that girl. Until now—'

'I know, I know. You have never known what love meant. Quite. Nevertheless, I stick to it that you would be well out of this perilous enterprise of trying to hitch up with a girl who appears to have the austere outlook of the headmistress of a kindergarten and will probably spend most of her married life rapping her husband on the knuckles with a ruler. But we mustn't sit yarning about your amours now. There are graver matters on which we have to rivet our attention.'

'Such as—?'

'My dear Pongo, Sally. Is it nothing to you that she is at this moment roaming Hampshire in her camiknickers? Where's your chivalry?'

Pongo bowed his head in shame. No appeal to the *preux chevalier* in him was ever wasted. The thought that he had clean forgotten about Sally was a knife in his bosom.

'Oh, golly. Yes, that's right. She'll catch cold.'

'If nothing worse.'

'And may be gathered in by Potter.'

'Exactly.'

'Blast him.'

'Yes, I confess to feeling a little cross with Constable Potter, and in the deepest and truest sense it will be all right with me if he trips over a footprint and breaks his damned neck. In trying to cope with Constable Potter one has the sense of being up against some great natural force. I wouldn't have thought so much zeal could have been packed into a blue uniform and a pair of number eleven boots. Well, see you shortly, Pongo.'

'Where are you going?'

'Out into the great open spaces,' said Lord Ickenham, picking up a flowered dressing gown. 'God knows where Sally is, but she can't have got far. As Potter said, she will be conspicuous.'

'Shall I come, too?'

'No,' said Lord Ickenham. 'We don't want the thing to look like one of those great race movements. You stay here and think calm, healing thoughts.'

He left the room, walking like one who intends not to let a twig snap beneath his feet, and Pongo leaned back against the cushion and closed his eyes.

'Healing thoughts!' he said to himself bitterly, and laughed one of his mirthless laughs.

But the human mind is capable of strange feats. You never know where you are with it. If questioned at the moment when the door had closed as to the chances of anything in the nature of a healing thought coming into a mind that was more like a maelstrom than a collection of grey cells, Pongo would have offered a hundred to eight against and been surprised if there had been any takers. Yet now, gradually, he discovered that one was beginning to shape itself.

As if painted in flame, the picture of the whisky decanter which he had left standing on the round table in the drawing room, at least half of its elixir still within it, started to rise before his mental retina, and he sat up, the light of hope dawning in his eyes. He had tested the magic properties of that decanter before, and they had in no way fallen short of his dreams, and now there came upon him the urge to test them again. Reason told him that he would never need one for the tonsils more than in the present pass to which he had been reduced. In fact, added Reason, the first thing any good specialist, seeing him, would recommend – nay, insist on – was a little something in a glass.

Thirty seconds later he had begun his journey to the promised land, and a couple of minutes after that was sitting in his favourite armchair with his feet up, almost calm again.

It was very pleasant in the quiet drawing room, very pleasant and restorative and soothing. At least, it was for perhaps a quarter of an hour. At the end of that period Sir Aylmer Bostock entered in his dressing gown. Tossing on his pillow after having had his beauty sleep twice broken, Sir Aylmer had bethought him of the decanter and it had drawn him like a magnet. Experience had taught him that the most stubborn insomnia can often be corrected by means of a couple of quick ones.

His emotions on beholding Pongo established at the fountainhead were sharp and poignant. Although he had been compelled to abandon his view of this young man as a rat of the underworld, he still considered him a rat, and the last thing he desired was a jolly party with him at half-past two in the morning, the glasses clinking and the conversation flowing free. Life, he was thinking, was difficult enough without finding Pongo under one's feet wherever one went. If Sir Aylmer Bostock after two days of his future son-in-law's society had been asked to sketch out a brief description of his ideal world, he would have replied that he was not a fussy man and did not expect perfection but that he did insist on one thing, that it should contain fewer and better Twistletons.

'Ugh!' he said. 'You!'

There are extraordinarily few good answers to the ejaculation 'You!' especially when preceded by the monosyllable 'Ugh!' Pongo could not think of any of them. The other's entry had caused him to repeat that sitting high jump of his, and on descending from the neighbourhood of the ceiling he had found his mind a blank. The best he could achieve was a nervous giggle.

This was unfortunate, for we have made no secret of Sir Aylmer Bostock's views on nervous gigglers. The ex-Governor had never actually fallen on a nervous giggler and torn him limb from limb, but that was simply because he had not wanted to get himself involved in a lot of red tape. But he definitely did not like them. He glared at Pongo, and as he glared observed the glass in the latter's hand, and it was as if someone had whispered in his ear, 'What is wrong with this picture?'

'Gar!' he exclaimed, once more calling on one of those tribal gods. 'I thought you told me you were a teetotaller.'

'Eh?'

'Teetotaller.'

'Oh, yes, that's right.'

'How the devil can you be a teetotaller, if you sit swigging whisky all the time?'

'Medicinal.'

'What?'

'I take a drop occasionally for my health,' said Pongo. 'Doctor's orders.'

There are moments in life when, after offering frank and manly explanations of our actions, we are compelled to pause and wonder if they have got by. This was one of them. And it was while Pongo was anxiously scrutinising his host's face and trying, without much success, to read in its rugged features an expression of childlike trust that Lady Bostock entered the room.

There are critics to whom it will seem one of those strained coincidences which are so inartistic that on this troubled night no fewer than six of the residents of Ashenden Manor should have been seized independently of each other with the idea of going to the drawing room in order to establish contact with the decanter placed there earlier in the evening by Jane, the parlourmaid, while others will see in the thing that inevitability which was such a feature of the best Greek tragedy. Aeschylus once said to Euripides, 'You can't beat inevitability,' and Euripides said he had often thought so, too.

Be that as it may, it was the decanter which had brought Lady Bostock to the spot. Finding a difficulty in getting to sleep after the recent strain upon her nerves, she had thought that a weak whisky and water might prove the specific which she needed.

She, too, was surprised on discovering that she had boon companions.

'Aylmer!' she said. 'You here? And Reginald?' The glass in Pongo's hand attracted her attention, producing reactions identical with those of her husband. 'I thought you were a tee-totaller, Reginald.'

Sir Aylmer snorted. A most unpleasant, cynical snort, a sort of nasal 'Oh, yeah.'

'He takes a drop occasionally for his health.'

'Oh, yes?'

'Yes,' said Sir Aylmer. 'Medicinal. Doctor's orders.' His intonation was so extremely disagreeable, suggesting as it did contempt, disgust and that revolted loathing which temperate men feel when confronted with the world's drink-sodden wrecks, that Pongo, though his sitting high jump had caused him to spill practically all the contents of his glass and he would much have liked to refill it, felt that this was not the moment. Stronger than his desire for one for the road was the passionate wish to be somewhere where Sir Aylmer and Lady Bostock were not.

'Well – er – good night,' he mumbled.

'You're leaving us?' said Sir Aylmer grimly.

'Er – yes. Good night.'

'Good night,' said Sir Aylmer.

'Good night,' said Lady Bostock.

There was an expression of concern on her face as the door closed. She looked like a horse that is worried about the quality of its oats.

'Oh, dear,' she said. 'I do hope Reginald is not a drinker.' A thought occurred to her, and she brightened. 'But, of course, I was forgetting. He isn't Reginald, is he? He's just somebody pretending to be Reginald.'

Sir Aylmer, though reluctant to present himself in the light of one who had been in error, felt obliged to put her abreast of his latest findings.

'Yes, he's Reginald. I've been into that matter, and it now seems pretty well established that he's Reginald all right. Apparently, at those dog races where Potter arrested him, he gave a false name and address.'

'That does not sound very nice.'

'It was not very nice. It wasn't nice at all. It was disgraceful and it throws a blinding light on the true character of Reginald Twistleton. Shows you what sort of a fellow he is. And as to him being a drinker, of course he's a drinker. You can tell it by those shifty eyes and that weak giggle. I knew there was something wrong with the young toad the first time I saw him. Dipsomaniac is written all over him. No doubt he has been absorbing the stuff like a sponge whenever our backs were turned. I don't suppose he has drawn a sober breath since he came here. God help Hermione, married to a chap like that. He'll be seeing pink snakes on the honeymoon. Orange spiders,' said Sir Aylmer, allowing his imagination free rein. 'Gamboge elephants. Purple penguins.'

It is never difficult to touch a mother's heart with this sort of thing. Lady Bostock uttered a stricken neigh.

'Hermione must be warned!'

'Exactly what I was about to suggest myself. You'd better write to her.'

'I'll go and see her.'

'Very well, go and see her.'

'Tomorrow morning!'

'The sooner, the better. Well, if you're going to London in the morning, you'd better go to bed and get some sleep. Can't imagine why you aren't there now.'

'I came down to get a weak whisky. I couldn't sleep.'

'I came to get a strong whisky. I couldn't sleep, either. How the devil can anyone be expected to sleep in a house where fools are incessantly breaking in on you, saying they're somnambulists, and policemen ring doorbells all the time? Did you get those women to bed?'

'Yes, dear. They kept giving their notices all the way upstairs.'

'Curse them. Say when, Emily.'

'When, oh dear, oh dear, oh dear.'

'What's the matter now?'

'I was only thinking of Reginald,' said Lady Bostock. 'I wonder if the gold cure would do any good.'

Unaware of the exact nature of what was being said about him by the parents of the girl he loved, but suspecting that his case might have come upon the agenda paper after his withdrawal, Pongo had tottered up the stairs to his room. While not in tiptop form, he found himself enjoying the novel sensation of being separated for a while from members of the human race, a race for which the events of the night had caused him to acquire a rather marked distaste. 'Alone at last,' he was saying to himself, as he opened the door.

A moment later he saw that he had been too optimistic. Seated on the bed was his Uncle Frederick, enjoying a mild cigar, and in the armchair, clad in a flowered dressing gown, a girl at the sight of whom his heart, already, as we have seen, on several occasions tonight compelled to rival the feverish mobility of a one-armed paperhanger with the hives, executed a leap and a bound surpassing all previous efforts by a wide margin.

'Ah, Pongo,' said Lord Ickenham. 'Come along in. Here's Sally. We climbed up the water pipe.'

3

It was not immediately that Pongo found himself able to speak. Strong emotion often has the effect of tying the vocal cords into a reefer knot, and he was in the grip of not one strong emotion, but two.

As always when confronted with some new manifestation of his uncle's activities, he was filled with a nameless fear, saying to himself, as so often in similar circumstances, 'What will the harvest be?' – and in addition to this nameless fear he was experiencing the embarrassment which cannot but come to a young man of sensibility when he encounters unexpectedly a former fiancée from whom he has severed relations in a scene marked on both sides by raised voices and harsh words.

Fortunately women handle these situations more adroitly than the uncouth male. In Sally's demeanour there was no suggestion that she found in this meeting any cause for discomfort. Her eyes, bright and beautiful as he had always remembered them, shone with a friendly light. Her voice, when she spoke, was cordial. And she accompanied her words with a dazzling smile.

'Hullo, Pongo.'

'Hullo, Sally.'

'It's nice to see you again.'

'What ho.'

'You look very well.'

'Oh, rather,' said Pongo.

He spoke absently, for he was distrait. What with going to New York to attend to his financial interests and getting engaged to Hermione Bostock and all the other excitements of what had recently been a full life, he had rather allowed the peculiar properties of Sally's smile to fade from his mind, and getting it between the eyes like this had had a shaking effect, inducing a feeling somewhat similar to that which must have come to Lord Ickenham's friend Bream Rockmeteller in the course of those distant Fourth of July celebrations.

Sally's smile . . .

That smile of Sally's . . .

Yes, he had forgotten just what it could do to your system, suddenly flashing out at you like the lights of a village pub seen through rain and darkness at the end of a ten-mile hike and transporting you into a world of cosiness and joy and laughter. He blinked, and not even his great love for Hermione Bostock could keep him from experiencing a momentary twinge of nostalgia, a swift pang of that self-reproach which comes to a man conscious of having been on a good thing and of having omitted to push it along.

The weakness passed. He thought – hard – of Hermione Bostock, and it did the trick. It was a Reginald Twistleton who was himself again, a strong, firm Reginald Twistleton with not a chink in his armour, who now put the question which he would have put a good deal earlier but for the mental upheaval which we have just been analysing.

'What's all this?' he asked, and Constable Potter himself, addressing a suspicious loiterer, could not have spoken in a colder, more level voice. 'What's the idea, Uncle Fred?'

'The idea?'

'What's Sally doing here?'

'Seeking sanctuary.'

'In my room?'

'Just for the time being, till we can make other arrangements.'

Pongo placed a hand on either side of his head to shore it up. That old, familiar sensation that it was coming unstuck had swept over him.

'Oh, God!'

'Why do you say "Oh, God!" my boy? What seems to you to be the difficulty?'

'How the dickens can she stay in my room?'

'Why not? You will have a shakedown in mine. I can't offer you a bed, but you remember that very comfortable *chaise longue*.'

'I don't mean that. I mean, well, dash it, what about people coming in?'

'Where?'

'Here.'

'When?'

'Tomorrow morning.'

'Nobody will come in tomorrow morning except the house-maid. And before nightfall I hope to get the poor child safely away. She tells me she stowed the car in the local garage. I shall take it out and drive over to Ickenham first thing, and bring her back some of my wife's reach-me-downs. She will then be free to go where she lists. A word,' said Lord Ickenham thoughtfully, 'which I have never been able to understand. Why lists? How do lists come into it? However, that is neither here nor there. Getting back to what you were saying, nobody is going to muscle in except the housemaid, and all that is needed, therefore, is to square the housemaid. I wonder if you have ever reflected that if only he could square the housemaid, every visitor at a country house would be able to take in paying guests and make a good deal of money.'

'And how are you going to square the housemaid?'

'Odd how when one keeps repeating that it sounds like one of those forgotten sports of the past. Squaring the housemaid. One can picture William the Conqueror being rather good at it. My dear Pongo, have no uneasiness. The housemaid is already squared. Perhaps I had better tell you the story from the beginning. It won't bore you, Sally?'

'Not at all, Uncle Fred.'

'Capital. Well, when I left you, Pongo, I started to make a systematic search of the grounds, exploring every avenue and leaving no stone unturned. I was handicapped by having no bloodhounds, another thing which one ought always to bring with one to a country house, but eventually I located Sally in the potting shed, watering the geraniums with her tears.'

'I wasn't,' said Sally indignantly, and Lord Ickenham rose, kissed the top of her head paternally and returned to the bed.

'I was only making a good story of it, my dear. Actually, your attitude was heroic. I was proud of you. She laughed, Pongo, when she heard my voice. Laughed heartily.'

'I wish I could.'

'Can't you? Not at this happy ending?'

'What do you mean, happy ending?'

'Well, it looks like a happy ending to me. I see Sally as a little storm-tossed boat that has put into harbour after the dickens of a gruelling from the winds and waves, and can now take it easy for a bit. Where was I, Sally?'

'Potting shed.'

'That's right. I found her in the potting shed. I draped her in the dressing gown, and we crept out into the night. Did you ever hear of Chingachgook?'

'No.'

'A red Indian of some celebrity in my younger days. I suppose nobody reads Fenimore Cooper now.'

'What about him?'

'I was only going to say that that was what we crept like; softly and silently, as if we were wearing moccasins. And while we were creeping, we heard voices.'

'And did I jump!'

'I, too. I soared up like a rocket. For one of the voices was Constable Potter's. The other was that of the housemaid, Elsie Bean. A rather pleasant feature of life at Ashenden Manor is the way you can always find housemaids sauntering about the grounds at half-past two in the morning. It was she who was doing most of the speaking. She seemed to be reproaching the officer for his professional activities. She was telling him that she had given her month's notice and that before her time expired he must make his decision about resigning from the Force. She said she hadn't any patience, and so alien did she appear to his aims and ideals that I felt that we had found a sympathiser. I was right. Presently, the constable left, his manner that of a man who has had his ears pinned back, and with a slight snort she turned, presumably to re-enter the house. It was at this point that we emerged and contacted her.'

'With a cheery "Hoy!"'

'With, as you say, a cheery "Hoy!" Well, after that everything went with the most delightful smoothness. I think she was a little surprised to see us – indeed, she stated later that that ghastly sound proceeding from the darkness had scared her out of a year's growth – but she soon recovered her poise and showed herself the soul of consideration. It was she who pointed out the water pipe and after I had helped Sally to climb it gave me that preliminary leg-up which a man needs at my time of life, if he is to negotiate water pipes successfully. I don't know when I have met a nicer girl, and I don't wonder you—'

'You don't wonder I what?'

'Oh, nothing. So here we are, thanks to her, and she has guaranteed that she will give us all the aid and comfort at her disposal. She said she would look in shortly and confer with us. I suppose she feels that there are one or two details which need discussing.'

Sally clasped her hands.

'My breakfast!'

'That, no doubt, was one of them.'

'I'm starving already.'

'Poor child. In a few minutes I will take you down to the larder and we will knock together a bite of supper which will keep you going till the morning. I could do with a couple of boiled eggs myself. These late hours give one an appetite. Ah, here is Miss Bean. Come in, Miss Bean. I think you know everybody. A cigarette?'

'Thank you, sir.'

'Give the lady a cigarette, Pongo. A chair, Miss Bean? and a footstool for your feet? That's right. And now, Miss Bean, tell us everything that is on your mind. I hope you have come to indicate to us in what way we may make some slight return for all your kindness tonight. Speaking for myself, if a fiver would be any good to you – and when I say a fiver I mean, of course, a tenner –'

Elsie Bean tossed her head, setting the curling pins leaping like Sir Aylmer Bostock's moustache.

'I don't want money,' she said, not actually referring to it as dross, but giving the impression that that was what she considered it. 'Thanking you all the same.'

'Not at all.'

'What I want,' said Elsie Bean, once more imparting life to the curling pins, 'is Harold bopped on the nose.'

She spoke with a strange intensity, her face hard and her blue eyes gleaming with a relentless light. That interview with her loved one in the garden seemed to have brought her to a decision. Here, you felt, was a housemaid who had been pushed just so far and could be pushed no further. Nor is the fact surprising. Tempers are quick in Bottleton East, and Constable Potter's way of replying 'Well, I dunno,' to her most impassioned pleadings would have irritated a far less emotional girl.

Lord Ickenham inclined his head courteously.

'Harold?'

'Harold Potter.'

'Ah, yes, our friend the constable. What did you say you wished done to his nose?'

'I want it bopped.'

'Struck, you mean? Socked? Given a biff?'

'R.'

189

'But why? Not that I want to be inquisitive, of course.'

'I was telling Mr Twistleton. There's only one way to make Harold be sensible and give up being a copper, and that's to dot him a good bop on the nose. Because he's nervous. He don't like being bopped on the nose.'

'Of course, of course. I see just what you mean. Your psychology is unerring. If I were a copper and somebody bopped me on the nose, I would hand in my resignation like a flash. The matter shall be attended to. Pongo—'

Pongo started convulsively.

'Now listen, Uncle Fred. All that's been arranged. This Bean and I have discussed it and are in full agreement that the bird to take the job on is her brother Bert. Bert, I may mention, is a chap who habitually sloshes slops on the napper with blunt instruments, so this will be a picnic to him.'

'But Bert doesn't come out till September.'

Lord Ickenham was shocked.

'Are you suggesting, Pongo, that this poor girl shall wait till September for the fulfilment of her hopes and dreams? It is obvious that time is of the essence and that we must rush to her assistance immediately. I, unfortunately, am a little too old to bop policemen on the nose, much as I should enjoy it, so the task devolves upon you. See to it as soon as possible.'

'But, dash it—'

'And don't say, "But, dash it." You remind me of our mutual ancestor, Sir Gervase Twistleton, who got a bad name in the days of the Crusades from curling up in bed and murmuring, "Some other time," when they asked him to come and do his bit at the Battle of Joppa. I am convinced that this matter could not be placed in better hands than yours, and I would suggest that you and Miss Bean have a talk about ways and means while Sally and I go down to the larder and forage. It might be best if we took the back stairs. Can you direct us to the back stairs, Miss Bean? At the end of the passage? Thank you. I don't suppose we shall have any trouble in finding the larder. Is there a gas range in the kitchen for egg-boiling purposes? Excellent. Every convenience. Then come along, Sally. I think I can promise you a blowout on lavish lines. I have already tested Mugsy's hospitality, and it is princely. I shouldn't wonder if in addition to eggs there might not be a ham and possibly even sausages.'

With a bow of old-world courtesy to Elsie Bean, Lord Ickenham escorted Sally from the room, speaking of sausages he had toasted at school on the ends of pens, and Pongo, who had folded his arms in a rather noticeable manner, found on turning to Miss Bean that her set face had relaxed.

'He's a nice old gentleman,' she said.

This seemed to Pongo such a monstrously inaccurate description of one who in his opinion was like a sort of human upas tree, casting its deadly blight on every innocent bystander who came within its sphere of influence, that he uttered a brassy 'Ha!'

'Pardon?'

'I said "Ha!"' said Pongo, and would have gone on to speak further, had there not at this moment occurred an interruption. Knuckles were rapping gently on the door, and through the woodwork there made itself heard a voice.

'Pongo.'

The voice of Bill Oakshott.

4

In the literature and drama which have come down to us through the ages there have been a number of powerful descriptions of men reacting to unpleasant surprises. That of King Claudius watching the unfolding of the play of *The Mouse Trap* is one of these, and writers of a later date than Shakespeare have treated vividly of the husband who discovers in an inner pocket the letter given to him by his wife to slip in the mail box two weeks previously.

Of all the protagonists in these moving scenes it is perhaps to Macbeth seeing the ghost of Banquo that one may most aptly compare Pongo Twistleton as he heard this voice in the night. He stiffened from the ankles up, his eyes rolling, his hair stirring as if beneath a sudden breeze, his very collar seeming to wilt, and from his ashen lips there came a soft, wordless cry. It was not exactly the Potter-Bean 'Coo!' and not precisely the 'Gar!' of Sir Aylmer Bostock, but a sort of blend or composite of the two. That intelligent Scottish nobleman, Ross, whom very little escaped, said, as he looked at Macbeth, 'His highness is not well,' and he would have said the same if he had been looking at Pongo.

Nor is his emotion hard to understand. When a sensitive young man, animated by a lively consideration for his personal well-being, has been told by a much larger young man of admittedly homicidal tendencies that if he does not abandon his practice of hobnobbing with housemaids in the drawing room at one-thirty in the morning he, the much larger young man, will scoop out his insides with his bare hands, he shrinks from the prospect of being caught by the other entertaining a housemaid in his bedroom at two-forty-five. If Pongo said 'Gar!' or it may have been 'Coo!' and behaved as if an old friend whom he had recently caused to be murdered had dropped in to dinner with dagger wounds all over him, he cannot fairly be blamed. Those hands of Bill Oakshott's seemed to rise before his eyes like dreadful things seen in a nightmare.

But it was only for an instant that he stood inactive. In times of crisis blood will tell, and he had the good fortune to belong to a family whose members, having gone through a lot of this sort of thing in their day, had acquired and transmitted to their descendants a certain technique. A good many Twistletons, notably in the eighteenth and early nineteenth centuries, had been constrained by circumstances to think quick on occasions just such as this and, having thought quick, to hide women in cupboards. It was to the cupboard, therefore, acting automatically in accordance with the family tradition, that Pongo now directed Elsie Bean.

'Slide in there!' he hissed. 'And not a sound, not a yip, not a murmur. A human life hangs on your silence.'

He closed the cupboard door, straightened his tie and drawing a deep breath called, 'Come in.' And it was while he was smoothing his hair and simultaneously commending his soul to God that Bill Oakshott entered.

'Oh, hullo,' he said.

'Hullo,' said Bill. 'I'm glad you're still up, Pongo. I – er – I wanted a word with you.'

The phrase is one that sometimes has an ominous ring, but it was not menacingly that Bill Oakshott employed it. His voice was soft, even winning, and Pongo was encouraged to see that though looking as large as ever, if not larger, he seemed pacific. Ross, or somebody like that who noticed things, would have said that Bill was embarrassed, and he would have been right.

It often happens that after talking to a boyhood friend like an elder brother a young man of normally kindly disposition, when he has had time to reflect, finds himself wondering if his tone during the interview was not a little brusque. It was so with Bill Oakshott. Musing in solitude and recalling the scene in the drawing room, it had seemed to him that some of his remarks had taken too anatomical a trend. It was to apologise that he had come to Pongo's bedroom, and he proceeded now to do so.

It would have suited Pongo better if he had put these apologies in writing and submitted them to him in the form of a note, but he accepted them in a generous spirit, though absently, for he was listening to a soft, rustling sound which had begun to proceed from the cupboard. It made him feel as if spiders were walking up and down his back. The celebrated Beau Twistleton, in the days of the Regency, had once had a similar experience.

Bill appeared to have heard it, too.

'What's that?' he asked, pausing in his remarks.

'Eh?'

'That sort of scratching noise. In the cupboard.'

Pongo wiped a bead of perspiration from his forehead.

'Mice,' he said.

'Oh, mice. Lots of them about.'

'Yes, quite a good year for mice,' said Pongo. 'Well, good night, Bill, old man.'

But Bill was not yet ready to leave. Like so many large young men, he was sentimental, and this disinclined him to rush these scenes of reconciliation. When he healed rifts with boyhood friends, he liked to assure himself that they were going to stay healed. He sat down on the bed, which creaked beneath his weight.

'Well, I'm glad everything's all right, Pongo. You're sure you're not offended?'

'Not at all, not a-tall.'

'I thought you might have got the impression that I thought you were a foul snake.'

'No, no.'

'I ought never to have suggested such a thing.'

'Not keeping you up, am I, Bill?'

'Not a bit. It was just that when I found you and Elsie Bean in the drawing room, I thought for a moment—'

'Quite.'

'You know how it is.'

'Oh, rather.'

'You see . . . I'd sock those mice, if I were you.'

'I will – tomorrow – with an iron hand. Regardless of their age and sex.'

'You see, your heads were a bit close together.'

'I was merely lighting her cigarette.'

'Of course, of course. I realise that now. I know that I can trust you.'

'Oh, rather.'

'I know that you love Hermione and will make her happy. You will look on it as a sacred duty.'

'You betcher.'

'Fine,' said Bill, clasping his hands and putting a good deal of soul into his expression. 'That's a bit of goose. I'm devoted to Hermione, Pongo.'

'Yes, you told me.'

'Hermione—'

'How about having a long talk about her in the morning?'

'Not now?'

'Bit late, isn't it?'

'Ah yes, I suppose you want to turn in. I was only going to say that Hermione is the . . . dash it, what are those things?'

'The berries?'

'Lodestars. She is the lodestar of my life. I've been crazy about her for years and years and years, and her happiness means everything to me. How wonderful she is, Pongo.'

'Terrific.'

'You don't find many girls like Hermione.'

'Very scarce.'

'So beautiful.'

'Ah.'

'So clever.'

'What ho.'

'You've read her novels, of course?'

Pongo could not repress a guilty start. The question was an awkward one. He was uncomfortably conscious of having devoted to *Murder in the Fog* hours of study which would have been better employed in familiarising himself with his loved one's output.

'Well, I'll tell you,' he said. 'Up to the moment of going to press, I haven't for one reason and another been able to smack into them to quite the extent I could wish. But she's given me her latest to read while I'm here, and I can see from the first page that it's the bezuzus. Strikes a new note, as you might say.'

'Which one is that?'

'I've forgotten the name, but I know it was called something.'

'How long has it been out?'

'Just published, I understand.'

'Ah, then I haven't seen it. Fine. That's a treat to look forward to. Isn't she amazing, Pongo? Isn't it extraordinary that she can write all those wonderful books—'

'Oh, rather.'

'—And still be a simple, healthy, out-of-doors country girl, never happier than when she is getting up at six in the morning and going for a long walk through the—'

Pongo started.

'Six in the morning?' He spoke in a thin, strained voice, and his jaw had fallen a little. 'She doesn't get up at six in the morning?'

'In the summer always.'

'And in winter?'

'Seven. I've known her to do a round and a half of golf before breakfast, and if she doesn't play golf it's a long walk through the woods and fields. I tell you, she's marvellous. Well, good night, Pongo, you'll be wanting to get to bed,' said Bill, and heaving himself up took his departure.

It was a pensive Pongo Twistleton who went to the door and listened and then went to the cupboard and extracted Elsie Bean. To say that Bill's words had weakened his great love would perhaps be going too far, for he still thought Hermione Bostock a queen among women and had no intention of replying in the negative when the clergyman said, 'Wilt thou, Reginald, take this Hermione to be thy wedded wife?' But the discovery that he was engaged to a girl who habitually got up at six in the morning, and would presumably insist on him getting up at that hour also, had definitely shaken him. His manner as he de-Beaned the cupboard was distrait, and when his guest complained of being in the final stages of suffocation he merely said, 'Oh, ah?'

His detachment displeased Elsie Bean. She displayed a captious spirit.

'What did I have to go killing myself in cupboards for? It was only Mr William.'

'Only!' said Pongo, unable to share this easy outlook. 'Do you realise that if he had found you here, he would have pulled my head off at the roots?'

'You don't say?'

'Not to mention scooping out my insides with his bare hands.'

'Coo! What a nut!'

'The word nut understates it. When roused – and finding

you on the premises would have roused him like nobody's business – he's a menace to pedestrians and traffic. Gosh!' said Pongo, struck with an idea. 'Why wouldn't he be the man to bop your Harold on the nose?'

'But you're going to do it.'

'In case I can't manage to get around to it, I mean. You know how full one's time is. I believe Bill would be just the chap you want.'

Elsie Bean shook her head.

'No, I asked him.'

'Asked him?'

'R. I met him walking in the garden after I'd helped that nice old gentleman up the water pipe. He said he wouldn't.'

'Why not?'

'He doesn't believe in bopping coppers on the nose.'

It was a prejudice which Pongo shared, but nevertheless he found himself exasperated. One never likes to see a man stifling his natural gifts. The parable of the talents crossed his mind.

'But how on earth do you expect me to do it?' he demanded peevishly. 'The way everybody talks, you'd think it was the simplest thing in the world to walk up to a fifteen-stone policeman and sock him on the beezer. I can't see the procedure. How does one start? One can't just go and do it. It wants leading up to. And even then—'

Elsie Bean seemed to appreciate his difficulty.

'I've been thinking about that,' she said. 'How would it be if you pushed him into the duck pond?'

'What duck pond?'

'The one outside the front gate.'

'But he may not go near the bally duck pond.'

'Yes, he will. He always does, when he's on his beat. He goes and stands there and spits into it.'

Pongo brightened a little. It would be idle to pretend that he found the picture which his companion had conjured up attractive, but it was less repellent than the other.

'Creep up behind him, you mean?'

'R.'

'And give him a hearty shove?'

'R.'

'Yes. Yes, I see what you mean. Well, there is much in what you say, and I will give the matter my attention. It may be that you have found the solution. Meanwhile, go and peer cautiously up and down the passage and see if there's anybody about. If there isn't, pick up your feet and streak for your dug-out like a flash.'

But before she could reach the door, it had opened to admit Lord Ickenham and Sally. Both looked greatly refreshed, the former in particular wearing the contented expression of a man who has been steeping himself in boiled eggs.

'As good a little meal as I have ever tasted,' he said. 'Really, Mugsy does one extraordinarily well. And now bed, don't you think? The evening is wearing along. You had better be putting a few things together, Pongo.'

Pongo did not reply. He was staring at Sally. Lord Ickenham approached him and drove a kindly finger into his ribs.

'Ouch!'

'Start packing, my boy.'

'Eh? Oh, right ho!'

'Just a few necessaries. I can lend you a razor and my great sponge, Joyeuse.' Lord Ickenham turned to Elsie Bean. 'You two have settled things, I hope?'

'Yes, sir. Mr Twistleton is going to push Harold into the duck pond.'

'Capital, capital,' said Lord Ickenham heartily. 'An excellent idea. You'll enjoy that, Pongo. Don't forget that in pushing policemen into duck ponds the follow through is everything.'

Pongo, mechanically filling a suitcase, again made no reply. Though he had ceased to stare at Sally, she still occupied his thoughts. The sight of her coming through the door had acted upon him like a powerful electric shock, for her eyes, the eyes of a girl refreshed with tea and eggs, had seemed, if possible, brighter than ever, and once more she had flashed upon him that smile of hers. And this time, though he had immediately thought of Hermione Bostock, it was only to be reminded of her habit of rising at six in the summer and at seven during the winter months.

He closed the suitcase, and stood waiting. Strange thrills were shooting through his streamlined body, and his heart, which had been comparatively inactive recently, was again jumping and bumping. That consciousness of not having pushed a good thing along was now very pronounced.

'Well, good night, Sally,' said Lord Ickenham.

'Good night, Uncle Fred. Good night, Pongo.'

'Eh? Oh, good night.'

'And thanks for the sanctuary.'

'Eh? Oh, not at all.'

'Good night, Miss Bean.'

'Good night, sir.'

'You will be turning in yourself shortly, no doubt? A thousand thanks once more for all your sympathy and kindness. The duck pond, eh?' said Lord Ickenham thoughtfully. 'Yes, admirable, admirable. Come along, Pongo.'

Halfway along the corridor Pongo paused. Lord Ickenham eyed him inquiringly.

'Forgotten something?'

'Eh? Oh, no. I was only thinking about Sally.'

'What about her?'

'She looked dashed pretty in that dressing gown.'

'Charming. By the way, she tells me she wants a lipstick. See to that tomorrow, will you.'

'Right ho,' said Pongo. 'Lipstick, one. Right.'

He resumed his progress musingly.

PART FOUR

X

I

If you motor to Wockley Junction in the morning, starting from Ashenden Manor reasonably soon after an earlyish breakfast, you can get an express train which deposits you on the arrival platform at Waterloo at twelve-forty-three. The passage of the hours in no way having weakened her determination to visit her child and make plain to her the bleakness of the future awaiting any girl rash enough to put on a white veil and walk down the aisle with her arm linked in that of Reginald Twistleton, Lady Bostock had done this. Bill Oakshott drove her to the junction, and she reached the block of flats where Hermione had her London residence shortly after one, just as Hermione, outside its front door, was about to step into her two-seater.

Privileged to direct a square look at this girl as she stood there in the almost unbelievable splendour of her new hat, her best frock and her carefully selected shoes, gloves and stockings, the dullest eye would have been able to see that she had what it takes. Her father might look like a walrus and her mother like something starting at a hundred to eight in the two-thirty race at Catterick Bridge, but Hermione herself, tall and dark, with large eyes, a perfect profile and an equally perfect figure, was an Oriental potentate's dream of what the harem needed.

Hearing Lady Bostock's bleating cry, she turned and stared, incredulity blended in her gaze with the natural dismay of a daughter who, having said goodbye to her mother on a

Monday afternoon after entertaining her for a week at her flat, sees her come bobbing up again on Wednesday morning.

'Mother!' she exclaimed in the rich contralto which for years had been stirring up Bill Oakshott's soul like an egg whisk. 'Whatever . . .?'

'Oh dear,' said Lady Bostock. 'Have you got to go? I came up specially to see you.'

'I must. I'm lunching at Barribault's and I'm late already. What did you want to see me about?'

'Oh dear, oh dear, oh dear. Reginald.'

'Reginald?'

'Yes, dear. Your father—'

A smouldering gleam came into Hermione's fine eyes. Those words 'Your father', taken in conjunction with the name of the man to whom she had plighted her troth, had aroused her suspicions. They could only mean, it seemed to her, that in defiance of her explicit instructions Sir Aylmer had not been treating her nominee like an ewe lamb. And she was a girl who when she said ewe lamb meant ewe lamb.

'What has Father been doing to Reginald?' she demanded sternly. 'Has he been barking at him?'

'No, no. Your father never barks. He sometimes raises his voice.'

'Has he been raising his voice, then?'

'Scarcely so that you could notice it. No, what has happened . . . Oh dear, it's such a long story.'

'Then I really can't wait to hear it now. I'm terribly late. And I'm lunching with a publisher.'

'Mr Popgood?'

Hermione laughed a short, dry laugh. In an association which had lasted three years Augustus Popgood, the sponsor of her books, had never offered her so much as a cheese straw. Nor had his partner, Cyril Grooly.

'No,' she said. 'This is a new one. He wrote to me a few days ago, saying that he would like to have me on his list and suggesting luncheon. He seems a most enterprising man, quite different from Popgood and Grooly. He is the head of a firm called Meriday House, a Mr Pointer or Punter or Painter. I couldn't make out the signature on his letter. Goodbye, Mother. I'll try to get back about three.'

'I'll wait for you, dear.'

'It's something important, you say?'

'Very, very important.'

'About Reginald?'

'Yes, dear. We find that he—'

'I'm sorry, Mother,' said Hermione. 'I must rush.'

She was not without a normal girl's curiosity, but she was also an ambitious young authoress who believed that there is a tide in the affairs of men which taken at the flood leads on to fortune, and there was awaiting her at Barribault's Hotel a publisher who, judging from his letter, was evidently a live wire endowed with pep and ginger and all the other qualities which ambitious young authoresses like to see in those responsible for the marketing of their books.

The car moved off. Seated at the wheel, she gave herself up to agreeable thoughts about this pushful Mr Pointer.

Or Punter.

Or possibly Painter.

2

Painter was the name. Not Pointer. Not Punter. Painter. It was Sally's brother Otis who was waiting for Hermione in the lobby of Barribault's Hotel, and at the moment when her two-seater joined the stream of traffic he had sprung from his chair, too nervous to sit any longer, and begun to stride to and fro, his eyes from time to time straying to his wristwatch. The coming luncheon marked a crisis in his affairs.

It was no mere coincidence that Otis Painter, in his capacity of publisher of the book beautiful, should have written to Hermione suggesting a meeting with a view to an agreement. The invitation had been the outcome of some very rapid thinking on his part.

Right from the start it had been plain to Otis Painter that if anything like a happy ending was to be achieved in that matter of the lawsuit which was brooding over him like a thunder cloud, Sir Aylmer Bostock would have to be pleaded with, and he had told Sally to tell Pongo to perform the task. And it was while he was in the grip of that unpleasant sinking feeling which always came to those who placed their affairs in Pongo's hands that he had happened upon the issue of the *Tatler* containing Hermione's photograph.

'Miss Hermione Bostock,' he read, 'daughter of Sir Aylmer and Lady Bostock of Ashenden Manor, Hants. In addition to being prominent in Society, Miss Bostock has written several novels under the pseudonym of Gwynneth Gould.'

The words had brought inspiration. His thoughts, as he gazed at the photograph and the caption beneath it, had run roughly as follows. And they seem to us to display an intelligence considerably above the average of what might have been expected in one who had been in his time both an interior decorator and a seller of antiques, besides running a marionette theatre in the Boulevard Raspail.

Q. Who is the best possible person to plead with an old crumb who is threatening to bring a ruinous suit for damages against a shaky young publishing firm?

A. Obviously the crumb's daughter, the apple of his eye to whom he can refuse nothing.

Q. Get hold of the daughter, then, and enlist her in one's cause?

A. Exactly.

Q. But how?

A. Easy. She's an author. Offer her a contract. Her interests will then be identical with those of her publisher, and she will exert her tremendous influence to save him from ruin. Better ask her to lunch.

Q. Right.

A. At Barribault's.

Q. *What?* Have you ever been to Barribault's and seen the prices on the right-hand side?

A. No good spoiling the ship for a ha'porth of tar. You can't swing a deal like this on bottled beer, a mutton chop and two veg.

So now Otis was pacing Barribault's lobby, wondering why his guest did not arrive and what the lunch was going to set him back when she did. A few thoughtful words about acidity might steer her off champagne, but at a place like this even hock was likely to inflict a ghastly gash on the wallet.

Watching Otis Painter walk to and fro with his mouth ajar and his knees clashing like cymbals, for he had the misfortune to suffer from adenoids and to be knock-kneed, a spectator would have been surprised to learn that he was so closely related to Sally. But just as daughters have a way of being easier on the eye than their fathers and mothers, so are sisters frequently more attractive than their brothers. Otis was a stout young man with a pink nose, horn-rimmed spectacles and short side-whiskers, who looked like something from the Anglo-Saxon colony on the east bank of the Seine.

It was, indeed, to the east bank of the Seine that he had migrated immediately after graduating from the college where he had received his education, having sprouted a soul and the side-whiskers simultaneously towards the end of his sopho-more year. From the *rive gauche* he had drifted to London, there to try various ventures with a uniform lack of success, and here he was, five years later, the directing executive of Meri-day House, formerly Ye Panache Presse, waiting in Barribault's lobby to give lunch to Hermione Bostock.

The hands of his watch were pointing to twenty-seven min-utes past one when through the glass of the outer door he saw the gaily apparelled official who stood on the threshold to scoop clients out of their cars and cabs suddenly stiffen himself; touch his hat convulsively and give his moustache a spasmodic twirl, sufficient indication that something pretty sensational was on its way in. And a moment later the door revolved and through it came a figure that made him catch his breath and regret that the pimple on the tip of his nose had not yielded to treatment that morning. There is nothing actually low and degrading about a pimple on the tip of the nose, but there are times when a sus-ceptible young man wishes he did not have one.

He stepped forward devoutly.

'Miss Gould?'

'Oh, how do you do, Mr Pointer?'

'Painter.'

'Punter?'

'Painter.'

'Oh, Painter. I hope I'm not late.'

'No, no. Cocktail?'

'No, thank you. I never drink.'

Otis started. The wallet in his hip pocket seemed to give a joyful leap.

'What, not even at lunch?'

'Only lemonade.'

'Come right in,' said Otis with an enthusiasm which he made no attempt to conceal. 'Come right along in.'

He led the way buoyantly towards the grill room. Lemonade, he happened to know, was half-a-crown.

3

It was probably this immediate striking of the right note that made the luncheon such a success. For that it was a success not even the most exacting critic could have disputed. From the first forkful of smoked salmon it went with all the swing of a Babylonian orgy or of one of those conferences between statesmen which are conducted throughout in a spirit of the utmost cordiality.

Too often when a publisher entertains an author at the midday meal a rather sombre note tinges the table talk. The host is apt to sigh a good deal and to choose as the theme of his remarks the hardness of the times, the stagnant condition of the book trade and the growing price of pulp paper. And when his guest tries to cheer him up by suggesting that these disadvantages may be offset by a spirited policy of publicity, he sighs again and says that eulogies of an author's work displayed in the press at the publisher's expense are of little or no value, the only advertising that counts being – how shall he put it – well, what he might perhaps describe as word-of-mouth advertising.

There was nothing of that sort here today. Otis scoffed at the idea that the times were hard. The times, in his opinion, were swell. So was the book trade. Not a trace of stagnation. And as for pulp paper, you might have supposed from the way he spoke that they gave him the stuff.

He then went on to sketch out his policy as regarded advertising.

Otis, said Otis, believed in advertising. When he found an author in whom he had confidence – like you, Miss Gould, if he might say so – the sky was the limit. A column here, a column there. That sort of thing. The cost? He didn't give a darn about the cost. You got it all back on the sales. His motto, he said, coming through smoothly with the only bit of French – except *Oo-la-la* – which had managed to stick from the old left bank days, was *L'audace, l'audace, et toujours l'audace.*

It was a statement of faith well calculated to make any young authoress feel that she was floating on a pink cloud over an ocean of joy, and that was how Hermione felt as she listened. The sensation grew even more acute as her host spoke of commissioning her next three books, sight unseen, and paying royalty on them at the rate of twenty per cent, rising to twenty-five above three thousand. Even when uttered by a man with adenoids the words were like the strains of some grand anthem.

It is possible that the reader of this chronicle, misled by Bill Oakshott's enthusiasm, may have formed an erroneous idea of Hermione Bostock's standing in the world of literature, for her career had been a good deal less triumphant than he had appeared to suggest. She had published three works of fiction through the house of Popgood and Grooly, of which the first two had sold eleven hundred and four and sixteen hundred and eight copies respectively. The last, just out, was reported by Popgood, a gloomy man, to be 'moving slowly'. Grooly, the optimist of the firm, spoke in brighter vein of a possible sale of two thousand.

But even if you strung along with sunny young Grooly you could not say that figures like these were anything but a poor return for a great deal of hard toil, and Hermione attributed them not to any lack of merit in the books themselves, for she knew their merit to be considerable, but to the firm's preference for keeping its money in the old oak chest instead of spending it on advertisements in the papers. She had once taken this matter up with the partners, and Popgood had said that it was no use advertising in the papers, because the only form of advertising that counted was . . . how should he put it?

'Word of mouth?' suggested Grooly.

'Word of mouth!' assented Popgood, looking gratefully at the ingenious phrase-maker.

Little wonder, then, that as Hermione drank in Otis's intoxicating words, soft music seemed to fill the air and even the directing executive of Meriday House became almost beautiful. She listened as if in a dream, and the more he talked the more she liked it. It was only as she was sipping her coffee (two shillings, but unavoidable) that anything crept into his remarks that suggested that all was not for the best in the best of all possible worlds. Quite suddenly, after an eloquent passage surcharged with optimism, he struck a minor chord.

'Yay,' he said, 'that's how I feel. I admire your work and I would like to take hold of your books and push them as they ought to be pushed. But—'

He paused, and Hermione, descending from her pink cloud, looked at him with concern. When a publisher has offered you twenty per cent rising to twenty-five above three thousand and has been talking spaciously of column spreads in all the literate Sunday papers, you do not like to hear him use that word 'but'.

'But——?' she echoed.

Otis removed his horn-rimmed spectacles, polished them and replaced them on a nose which an excellent luncheon had turned from pink to scarlet. He also touched his pimple and polished that, and with a pudgy hand stroked his starboard whisker. The interview had reached its crux, and he wished to reflect before proceeding.

'But . . . Well, the fact is,' he said, 'there's a catch. I'm not so sure I'm going to have the money to do it with. I may go bankrupt before I can start.'

'What!'

'You see, I'm faced with a darned nasty legal action, and my lawyer tells me the damages may be very heavy.'

'But why do you speak as if you were certain to lose?'

'I am, if it ever comes into court. And I don't see how I'm going to stop it coming into court. This man Bostock——'

'Bostock?'

'Sir Aylmer Bostock. He used to be Governor of one of those African colonies, and he wrote his Reminiscences and got me to publish them——'

'But that was Ye Panache Presse.'

'I changed the name to Meriday House. Crisper. Why, say,' said Otis with natural surprise, 'you speak as if you know all about it. You do? Extraordinary how these things get around. Well, if you've heard what happened, I don't have to explain. The point is that this Bostock is showing a very vindictive spirit. And, as I say, if the thing comes into court, I shall be ruined.'

'Ah!' said Hermione.

Lord Ickenham, looking at this girl's photograph, had given it as his opinion that she was a potential eye-flasher. He had been correct. Her eyes were flashing now, and in that simple 'Ah!' there was all the sinister significance of Constable Potter's 'Ho!'

In earlier portions of this chronicle reference was made to the emotions of wolves which overtake sleighs and find no Russian peasant aboard and of tigers deprived of their Indian coolie just as they are sitting down to lunch. More poignant even than these are the feelings of a young authoress who, having just been offered twenty per cent rising to twenty-five above three thousand by a publisher who believes in column spreads in all the literate Sunday papers, learns that her father is planning to rob that publisher of the means to publish.

Hermione rose, grim and resolute.

'Don't worry, Mr Painter. I will see that the suit does not come into court.'

'Eh?'

'I ought to have told you earlier that Gwynneth Gould is merely my pen-name. I am Hermione Bostock. Sir Aylmer's daughter.' Otis was almost too amazed for words.

'His *daughter*? Well, fancy that. Well, I'll be darned. What an extraordinary thing.'

'I will talk to Father. I will drive down and see him at once.'

'How would it be if you took me along? In case you needed help.'

'I shall not need help.'

'Still, I'd like to be on the spot, to hear the good news as soon as possible.'

'Very well. While I am seeing Father, you can wait at the inn. So if you are ready, Mr Painter, let us be going. My car is outside.'

It was as they were nearing Guildford at sixty miles an hour, for she was a girl who believed that accelerators were made to be stepped on, that a thought which for some time had been groping about the exterior of Hermione's mind, like an inebriated householder fumbling with his latch-key, suddenly succeeded in effecting an entrance, and she gave a gasp.

'Pardon?' said Otis, who also had been gasping. He was finding his companion's driving a novel and terrifying experience.

'Nothing,' said Hermione. 'Just something I happened to remember.'

It was the circumstance of her mother's visit that she had happened to remember, that devoted mother who had now been waiting three hours at her flat to tell her something about Reginald. For an instant she was conscious of a twinge of remorse. Then she told herself that Mother would be all right. She had a comfortable chair and all the illustrated papers.

She pressed her foot on the accelerator, and Otis shut his eyes and commended his soul to God.

XI

I

The afternoon sun, slanting in through the French window of what until the previous night had been Pongo's bedroom, touched Sally's face and woke her from the doze into which she had fallen. She rose and stretched herself, yawning.

The French window opened on a balcony, and she eyed it wistfully. It would have been pleasant on so fine a summer day to go and sit on that balcony. But girls who are known, if only slightly, to the police must be prudent. The best she could do was to stand behind the curtain and from this observation post peer out at the green and golden world beyond.

Soon exhausting the entertainment value of a patch of gravel and part of a rhododendron bush, she was about to return to the *chaise longue*, when there appeared on the patch of gravel the tall, distinguished figure of Lord Ickenham, walking jauntily and carrying a small suitcase. He passed from view, and a moment later there was a thud as the suitcase fell on the balcony.

Her heart leaped. An intelligent girl, she realised that this must mean clothes. The fifth Earl might have his frivolous moments, but he was not the man to throw suitcases on to balconies in a spirit of mere wantonness. She crawled cautiously on all fours and possessed herself of the rich gift.

Her confidence had not been misplaced. It was clothes, and she hastened to put on what she recognised as a white sports dress and red jacket belonging to Lady Ickenham with all the eagerness of a girl who likes to look nice and for some little time has had to get along with a man's flowered dressing gown. And it was as she stood examining herself contentedly in the mirror that Lord Ickenham entered.

'So you got them all right?' he said. 'Not a bad shot for a man who has jerked very little since the old soda days. But if you have once jerked soda, you never really lose the knack. I like that red coat. Rather dressy.'

Sally kissed him gratefully.

'You're an angel, Uncle Fred. Nobody saw you, I hope?'

'Not a soul. The enemy's lines were thin and poorly guarded. Your hostess went to London soon after breakfast, and Mugsy is over at a neighbouring village, trying to sell someone a cow, I understand.'

Sally started.

'Then why not do it now? Get the bust, I mean.'

'My dear child, you don't suppose that idea did not occur to me? My first move on learning that the coast was clear was to make a beeline for the collection room, only to discover that Mugsy had locked the door and gone off with the key. As I was saying to Pongo last night, there is a streak of low cunning in Mugsy's nature which one deplores. Still, don't worry. I'm biding my time. That's the sort of man I'm, as the song says. I shall arrange everything to your full satisfaction quite shortly.'

'Says you.'

'Sally! Don't tell me you're losing confidence in me.'

'Oh, darling Uncle Fred, of course not. Why did I speak those harsh words? Consider them unsaid.'

'They are already expunged from my memory. Yes, you look charming in that coat. Quite a vision. No wonder Pongo loves you.'

'Not any more.'

'More than ever. I was noticing the way his eyes came popping out last night every time they rested on you. Did you ever see a prawn in the mating season? Like that. And one of the last things he said to me was, "She looked dashed pretty in that dressing-gown." With a sort of catch in his voice. That means love.'

'If he thought I looked pretty in a dressing gown made for a man of six feet two, it must mean something.'

'Love, my dear. Love, I tell you. All the old fervour has started gushing up again like a geyser. He worships you. He adores you. He would die for one little rose from your hair. How are conditions at your end?'

'Oh, I haven't changed.'

'You love him still?'

'I'm crazy about him.'

'That's satisfactory. Though odd. I'm very fond of Pongo. In fact, except for my wife and you and my dog, George, I can think of nobody of whom I am fonder. But I can't understand anyone being crazy about him. How do you do it?'

'It's quite easy, bless his precious heart. He's a baa-lamb.'

'You see him from that angle?'

'I always have. A sweet, woolly baa-lamb that you want to stroke and pet.'

'Well, you may be right. You know more about baa-lambs than I do. But this is official. If I were a girl and he begged me for one little rose from my hair, I wouldn't give it him. He'd have a pretty thin time trying to get roses out of me. Still, the great thing is that you love him, because I have an idea that he will very soon be at liberty to pay his addresses to you. This engagement of his can't last.'

'You certainly do spread sweetness and light, don't you, Uncle Fred?'

'I try to.'

'Tell me more. I could listen for ever. Why do you think the engagement won't last?'

'How can it? What on earth does a girl like Hermione Bostock want to marry Pongo for?'

'Maybe she likes baa-lambs, too.'

'Nonsense. I've only seen her photograph, but I could tell at a glance that what she needs is a large, solid, worshipping husband of the huntin', shootin' and fishin' type, not a metropolitan product like Pongo. Her obvious mate is her cousin, Bill Oakshott, who has been devoted to her for years. But he's too mild in his methods. He doesn't tell his love, but lets concealment like a worm i' the bud feed on his damask cheek. You can't run a business that way. I intend to have a very serious talk with young William Oakshott next time I see him. In fact, I'll go and try to find him now.'

'No, don't go yet. I want to tell you about Pongo.'

'What about him?'

'He's worried to death, the poor pet. My heart aches for him. He was in here not long ago, and he just sat in a chair and groaned.'

'You're sure he wasn't singing?'

'I don't think so. Would he have buried his face in his hands, if he had been singing?'

'No. You're perfectly right. That is the acid test. I have heard Pongo sing on several occasions at our village concert, and it is impossible to mistake the symptoms. He sticks his chin up and throws his head back and lets it go in the direction of the ceiling at an angle of about forty-five. And very unpleasant it is, especially when the song is "Oh, My Dolores, Queen of the Eastern Sea", as too often happens. So he groaned, did he? Why?'

'He doesn't like this idea of pushing the policeman into the duck pond.'

'Doesn't *like* it? Not when he knows it's going to bring happiness and wedding bells to the divine Bean?'

'The impression he gave me was that he wasn't thinking much about the divine Bean and her wedding bells.'

'Looking at the thing principally in the light of how it was going to affect good old Twistleton?' Lord Ickenham sighed. 'Young men are not what they were in my day, Sally. We were all Galahads then. Damsels in distress had merely to press a button, and we would race up with our ears flapping, eager to do their behest. Well, we can't have him backing out. We owe a debt of honour to Miss Bean, and it must be paid. And, dash it, what's he making such heavy weather about? It isn't as if this duck pond were miles away across difficult country.'

A strange look had come into Sally's face, the sort of resolute look you might have surprised on the faces of Joan of Arc or Boadicea.

'Where is it?' she asked. 'He didn't tell me.'

'Outside the front gate. A mere step. And I was speaking to Miss Bean this morning, and she tells me that when Potter arrives there on his beat he always stands beside it for an appreciable space of time, spitting and, one hopes, thinking of her. What simpler and more agreeable task could there be than to saunter up behind a spitting policeman, at a moment when he is wrapped in thought, and push him into a pond? To further the interests of a girl like La Bean, the finest housemaid that ever flicked a duster, I would have pushed twenty policemen into twenty ponds when I was Pongo's age.'

'But Pongo has such a rare, sensitive nature.'

'So had I a rare, sensitive nature. It was the talk of New York. Well, if the thing is to be done today, he ought to be starting. It is at just about this hour, I am informed, that Potter rolls along. Where is he?'

'I don't know. He drifted out.'

'I must find him at once.'

'Just a minute,' said Sally.

The resolute expression on her face had become more noticeable than ever. In addition to looking like Joan of Arc and Boadicea, she could now have been mistaken in a dim light for Jael, the wife of Heber, and Lord Ickenham, pausing on his way to the door, was impressed and vaguely disturbed.

'What's the matter?' he asked. 'You have a strained air. You aren't worrying about Pongo?'

'Yes, I am.'

'But I keep assuring you that the task before him is both simple and agreeable.'

'Not for Pongo. He's a baa-lamb. I told you that before.'

'But why should the circumstance of being a baa-lamb unfit a man for pushing policemen into ponds?'

'I don't know. But it does. I've studied this thing of pushing policemen into ponds, Uncle Fred, and I'm convinced that what you need, to get the best results, is a girl whose clothes the policeman tore off on the previous night.'

'Good God, Sally! You don't mean—?'

'Yes, I do. My mind is made up. I'm going to pinch hit for Pongo, and, if it interests you to know it, it is a far, far better thing that I do than I have ever done. Goodbye, Uncle Fred. See you later.'

She disappeared on to the balcony, and a scrabbling sound told Lord Ickenham that she was descending the water pipe. He went out, and was in time to see her vanish into the bushes on the other side of the terrace. For some moments he stood there staring after her, then with a little sigh, the sigh too often extorted from Age by the spectacle of Headstrong Youth doing its stuff, passed thoughtfully from the room. Making his way downstairs, still pensive, he reached the hall.

Bill Oakshott was there, balancing a walking stick on the tip of his nose.

2

That the young squire of Ashenden in essaying this equilibristic feat had not been animated by a mere spirit of frivolity, but was endeavouring rather, as men will in times of mental stress, to divert his thoughts from graver issues, was made clear by a certain touch of the careworn in his manner. It is not easy to look careworn when you are balancing a walking stick on the tip of your nose, but Bill Oakshott contrived to do so.

At the sight of Lord Ickenham he brightened. Ever since he had escorted Lady Bostock to Wockley Junction that morning he had been wanting to see and seek counsel from one on whose judgment he had come to rely, and owing to the fact of having been obliged to fulfil a long-standing luncheon engagement with friends who lived on the Wockley road he had had no opportunity of approaching him earlier.

'Oh, there you are,' he said. 'Fine.'

Lord Ickenham reluctantly put Sally's affairs to one side for the time being. The sight of this massive youth had reminded him that he had a pep talk to deliver.

'The word "fine",' he replied, 'is happily chosen, for I, too, have been looking forward to this encounter. I want to speak to you, Bill Oakshott.'

'I want to speak to *you*.'

'I have much to say.'

'So have I much to say.'

'Well, if it comes to a duet, I'll bet I can talk louder and quicker than you, and I am willing to back this opinion with notes, cash or lima beans. However, as I am your guest, I suppose courtesy demands that I yield the floor. Proceed.'

Bill marshalled his thoughts.

'Well, it's like this. After breakfast this morning, I drove my aunt to Wockley to catch the express to London. I was feeling a bit tired after being up so late last night, so I didn't talk as we tooled along, just kept an eye on the road and thought of this and that.'

Lord Ickenham interrupted him.

'Skip all this part. I shall be able to read it later, no doubt, in your autobiography, in the chapter headed "Summer Morning Outings with My Aunt". Spring to the point.'

'Well, what I was going to say was that I was keeping an eye on the road and thinking of this and that, when she suddenly said, "Dipsomaniac."'

'Why did she call you a dipsomaniac?'

'She didn't. It turned out she was talking about Pongo.'

'Pongo, egad? Was she, indeed?'

'Yes. She said, "Dipsomaniac". And I said, "Eh?" And she said, "He's a dipsomaniac." And I said, "Who's a dipsomaniac?" And she said, "Reginald Twistleton is a dipsomaniac. Your uncle says he has not been sober since he got here."'

Lord Ickenham drew in his breath with a little hiss of admiration.

'Masterly!' he said. 'Once again, Bill Oakshott, I must pay a marked tribute to your narrative gifts. I never met a man who could tell a story better. Come clean, my boy. You are Sinclair Lewis, are you not? Well, I'm convinced you're someone. So your aunt said, "Dipsomaniac", and you said, "Eh?" and she said . . .

and so on and so forth, concluding with this fearless *exposé* of Pongo. Very interesting. Did she mention on what she based the charge?'

'Oh, rather. Apparently she and Uncle Aylmer found him swigging whisky in the drawing room.'

'I would not attach too much importance to that. Many of our noblest men swig whisky in drawing rooms. I do myself.'

'But not all night. Well, you might say all night. What I mean is, I found Pongo in the drawing room, swigging away, at about one o'clock this morning, and my aunt and uncle appear to have found him there, still swigging, at half-past two. That makes one and a half hours. Give him say half an hour before I came in, and you get two hours of solid swigging. And after my aunt and uncle left he must have started swigging again. Because he was unquestionably stinko after breakfast.'

'I decline to believe that anyone could get stinko at breakfast.'

'I didn't say he did get stinko at breakfast. You're missing the point. My theory is that he swigged all night, got stinko round about six a.m. and continued stinko till the incident occurred.'

'To what incident do you allude?'

'It happened just after breakfast. My aunt was waiting for me to bring the car round, and Uncle Aylmer made some unpleasant cracks about the hat she was wearing. So she went up to her room to get another, and as she reached the door she heard someone moving about inside. When she went in, there was nobody to be seen, and then suddenly there came a sneeze from the wardrobe, and there was Pongo, crouching on the floor.'

'She was sure?'

'Sure?'

'It wasn't a shoe or a bit of fluff?'

'No, it was Pongo. She says he smiled weakly and said he

had looked in to borrow her lipstick. He must have been as tight as an owl. Because, apart from anything else, a glance at Aunt Emily should have told him she hasn't got a lipstick. And what I've been trying to make up my mind about is, oughtn't Hermione to be warned? Isn't it a bit thick to allow her to breeze gaily into a lifelong union with a chap who's going to spend his married life sitting up all night getting stinko in the drawing room? I don't see how a wife could possibly be happy under such conditions.'

'She might feel rather at a loose end, might she not? But you are misjudging Pongo in considering him a non-stop swigger. As a general thing he is quite an abstemious young man. Only in exceptional circumstances does he go on anything which a purist would call a bender. At the moment he is under a severe nervous strain.'

'Why?'

'For some reason he always is when we visit a house together. My presence – it is difficult to explain it – seems to do something to him.'

'Then you don't feel that Hermione ought to be told?'

'I will have to think it over. But,' said Lord Ickenham, fixing his young friend with a penetrating eye, 'there is something she must be told – without delay, and by you, Bill Oakshott.'

'Eh?'

'And that is that you love her and would make her yours.'

'Eh?'

'Fight against this tendency to keep saying "Eh". You do love her, do you not? You would make her yours, wouldn't you? I have it from an authoritative source that you have been thinking along those lines for years and years.'

Bill had turned a pretty vermilion. He shuffled his feet.

'Why, yes,' he admitted, 'that's right, as a matter of fact. I have. But how can I tell her I would make her mine? She's engaged to Pongo.'

'What of it?'

'You can't go barging in on a girl, telling her you would make her yours, when she's engaged to another chap.'

'Of course you can. How about Young Lochinvar? He did it, and was extremely highly thought of in consequence. You are familiar with the case of Young Lochinvar?'

'Oh, yes. I used to recite the poem as a kid.'

'It must have sounded wonderful,' said Lord Ickenham courteously. 'I myself was best at "It wath the thschooner Hethperuth that thailed the thtormy theas." Well, let me tell you something, my dear chap. You need have no morbid scruples about swinging Hermione Bostock on to your saddle bow, as far as Pongo is concerned. He's in love with somebody else. Do you remember me speaking at our first meeting of a girl I had been hoping he would marry? I don't think I mentioned it then, but he was at one time engaged to her, and all the symptoms point to his wanting to be again. The last time I saw them together, which was quite recently, I received the distinct impression that he would die for one little rose from her hair. So you can go ahead without a qualm. Miss Bostock is in London, I understand. Pop up there and pour your heart out.'

'M'm.'

'Why do you say "M'm"?'

Once again Bill Oakshott shuffled his feet, producing on the parquet floor a sound resembling waves breaking on a stern and rockbound coast.

'It's so difficult.'

'What, to pour your heart out? Nonsense.'

'Well, I've been trying to do it for nine years, but not a ripple. I can't seem to get started.'

Lord Ickenham reflected.

'I think I see where the trouble lies. You have made the mistake of brooding in advance too much, with the result that you have pottered about and accomplished nothing. Swiftness and decision are what is needed. Don't hesitate. Have at her. Sweep her off her feet. Take her by storm.'

'Oh, yes?' said Bill flatly, and Lord Ickenham laid a kindly hand on his shoulder. He knew what was passing in the young man's mind.

'I can understand your feeling a little nervous,' he said. 'When I saw Hermione Bostock's photograph, I was struck at once by something formidable in her face, a touch of that majestic inaccessibility which used to cramp the style of diffident young Greek shepherds in their relations with the more dignified of the goddesses of Mount Olympus. She is what in my day would have been called a proud beauty. And that makes it all the more necessary to take a strong line from the start. Proud beauties have to be dominated.'

'But, dash it, Pongo can't have dominated her.'

'True. But Pongo, so I am informed, is a baa-lamb. Baa-lambs get their results by different methods.'

'You don't think I'm a baa-lamb?'

'I fear not. You're too large, too robust and ruddy of countenance, too obviously a man who does his daily dozen of a morning and likes roly-poly pudding for lunch. Where a Pongo can click by looking fragile and stammering words of endearment, you must be the whirlwind wooer, or nothing. You will have to behave like the heroes of those novels which were so popular at one time, who went about in riding breeches and were not above giving the girl of their choice a couple with a hunting crop on the spot where it would do most good. Ethel M. Dell. That's the name I was trying to think of. You must comport yourself like the hero of an Ethel M. Dell novel. Buy her works, and study them diligently.'

A firm look came into Bill's face.

'I'm not going to sock her with a hunting crop.'

'It would help.'

'No. Definitely no.'

'Very well. Cut business with hunting crop. Then what you must do is stride up to the girl and grab her by the wrist.'

'Oh, gosh!'

'Ignoring her struggles, clasp her to your bosom and shower kisses on her upturned face. You needn't say much. Just "My mate!" or something of that sort. Well, think it over, my dear fellow. But I can assure you that this method will bring home the bacon. It is known as the Ickenham System, and it never fails. And now I fear I must be leaving you. I'm looking for Pongo. You don't happen to know where he is?'

'I saw him half an hour ago walking up and down on the tennis lawn.'

'With bowed head?'

'Yes, I believe his head was bowed, now you mention it.'

'I thought as much. Poor lad, poor lad. Well, I have tidings for him which will bring it up with a jerk. So goodbye for the moment. Oh, by the way,' said Lord Ickenham, reappearing like a benevolent Cheshire cat, 'in grabbing the subject by the wrist, don't behave as if you were handling a delicate piece of china. Grip firmly and waggle her about a bit.'

He disappeared again, and Bill could hear him trolling an old love song of the early nineteen hundreds as he started for the tennis lawn.

On a shy and diffident young man, accustomed for years just to shuffle his feet and look popeyed when in the presence of the girl he loves, a pep talk along the lines of that delivered by Lord Ickenham has much the same effect as a plunge into icy water on a cold morning. First comes the numbing shock, when everything turns black and the foundations of the soul seem to start reeling. Only later does there follow the glowing reaction.

For some appreciable time after his mentor had taken his departure, Bill stood congealed with horror as he contemplated the picture which the other had limned for him. The thought of showering kisses on Hermione Bostock's upturned face set his spine crawling like something in the Snake House at the Zoo. The idea of grabbing her by the wrist and waggling her about a bit made him feel as he had once felt at his private school after eating six ice-creams in a quarter of an hour because somebody bet him he wouldn't.

And then suddenly, with considerable astonishment, he found that horror had given way to a strange exhilaration. He could now appreciate the solid merits of this Ickenham system, chief among which was the fact that it placed the wooing of Hermione Bostock on the plane of physical action. Physical action was his dish. Give him something to do with his hands, and he knew where he was.

So simple, too. Nothing intricate or elaborate about it. Run over it once more, just to make sure one hadn't forgotten anything.

Stride up and grab?

Easy.

Waggle about?

Pie.

Clasp to bosom and s.k. on upturned f.?

No difficulty there.

Say, 'My mate'?

About that he was not so sure. It seemed to him that Lord Ickenham, brilliant as an arranger of stage business, had gone astray as regarded dialogue. Wouldn't a fellow be apt to feel a bit of a chump, saying, 'My mate'? Better, surely, just to pant a good deal? Yes, that was the stuff. Stride, grab, waggle, clasp, kiss, pant. Right.

Under the stress of intense thought he had started to walk up and down the hall, his head bent over the fingers on which he was ticking off the various items on the list, and it was as he unconsciously accelerated his pace on getting that inspiration about panting that a bumping sensation and a loud roar of anguish told him that there had been a traffic accident.

Narrowing his gaze, he saw that he had rammed something substantial and white-moustached, and narrowing it still further identified this as his uncle, Sir Aylmer Bostock. And he was about to offer suitable apologies, when all thought of injured uncles was wiped from his mind and his heart leaped within him like an adagio dancer trying out a new step. Behind Sir Aylmer, looking more unbelievably beautiful even than he had remembered her, stood Hermione.

Hermione smiled upon him dazzlingly. She was in the sunniest of moods. After dropping Otis at the Bull's Head in the High Street, she had arrived at the front door just in time to see her father driving up, and such was the force of her personality that she had settled that little matter of the proposed legal action of Bostock *v.* Painter in something under two minutes and a quarter. The future of the publishing firm of Meriday

House, in so far as concerned civil actions on the part of the late Governor of Lower Barnatoland, was secure.

So she smiled dazzlingly. In an amused, sisterly way she had always been devoted to dear old Bill, and she was glad to see him again.

'Hullo, Bill,' she said.

Bill found speech.

'Oh, hullo, Hermione.'

Sir Aylmer also found speech.

'What the devil are you doing, you great clumsy oaf,' he said, standing on one leg and submitting the other to a system of massage, for the impact had been severe. 'Charging about the place like a damned rhinoceros. Why can't you look where you're going?'

Bill was staring at Hermione. In a dim way he was aware that words were proceeding from this old blighter, but he was unable to concentrate on their import.

'Oh, rather,' he said.

'What do you mean, oh, rather?'

'Yes, isn't it?' said Bill.

To a man who was good at snorting and to whom snorts came easily there was only one answer to this sort of thing. Sir Aylmer snorted, and stumped into the collection room, telling himself that he would go into the matter later on when his nephew seemed more in the mood. Useless to waste good stuff on one who, always deficient in intellect, seemed now to be suffering from some form of mental paralysis.

Hermione continued cordial.

'So you're back, Bill. It's jolly seeing you again. How was Brazil?'

'Oh, fine.'

'Have a good time?'

'Oh, yes, fine, thanks.'

'You're very sunburned. I suppose you had lots of adventures?'

'Oh, rather.'

'Snakes and so on?'

'Oh, yes.'

'Well, you must tell me all about it later. I've got to hurry off now. I have to see a friend of mine at the inn.'

Bill cleared his throat.

'Er – just a second,' he said.

This, he was telling himself, was the moment. Now, if ever, was his opportunity of putting the Ickenham system into practice. Here they were, alone together. A single stride would place him in a position to grab. And he was already panting. More ideal conditions could scarcely have been asked for.

But he found himself unable to move. All through those weary months in Brazil the image of this girl had been constantly before his mental eye, but now that he was seeing her face to face her beauty numbed him, causing trembling of the limbs and that general feeling of debility and run-down-ness which afflicts so many people nowadays and can be corrected only by the use of such specifics as Buck-u-Uppo or Doctor Smythe's Tonic Swamp Juice.

Had he had a bottle – nay, even a tablespoonful – of the tonic swamp juice handy, all might have been well. Lacking it, he merely shuffled his feet and looked popeyed, just as he had been doing for the last nine years.

'Well?' said Hermione.

('Stride, grab, waggle, clasp, kiss, pant,' urged Bill's better self. But his limbs refused to move.)

'Well?'

'Hermione.'

'Yes?'

'Hermione.'

'Well?'

'Oh, nothing,' said Bill.

He found himself alone. From outside came the sound of a car getting into gear and moving off. She had gone.

Nor could he blame her. Reviewing the late scene, recalling that horrible, bleating voice with its hideous resemblance to that of a BBC announcer, he shuddered, marvelling that any being erect upon two legs and bearing the outward semblance of a man could have shown himself so wormlike a poltroon.

Writhing in anguish, he thought for a moment of bumping his head against the wall, but on reflection decided against this. No sense in dinting a good wall. Better to go to his room, fling himself on the bed and bury his face in the pillow. He did so.

4

Anxious to get to the Bull's Head and inform Otis as soon as possible of the happy outcome of her interview with her father, Hermione had started up her car and driven off with the minimum of delay. Had she postponed her departure for as long as a minute, she would have observed a wild-eyed young man without a hat making for the house from the direction of the tennis lawn at a feverish canter, his aspect that of a young man who has taken something big. Once before in the course of this chronicle we have heard Reginald Twistleton compared to a cat on hot bricks. It was of a cat on hot bricks that he would have reminded an onlooker now.

Skimming across the terrace, he reached the house and plunged over the threshold. Skimming across the hall, he flew up the stairs. Skimming along the first-floor corridor, he burst into what had formerly been his bedroom, and Sally, who was reclining on the *chaise longue* like an Amazon resting after an important battle, rose as he entered. Indeed, she shot up as if a gimlet had suddenly penetrated the cushions and embedded itself in her person. She was a girl of poise, who did not easily lose command of herself, but after pushing policemen into ponds even girls of poise experience a certain tautness of the nerves, and the abrupt opening of the door had given her a momentary impression that here came Constable Potter.

Recognising her visitor, she became calmer, though still inclined to gasp.

'Oh, Pongo!' she said.

'Oh, Sally!' said Pongo.

To say that the story which Lord Ickenham had related to him on the tennis lawn, before going off to the Bull's Head for a drop of beer and a chat with the boys about Brazil, had stirred Reginald Twistleton would be to indicate but feebly the turmoil which it had created in his bosom. It had caused him to run what is known as the gamut of the emotions, prominent among them gratitude to a girl who could thus risk all on his behalf, shame that his own pusillanimity had rendered her stupendous act of heroism necessary and, above all, a surge of love such as he had never felt before – and he had been falling in love with fair regularity ever since his last summer but one at Eton.

His honourable obligations to Hermione Bostock had passed completely from his mind. He had no other thought than to find Sally and notify her of the trend of his views. Precisely as Bill Oakshott had done, he contemplated a future in which he would stride, grab and waggle, clasp, kiss and pant. With this difference, that whereas Bill, as we have seen, had planned to behave like an osteopath handling a refractory patient, he, Pongo, saw the set-up more in the light of abasing himself at a shrine. The word 'grab' is wrong. So is the word 'waggle'. But 'clasp', 'kiss' and 'pant' may stand.

He was panting now, and he lost no time in proceeding to the other items on the programme which he had sketched out. Bill Oakshott, had he been present, would have received a valuable object lesson on how this sort of thing should be done.

'Oh, Sally!' he said.

'Oh, Pongo!' said Sally.

Time stood still. In the world outside people were going about their various occupations. Constable Potter was in his cottage, changing into a dry uniform. Lord Ickenham, humming a gay stave, was striding along the road to the village. Hermione, half a mile ahead of him, was driving along the same road. Sir Aylmer was messing about with his African curios. Bill Oakshott was burying his face in his pillow. And up in London Lady Bostock, in her daughter's flat, had finished the illustrated papers and fallen into a light doze.

But Pongo and Sally were alone together in a world of their own, enjoying the scent of the violets and roses which sprouted through the bedroom floor and listening to the soft music which an orchestra of exceptional ability, consisting chiefly of harps and violins, was playing near at hand. Of Constable Potter, of Lord Ickenham, of Sir Aylmer Bostock, of Lady Bostock, of Bill Oakshott and of Hermione they recked nothing; though the time was to come when they, particularly Pongo, would be obliged to reck of the last named quite a good deal.

Presently Pongo, adjusting his arm more comfortably about Sally's waist, for they were now sitting side by side on the *chaise longue*, began to speak remorsefully of the past, featuring in his observations the criminal idiocy of the oaf Twistleton, that abysmal sap who had allowed himself to be parted from the only girl on earth whom a discriminating man could possibly wish to marry. He contemplated with unconcealed aversion this mutton-headed Twistleton.

'Gosh, what a chump I was!'

'Not such a chump as me.'

'Much more of a chump than you. No comparison.'

'It was all my fault.'

'No, it wasn't.'

'Yes, it was.'

'It wasn't.'

'It was.'

The dispute threatened to become heated, but just as Pongo was about to say 'It wasn't' again he suddenly paused, and into his sensitive features there crept that look of horror and apprehension which they had worn fourteen hours earlier, on the occasion when Bill Oakshott's knocking had sounded in the silent night.

'What's the matter, precious?' asked Sally solicitously.

Pongo gulped.

'Oh, nothing. At least, nothing much, I just happened to think of Hermione.'

There was a pause. A quick twinge of anxiety and alarm shot through Sally. Much – indeed, her life's happiness – depended on the exact extent to which the Twistletons regarded their word as their bond.

'Oh, Hermione?' she said. 'You don't mean you're too honourable to break off the engagement?'

Pongo gulped again.

'Not too honourable exactly, but . . . You've never met Hermione, have you? Well, it's difficult to explain, but she isn't a frightfully easy girl to break off engagements with. It's a little hard to know how to start.'

'I should just go to her and tell her frankly that you find you have made a mistake.'

'Yes, that's one way.'

'Or you could write her a letter.'

Pongo gave a start, like some strong swimmer in his agony who hears a splash and observes that somebody has thrown him a lifebelt.

'A letter?'

'You might find it less embarrassing.'

'I might,' said Pongo, and, quivering with gratitude to his helpmeet for her timely suggestion, he clasped her to his bosom and showered kisses on her upturned face.

This would probably have gone on for some time, had not Elsie Bean at this moment entered softly with a tray in her hands containing a teapot, a cup, some slices of buttered toast and a piece of cake.

'Tea,' said Elsie, and Pongo, soaring ceilingwards, came down and regarded her wrathfully.

'Why the dickens can't you blow your horn?' he demanded with a good deal of heat.

Elsie remained unmoved. The passionate scene which she had interrupted had made little impression upon her. It was the sort of thing that was happening all the time in Bottleton East.

'Tea, toast and a bit-er-cake,' she said. 'Have you pushed Harold into the pond yet, Mr Twistleton?'

Sally took charge of the situation in her competent way.

'Of course he has pushed him into the pond. He said he would, didn't he? You don't suppose Mr Twistleton would fail you?'

'Did he go in with a splash?'

'With a terrific splash. You could hear it for miles.'

'Coo. Well, I'm sure I'm very much obliged to you, Mr Twistleton. Have you seen Miss Hermione?'

Pongo leaped an inch or two.

'She isn't here?'

'Yes, she is. I saw her drive up in her car.'

Pongo remained silent for a space. He was clutching his head.

'I think I'll go and walk up and down on the tennis lawn for a while,' he said. 'This wants brooding over.'

With a brief groan he left the room, once more with that suggestion in his manner of a cat on hot bricks, and Elsie followed him with a critical eye.

'Nice young gentleman, Mr Twistleton,' she said. 'A bit barmy, isn't he?'

'A bit,' agreed Sally. 'I love it.'

5

The Bull's Head was still standing in its old place in the High Street when Hermione drove up, but Otis was no longer on the premises. She was informed that he had stepped out some little time previously, but whither he had stepped was not known. Annoyed, for no girl bringing the good news from Aix to Ghent likes to find Ghent empty when she gets there, Hermione returned to her two-seater and started to drive back along the road by which she had come. It had occurred to her that, now that she was in the Ashenden Manor neighbourhood, she ought to take the opportunity of exchanging a few words with her betrothed. It was the first time since lunch that she had given him a thought.

But her annoyance did not last long, nor did the desire to seek out Pongo. She had just reached the first milestone when something seemed to hit her between the eyes. It felt like a thunderbolt, but actually it was the central idea for the first of that series of three novels at twenty per cent rising to twenty-five above three thousand which Otis Painter would now be in a position to publish. This sort of thing is always happening to authors. They are driving along or walking along or possibly just sitting in a chair, their minds a blank, when all of a sudden – *bing*.

And the first thing an author learns is that it is fatal on these occasions to pigeonhole the inspiration away at the back of the mind, trusting that memory will produce it when required. Notes must be made immediately. Drawing up her two-seater at the side of the road, Hermione found an old envelope and began to write. She wrote rapidly, breathing tensely through the nose.

At about the same moment Lord Ickenham reached the Bull's Head and turned in at the door of the saloon bar.

6

It was with the easy assurance of one confident of his welcome that Lord Ickenham entered the saloon bar, for on his previous visit there he had had an outstanding social success. The stout blonde behind the counter, her uncle the landlord (Jno. Humphreys, licensed to sell ales, wines and spirits) and quite a number of the inn's clients had hung upon his lips. It is not often given to the natives of remote Hampshire hamlets to sit at the feet of a man who knows Brazil like the back of his hand, who has looked his alligator in the eye and made it wilt and who can talk of his adventures fluently and well.

Today he saw that his audience was to be smaller. Indeed, at the moment only the barmaid was present. He seemed to have struck one of those slack periods which come to all saloon bars. With the best will in the world English villagers cannot be drinking all the time, and this appeared to be one of the times when those of Ashenden Oakshott had decided to allow their gullets a brief respite, no doubt on the *reculer pour mieux sauter* principle.

But your true artist will always give of his best, however thin the house. As Lord Ickenham placed an elbow on the counter and requested the stout blonde to start pouring, there was no suggestion in his manner that he was going to walk through his part. He resumed his saga of life on the Lower Amazon as if he had been addressing a crowded hall, and the barmaid listened with all the impressment which she had shown on the previous day.

'Well, I do call that a pity,' she said, as he paused for an instant to raise his tankard.

'A pity?' said Lord Ickenham, a little hurt, for he had been speaking of the occasion when a puma had only just failed to add him to its bill of fare. 'Ah, I see. You are looking at the incident from the puma's viewpoint, and your womanly sympathy has been aroused by its failure to get the square meal for which it had been budgeting. Yes, it was tough on the puma. I remember noticing at the time that the animal's eyes were wet with unshed tears.'

'A pity you should have missed that gentleman, I mean. There was a gentleman in here for a quick one not five minutes ago,' explained the barmaid, 'who was telling me he had just come from Brazil. He'd have liked to meet you.'

Lord Ickenham gave her to understand that this was an almost universal aspiration on the part of his fellow men, but privately he was relieved that he had not arrived five minutes earlier. In his present rather delicate circumstances he greatly preferred to avoid gentlemen who had just come from Brazil.

'Too bad,' he said. 'One of the boys, eh? It would have been delightful to have got together and swapped yarns.'

'Why, here he is,' said the barmaid.

The door had opened, revealing an elderly man of square build with a pugnacious, sunburned face. Such was the excellence of the Bull's Head beer that those who went out after having a quick one nearly always came homing back again to have another.

'This is the gentleman I was speaking of. Excuse me, sir,' said the barmaid, addressing the gentleman, who had approached the counter and placed an elbow on it and was now licking his lips in quiet anticipation, 'here's a gentleman you ought to know, you being from Brazil. He knows more about Brazil than you could shake a stick at. Major Plank, the great explorer.'

At this moment a voice from without, recognisable as that of Jno. Humphreys, licensed to sell ales, wines and spirits, made itself heard. It was bellowing 'Myrtle', and the barmaid, whose parents had inflicted that name on her, vanished with a brief 'Excuse me.' The voice had been urgent, and it was evident that stern experience had taught this niece that her Uncle Jno. was a man who did not like to be kept waiting.

'Tell him about the puma, Major Plank,' she said, pausing for an instant in her flight.

Normally, Lord Ickenham would have done this without delay, for he enjoyed telling people about pumas and knew that he was good at it. But one of the things which a man of the world learns early in his career is that there are times when it is best to keep silent on the subject of these fascinating fauna.

The gentleman was looking at him fixedly, and in his eye there was no spark of the encouraging light which indicates a willingness to be informed about pumas. There have been some bleak and fishy eyes scattered through this chronicle – those of Coggs, the butler at Ickenham Hall, spring to the mind – but none bleaker and fishier than the gentleman's at this juncture.

'Plank?' he said, speaking raspingly. 'Did I hear her call you Major Plank?'

'That's right,' said Lord Ickenham. 'Major Plank.'

'Are you Major Brabazon-Plank, the explorer?'

'I am.'

'So am I,' said the gentleman, evidently rather impressed by the odd coincidence.

XII

I

When two strong men stand face to face, each claiming to be Major Brabazon-Plank, it is inevitable that there will be a sense of strain, resulting in a momentary silence. There was on this occasion. Lord Ickenham was the first to speak.

'Oh, are you?' he said. 'Then you owe me two bob.'

His companion blinked. The turn the conversation had taken seemed to have surprised him.

'Two bob?'

'If you have nothing but large bills, I can give you change.'

Major Plank's mahogany face took on a richer hue.

'What the devil are you talking about?'

'Two bob.'

'Are you crazy?'

'It is a point on which opinions differ. Some say yes. I maintain no. Two bob,' said Lord Ickenham patiently. 'It is useless for you to pretend that you do not owe me that sum, Bimbo. You took it off me forty-three years ago as we were crossing the cricket field one lovely summer evening. "Barmy," you said, "would you like to lend me two bob?" And I said, "No, but I suppose I'll have to," and the money changed hands.'

Major Plank clutched the counter.

'Bimbo? Barmy? Cricket field?' He stared with terrific concentration, and his face suddenly cleared. 'Good God! You're Barmy Twistleton.'

'I was in those days, but I've come on a lot since then, Bimbo. You see before you Frederick Altamont Cornwallis, fifth Earl of Ickenham, and one of the hottest earls that ever donned a coronet. The boy you knew as a wretched Hon. is now a peer of the realm, looked up to like the dickens by one and all. Just mention to anyone that you know Lord Ickenham, and they'll fawn on you and stand you lunch.'

Major Plank took an absent sip from the tankard.

'Barmy Twistleton!' he murmured. It was plain that the encounter had affected him greatly. 'But why did you tell that girl you were me?'

'One has to say something to keep the conversation going.'

'Barmy Twistleton. Well, I'll be damned. After all these years. I wouldn't have recognised you.'

'Exactly what Mugsy Bostock said when we met. You remember Mugsy Bostock? Did you know that he lived in these parts?'

'I knew his nephew, Bill Oakshott, did. I motored down to see him.'

'You aren't on your way to Ashenden Manor?'

'Yes.'

'Turn round and go back, Bimbo,' said Lord Ickenham, patting his shoulder kindly. 'You must not visit Ashenden Manor.'

'Why not?'

'Because I am already in residence there under your name. It would confuse Mugsy and give him a headache if he were confronted with a couple of us. No doubt you will say that you can't have too many Brabazon-Planks about the home, but Mugsy wouldn't look at it that way. He would get bewildered and fret.'

Major Plank took another sip at the tankard, and when Lord Ickenham mentioned that he had paid for its contents and that if his old friend proposed to treat it as a loving cup he would be obliged to charge him a small fee, seemed disinclined to go into the matter. It was the earlier portion of the conversation that was engaging his mind.

'You're staying with Mugsy under my name?'

'Exactly.'

'He thinks you're me?'

'Precisely.'

'Why?' said Major Plank, going right to the core of the problem. 'Why are you staying with Mugsy under my name?'

'It's a long story, Bimbo, and would bore you. But have no uneasiness. Just say to yourself, "Would my old crony do this without a motive?" and "Is his motive bound to be a good one?" The answers to these questions are "No" to the first, "Yes" to the second.'

Major Plank relapsed into a sandbagged silence. His was a slow mind, and you could almost hear it creaking as it worked.

'Good God!' he said again.

And then abruptly the full horror of the situation seemed to come home to him. No doubt he had been diving into the past and had brought memories of the boy Twistleton to the surface. It was not for nothing that this man before him had been called 'Barmy' at school. He had applied himself absently to the tankard once more, and his eyes above it suddenly grew round and wrathful.

'What the devil do you mean by staying with people under my name?'

'It's a good name, Bimbo. Got a hyphen and everything.'

'You'll ruin my reputation.'

'On the contrary. The image which I have been building up in the minds of all and sundry is that of what I should describe as a super-Plank or Plank *plus*. You ought to think

246

yourself lucky that a man like me has gone out of his way to shed lustre on your name.'

'Well, I don't. So you had better get back to Mugsy's and start packing, quick. Because as soon as I've had some more of this excellent beer I'm coming up there to expose you.'

'Expose me?' Lord Ickenham's eyebrows rose reproachfully. 'Your old friend?'

'Old friend be damned.'

'A fellow you used to throw inked darts at?'

'Inked darts have nothing to do with the case.'

'And who once lent you two bob?'

'Curse the two bob.'

'You're a hard man, Bimbo.'

'No, I'm not. I've a right to think of my reputation.'

'I have already assured you that it is in safe hands.'

'God knows what you may not have been up to. If I don't act like lightning, my name will be mud. Listen,' said Major Plank, consulting his watch. 'I shall start exposing you at five sharp. That gives you twenty-three minutes. Better look slippy.'

Lord Ickenham did not look slippy. He stood regarding the friend of his youth with the same gentle commiseration which he had displayed when dealing, in somewhat similar circumstances, with Constable Potter. Essentially kind-hearted, he disliked being compelled to thwart these eager spirits who spoke so hopefully of exposing him. But it had to be done, so with a sigh he embarked on the distasteful task.

'Dismiss all ideas of that sort from your mind, Bimbo. It is hopeless for you to dream of exposing me. Bill Oakshott has told me all about you.'

'What do you mean?'

'You are a man with an Achilles heel, a man with a fatal chink in your armour. You suffer from a strongly marked baby phobia. If anyone points a baby at you, Bill tells me, you run like a rabbit. Well, if you betray my little secret to Mugsy, you will immediately find yourself plunging into a foaming sea of them. A fete is taking place here shortly, and among its numerous features is a contest for bonny babies. And here is the point. In my capacity of Major Brabazon-Plank I have undertaken to act as judge of it. You begin to see the hideous peril confronting you? Eliminate me, and you automatically step into my place.'

'Why?'

'Because, my dear fellow, some variety of Brabazon-Plank has got to judge those bonny babies. This has been officially announced, and the whole village is agog. And after my departure you will be the only Brabazon-Plank available. And if you imagine that Mugsy, a determined man, and his wife, a still more determined woman, will let you sneak away, you are living in a fool's paradise. You haven't a hope, Bimbo. You will be for it.'

His pitiless clarity had its effect. Major Plank's tan was so deep that it was impossible to say whether or not he paled beneath it, but he shuddered violently and in his eyes was the look that comes into the eyes of men who peer into frightful abysses.

'Why don't they get the curate to do it?' he cried, plainly struggling with a strong sense of grievance. 'When we had these damned baby competitions at Lower Shagley, it was always the curate who judged them. It's what curates are for.'

'The curate has got measles.'

'Silly ass.'

'An unsympathetic thing to say of a man who is lying on a bed of pain with pink spots all over him, but I can make allowances for your feelings, appreciating how bitter a moment this must be for you, my poor old Bimbo. I suppose there is nothing much more sickening than wanting to expose a fellow and not being able to, and I would love to help you out if I could. But I really don't know what to suggest. You might . . . No, that's no good. Or . . . No, I doubt if that would work, either. I'm afraid you will have to give up the idea. The only poor consolation I can offer you is that it will be all the same in another hundred years. Well, my dear chap, it's been delightful running into you again after all this time, and I wish I could stay and chat, but I fear I must be pushing along. You know how busy we Brabazon-Planks always are. Look me up some time at my residence, which is quite near here, and we will have a long talk about the old school days and Brazil and, of course,' said Lord Ickenham indulgently, 'any other subject you may wish to discuss. If you can raise it by then, bring the two bob with you.'

With another kindly pat on the shoulder he went out, and Major Plank, breathing heavily, reached for the tankard and finished its contents.

2

The plot of Hermione's novel was coming out well. As so often happens when an author gets the central idea for a story and starts to jot it down, all sorts of supplementary ideas had come trooping along, demanding to be jotted down too. It was not many minutes before the envelope proved quite inadequate to contain the golden thoughts which were jostling one another in her brain, and she had just started to use the back of her motor licence when, looking up, she perceived approaching an elderly man of distinguished appearance, who raised his hat with an old-world polish.

'Good afternoon,' he said.

In this lax age in which we live, it not infrequently happens to girls of challenging beauty to find themselves approached by hat-raising strangers of the opposite sex. When Hermione Bostock had this experience, her manner was apt to become a little brusque, so much so that the party of the second part generally tottered off feeling as if he had incurred the displeasure of a wild cat. It is a tribute, therefore, to Lord Ickenham's essential respectability that he gave her pause. Her eyebrows quivered slightly, as if about to rise, but she made no move to shoot the works.

'Miss Bostock, I believe? My name is Brabazon-Plank. I am a guest at your father's house.'

This, of course, made it all quite different. One of the gang. Hermione became cordial.

'Oh, how do you do?'

'How do you do? Could you spare me a moment?'

'Why, of course. How odd that you should have known who I was.'

'Not at all. Yours, if I may say so, are features which, once seen, cannot be forgotten. I have had the privilege of studying a photograph of you.'

'Oh, yes, the one in the *Tatler*.'

'Not the one in the *Tatler*. The one which your cousin, William Oakshott, carries always next to his heart. I should explain,' said Lord Ickenham, 'that I was the leader of the expedition up the Amazon of which Bill Oakshott was so prominent a member, and every time he got a touch of fever he would pull your photograph out and kiss it, murmuring in a faint voice, "I love her, I love her, I love her." Very touching, I thought it, and so did all the rest of the personnel of the expedition. It made us feel finer, better men.'

Hermione was staring. Had she been a less beautiful girl, it might have been said that she goggled. This revelation of a passion which she had never so much as suspected had come as a complete surprise. Looking on Bill as a sort of brother, she had always supposed that he looked on her as a sort of sister. It was as if she had lived for years beside some gentle English hill and suddenly discovered one morning that it was a volcano full to the brim of molten lava.

'And don't get the idea,' proceeded Lord Ickenham, 'that he spoke thus only when running a temperature. It was rare for half an hour to pass without him whipping out your photograph and kissing it. So you see he did not forget you while he was away, as so many young men are apt, once they are abroad, to forget the girl to whom they are engaged. His heart was always true. For when he said, "I love her, I love her, I love her," it seemed to me that there was only one construction that could be placed on his remarks. He meant that he loved you. And may I be allowed to say,' went on Lord Ickenham with a paternal smile, 'how delighted I am to meet you at last and to see at a glance that you are just the girl for him. This engagement makes me very happy.'

'But—'

'He will be getting a prize. And so, my dear, will you. I know few men whom I respect more than William Oakshott. Of all my circle he is the one I would choose first to be at my side in the event of unpleasantness with an alligator. And while it may be argued, and with perfect justice, that the part which alligators play in the average normal married life is not a large one, it is no bad thing for a girl to have a husband capable of putting them in their place. The man who can prop an alligator's jaws open with a stick and then, avoiding its lashing tail, dispatch it with a meat axe is a man who can be trusted to help fire the cook. So no one will rejoice more heartily than I when the bells ring out in the little village church and you come tripping down the aisle on Bill Oakshott's sinewy arm. This will happen very shortly, I suppose, now that he is back with you once more?'

He paused, beaming benevolently, and Hermione, who had made several attempts to speak, at last found herself able to do so.

'But I am not engaged to Bill.'

'Nonsense. You must be. How about all that "I love her, I love her, I love her" stuff?'

'I am engaged to someone else. If you are staying at the house, you will have met him.'

Lord Ickenham gasped.

'Not the pinhead Twistleton?'

Something of the chill which hat-raising strangers usually induced crept into Hermione's manner.

'His name is Reginald Twistleton,' she said, allowing her eyes to flash for a moment. 'I am sorry you consider him a pinhead.'

'My dear girl, it isn't that I consider him a pinhead. Everyone considers him a pinhead. Walk into any gathering where he is a familiar figure and say to the first man you meet, "Do you know Reginald Twistleton?" and his reply will be, "Oh, you mean the pinhead?" Good heavens, child, you mustn't dream of marrying Reginald Twistleton. Even had you not a Bill Oakshott on your waiting list, it would be madness. How could you be happy with a man who is always getting arrested at dog races?'

'What!'

'Incessantly, you might say. *And* giving a false name and address.'

'You're talking nonsense.'

'My dear, these are well-documented facts. If you don't believe me, creep up behind this young Twistleton and shout, "Yoo-hoo, Edwin Smith, 11, Nasturtium Road, East Dulwich!" in his ear and watch him jump. Well, I don't know what you think, but to my mind there is something not very nice in going to dog races at all, for the people you meet there must be very mixed. But if a young man does go to dog races, I maintain that the least he can do is to keep from behaving in so disorderly a manner that he gets scooped in by the constabulary. And if you are going to try to excuse this Twistleton on the ground that he was intoxicated at the time, I can only say that I am unable to share your broad-minded outlook. No doubt he was intoxicated, but I can't see that that makes it any better. You knew, by the way, I suppose, that he is a dipsomaniac?'

'A *what*?'

'So your father tells me.'

'But Reginald is a teetotaller.'

'While your eye is on him, perhaps. But only then. At other times he shifts the stuff like a vacuum cleaner. You should have been here last night. He stole down when everyone was in bed and threw a regular orgy.'

Hermione had been intending to put an end to this conversation by throwing in her clutch and driving off with a stiff word of farewell, but now she saw that she would have to start later. A girl who has been looking on the man of her choice as a pure white soul and suddenly discovers that he is about as pure and white as a stevedore's undervest does not say, 'Oh, yes? Well, I must be off.' She sits rigid. She gasps. She waits for more.

'Tell me everything,' she said.

As Lord Ickenham proceeded to do so, the grim expression

on Hermione Bostock's lovely face became intensified. If there is one thing a girl of ideals dislikes, it is to learn that she has been nursing a viper in her bosom, and that Reginald Twistleton was a Grade A viper, with all the run-of-the-mill viper's lack of frankness and square shooting, seemed more manifest with every word that was spoken.

'Oh!' she said.

'*Well!*' she said.

'Go on,' she said.

The story wore to its conclusion. Lord Ickenham ceased to speak, and Hermione sat gazing before her with eyes of stone. She was doing something odd with her teeth which may have been that 'grinding' we read about.

'Of course,' said Lord Ickenham, ever charitable, 'he may simply be off his head. I don't know if you know anything of his family history, but he tells me he is the nephew of Lord Ickenham; a fact, surely, that makes one purse the lips dubiously. Do you know Lord Ickenham?'

'Only by reputation.'

'And what a reputation! There is a strong body of opinion which holds that he ought to have been certified years ago. I understand he is always getting flattering offers from Colney Hatch and similar establishments. And insanity so often runs in families. When I first met this young man Twistleton, I received a distinct impression that he was within a short jump of the loony bin, and that curious incident this morning, of which Bill Oakshott was telling me, has strengthened this view.'

Hermione quivered. She had not supposed that there was to be an Act Two.

'Curious incident?'

'It took place shortly after breakfast. Lady Bostock, going to her room, heard movements within, looked in the wardrobe and found Reginald Twistleton in it, crouching on the floor. His explanation was that he had come to borrow her lipstick.'

Hermione gripped her motor licence till the knuckles stood out white under the strain. Act One had stirred her profoundly, but Act Two had topped it.

In speaking of the dislike which high-principled girls have for vipers, we omitted to mention that it becomes still more pronounced when they discover that they use lipstick. That this erstwhile idol of hers should have feet of clay was bad, but that in addition to those feet of clay he should have, at the other end, a mouth that apparently needed touching up from time to time was the pay-off. People still speak of the great market crash of 1929, asking you with a shudder if you remember the way US Steel and Montgomery Ward hit the chutes during the month of October: but in that celebrated devaluation of once gilt-edged shares there was nothing comparable to the swift and dizzy descent at this moment of Twistleton Preferred.

Hermione's teeth came together with a click.

'I shall have a talk with Reginald!'

'I should. I think you owe it to yourself to demand an explanation. One wonders if Reginald Twistleton knows the difference between right and wrong.'

'I'll tell him,' said Hermione.

Lord Ickenham watched her drive off, well content with the way she stepped on the gas. He liked to see her hurrying to the tryst like that. The right spirit, he considered.

He climbed the five-barred gate at the side of the road and lowered himself on to the scented grass beyond it. His eyes fixed on the cloudless sky, he thought how pleasant it was to spread sweetness and light and how fortunate he ought to reckon himself that he had been granted this afternoon such ample opportunity of doing so. If for an instant a pang of pity passed through him as he pictured the meeting between Pongo and this incandescent girl, he suppressed it. Pongo – if he survived – would surely feel nothing but a tender gratitude towards an uncle who had laboured so zealously on his behalf. A drowsiness stole over him, and his eyelids closed in sleep.

Hermione, meanwhile, had reached the house and come to a halt outside its front door with a grinding of brakes and a churning of gravel. And she was about to enter, when from the room to her left she heard her father's voice.

'GET OUT!' it was saying, and a moment later Constable Potter emerged, looking like a policeman who has passed through the furnace. She went to the window.

'Father,' she said, 'do you know where Reginald is?'

'No.'

'I want to see him.'

'Why?' asked Sir Aylmer, as if feeling that such a desire was morbid.

'I intend,' said Hermione, once more grinding her teeth, 'to break off our engagement.'

A slender figure pacing the tennis lawn caught her eye. She hastened towards it, little jets of flame shooting from her nostrils.

3

Down at the Bull's Head the girl Myrtle, her conversation with her uncle concluded, had returned to her post in the saloon bar. The gentleman was still at the counter, staring fixedly at the empty tankard, but he was alone.

'Hullo,' she said disappointedly, for she had been hoping to hear more about Brazil, where might is right and the strong man comes into his own. 'Has Major Plank hopped it?'

The gentleman nodded moodily. A shrewder observer than the barmaid would have sensed that the subject of Major Plank was distasteful to him.

'Did he tell you about the puma? No? Well, it was very interesting. It was where he was threading his way through this trackless forest, gathering Brazil nuts, when all of a sudden what should come along but this puma. Pardon?'

The gentleman, who beneath his breath had damned and blasted the puma, did not repeat his observation, but asked for a pint of bitter.

'Would have upset me, I confess,' proceeded the barmaid. 'Yessir, I don't mind saying I'd have been scared stiff. Because pumas jump on the back of your neck and chew you, which you can't say is pleasant. But Major Plank's what I might call intrepid. He had his gun and his trusty native bearer—'

The gentleman repeated his request for bitter in a voice so forceful that it compelled attention. Haughtily, for his tone had offended her, the barmaid pulled the beer handle and delivered the goods, and the gentleman, having drunk deeply, said, 'Ha!' The barmaid said nothing. She continued piqued.

But pique is never enough to keep a barmaid silent for long. Presently, having in the meantime polished a few glasses in a marked manner, she resumed the conversation, this time selecting a topic less calculated to inflame the passions.

'Uncle John's in a rare old state.'

'Whose Uncle John?'

'My Uncle John. The landlord here. Did you hear him shouting just now?'

The gentleman, mellowed by beer, indicated with an approach to amiability that Jno. Humphreys's agitation had not escaped his notice. Yes, he said, he had heard him shouting just now.

'So I should think. You could have heard him at Land's End. All of a doodah, he is. I must begin by telling you,' said the barmaid, falling easily into her stride, 'that there's a big fete coming on here soon. It's an annual fete, by which I mean that it comes on once a year. And one of the things that happens at this annual fete is a bonny baby competition. Pardon?'

The gentleman said he had not spoken.

'A bonny baby competition,' resumed the barmaid. 'By which I mean a competition for bonny babies. If you've got a bonny baby, I mean to say, you enter it in this bonny baby competition, and if the judge thinks your bonny baby is a bonnier baby than the other bonny babies, it gets the prize. If you see what I mean?'

The gentleman said he saw what she meant.

'Well, Uncle John had entered his little Wilfred and was fully expecting to cop. In fact, he had as much as a hundred bottles of beer on him at eight to one with sportsmen in the village. And now what happens?'

The gentleman said he couldn't imagine.

'Why, Mr Brotherhood, the curate, goes and gets the measles, and the germs spread hither and thither, and now there's so many gone down with it that the vicar says it isn't safe to have the bonny baby competition, so it's off.'

She paused, well satisfied with the reception of her tale. Her audience might have been hard to grip with anecdotes of Major Plank among the pumas, but he had responded admirably to this simpler narrative of English village life. Though oddly, considering that the story was in its essence a tragic one, the emotion under which he was labouring seemed to be joy.

Quite a sunny look had come into his eyes, as if weights had been removed from his mind.

'Off,' said the barmaid. 'By which I mean that it won't take place. So all bets are null and void, as the expression is, and Uncle John won't get his bottles of beer.'

'Too bad,' said the gentleman. 'Can you direct me to Ashenden Manor?'

'Straight along, turning to the right as you leave the door.'

'Thank you,' said the gentleman.

XIII

I

That Constable Potter, having returned to his cottage and changed into a dry uniform, should then have proceeded without delay to Ashenden Manor to see Sir Aylmer Bostock was only what might have been expected. Sir Aylmer was the chairman of the local bench of magistrates, and he looked upon him as his natural protector. The waters of the pond had scarcely closed over his head before he was saying to himself that here was something to which the big chief's attention would have to be drawn.

He was unaware that in seeking an audience at this particular time he was doing something virtually tantamount to stirring up a bilious tiger with a short stick. No warning voice whispered in his ear, 'Have a care, Potter!' adding that as the result of having been compelled to withdraw a suit for damages to which he had been looking forward with bright anticipation for weeks his superior's soul was a bubbling maelstrom of black malignity and that he was far more likely to bite a policeman in the leg than to listen patiently to his tales of woe.

The realisation that this was so came, however, almost immediately. He had been speaking for perhaps a minute when Sir Aylmer, interrupting him, put a question.

'Are you tight, you bloodstained Potter?' asked Sir Aylmer, regarding him with a sort of frenzied loathing. When a man has come to his collection room to be alone with his grief, to brood on the shattering of his hopes and to think how sweet life might have been had he had one of those meek, old-fashioned daughters who used to say, 'Yes, Papa!', the last thing he wants is policemen clumping in with complicated stories. 'What on earth are you talking about? I can't make head or tail of it.'

Constable Potter was surprised. He was not conscious of having been obscure. It also came as a shock to him to discover that he had misinterpreted the twitching of his audience's limbs and the red glare in that audience's eye. He had been attributing these phenomena to the natural horror of a good man who hears from another good man of outrages committed on his, the second good man's, person and it seemed now that he had been mistaken.

'It's with ref to this aggravated assault, sir.'

'What aggravated assault?'

'The one I'm telling you about, sir. I was assaulted by the duck pond.'

The suspicion that the speaker had been drinking grew in Sir Aylmer's mind. Even Reginald Twistleton at the height of one of his midnight orgies might have hesitated, he felt, to make a statement like that.

'By the duck pond?' he echoed, his eyes widening.

'Yes, sir.'

'How the devil can you be assaulted by a duck pond?'

Constable Potter saw where the misunderstanding had arisen. The English language is full of these pitfalls.

'When I said "by the duck pond", I didn't mean "by the duck pond", I meant "by the duck pond". That is to say,' proceeded Constable Potter, speaking just in time, '"near" or "adjacent to", in fact "on the edge of". I was the victim of an aggravated assault on the edge of the duck pond, sir. Somebody pushed me in.'

'Pushed you in?'

'Pushed me in, sir. Like as it might have been someone what had a grudge against me.'

'Who was it?'

'A scarlet woman, sir,' said Constable Potter, becoming biblical. 'Well, what I mean to say, she was wearing a red jacket and a kind of red thingummy round her head, like as it might have been a scarf.'

'Was it a scarf?'

'Yes, sir.'

'Then why say "like as it might have been" one? I have had to speak before, from the bench, of the idiotic, asinine way in which you blasted policemen give your evidence. Did you see this woman?'

'Yes and no, sir.'

Sir Aylmer closed his eyes. He seemed to be praying for strength.

'What do you mean, yes and no?'

'I mean to say, sir, that I didn't actually see her, like as it might have been see. I just caught sight of her for a moment as she legged it away, like as it might have been a glimp.'

'Do you mean glimpse?'

'Yes, sir.'

'Then say glimpse. And if you use that expression "like as it might have been" once more, just once more, I'll . . . Could you identify this woman?'

'Establish her identity?' said Constable Potter, gently corrective. 'Yes, sir, if I could apprehend her. But I don't know where she is.'

'Well, I've not got her.'

262

'No, sir.'

'Then why come bothering me? What do you expect me to do?'

Broadly speaking, Constable Potter expected Sir Aylmer to have the countryside scoured and the ports watched, but before he could say so the latter had touched on another aspect of the affair.

'What were you doing by the duck pond?'

'Spitting and thinking, sir. I generally pause there when on my beat, and I had just paused this afternoon when the outrage occurred. I heard something behind me, like as it might have been a footstep, and the next moment something pushed me in the small of the back, like as if it might have been a hand—'

'GET OUT!' said Sir Aylmer.

Constable Potter withdrew. Crossing the terrace, he made for the bushes on the other side and there, lighting his pipe, stood spitting and thinking. And we make no secret of the fact that his thoughts were bitter thoughts and his expectoration disillusioned.

Just as a boy's best friend is his mother, so is a policeman's prop and stay the chairman of the local bench of magistrates. When skies are dark, it is the thought of the chairman of the local bench of magistrates that brings the sun smiling through, and it is to the chairman of the local bench of magistrates that he feels he can always take his little troubles and be sure of support and sympathy. Who ran to catch me when I fell and would some pretty story tell and kiss the place to make it well? The chairman of the local bench of magistrates. That is the policeman's creed.

Anyone, therefore, who when a boy ever went running to his mother with a tale of wrongs and injuries and instead of condolences received a kick in the pants will be able to appreciate this officer's chagrin as he passed the late scene under mental review. Sir Aylmer's attitude had hurt and disappointed him. If this was how a constable's legitimate complaints were received by those whose duty it was to comfort and console, then Elsie, he felt, was right and the quicker he left the Force, the better.

If you had approached Harold Potter as he stood there in his bush, smoking his pipe and spitting bitterly, and had said, 'Well, Constable Potter, how are you feeling?' he would have replied that he was feeling fed up. And there is little doubt that this black mood would have grown in intensity, had not something happened which abruptly wrenched his thoughts from their contemplation of the policeman's unhappy lot.

Through the branches before him he had a good view of the front of the house, and at this moment there appeared on the balcony of one of the windows on the first floor a female figure in a red jacket, wearing upon its head a red thingummy, like as it might have been a scarf. It came to the balcony rail, looked left and right, then went back into the room.

The spectacle left Harold Potter gaping. A thrill ran through him from the base of the helmet to the soles of his regulation boots. He started to say 'Cool!' but the word froze on his moustache.

Harold Potter was a man who could reason. A mystery woman in a red jacket had pushed him into the duck pond. A mystery woman in a red jacket was in that room on the first floor. It did not take him long to suspect that these two mystery women might be one and the same.

But how to make sure?

It seemed to him that there lay before him the choice between two courses of action. He could go and report to Sir

Aylmer, or he could pop along to the potting shed, where there was a light ladder, secure this light ladder, take it to the side of the house, prop it up and climb to that first-floor window and peer in. A steady look at close range would establish the identity of the red-jacketed figure.

He did not hesitate long between these alternative plans. Rejecting almost immediately the idea of going and reporting to Sir Aylmer, he knocked out his pipe and started for the potting shed.

2

Sally, her tea and buttered toast long since consumed, had begun to feel lonely. It was quite a time now since Pongo had left her, and she yearned for his return. Seated on the *chaise longue*, she thought what a baa-lamb he was and longed for him to come back so that she could go on stroking his head and telling him how much she loved him.

An odd thing, this love, and one about which it is futile to argue. If individual A finds in individual B a glamour which escapes the notice of the general public, the general public has simply got to accept the situation without protest, just as it accepted without protest, though perhaps with a silent sigh of regret, the fact of Mr Brotherhood, the curate, getting measles.

Seeing Sally sitting on the *chaise longue* with clasped hands and starry eyes, her heart overflowing with love for Pongo, it would have been useless for a discriminating third party to tap her on the shoulder and try to persuade her that there was nothing in the prospect of a lifelong union with Reginald Twistleton to get starry-eyed about. Fruitless to attempt to sketch for her a picture of Reginald Twistleton as seen by the cooler-headed. She was in love, and she liked it.

The only cloud that darkened her sky was the fear lest a shrewd girl like Hermione Bostock, having secured such a prize, might refuse to relinquish it, but she need have had no anxiety. Hermione was relinquishing the prize at that very moment. When, some twenty minutes after he had left it, Pongo re-entered the room, there was a dazed look on his face as if he had recently been mixed up with typhoons, water-spouts and other Acts of God, but in his eyes shone the light which comes into the eyes of men who have found the blue bird.

Sally was not able to detect this immediately, her vision being obscured by the handkerchief with which he was mopping his forehead, and her first words were reproachful.

'Oh, angel, what a time you've been.'

'Sorry.'

'I went out on to the balcony just now to see if I could see you, but you weren't in sight. I know you had to brood, but need you have brooded so long?'

Pongo lowered the handkerchief.

'I wasn't brooding,' he said. 'I was chatting with Hermione.'

Sally gave a jump.

'Then you found her?'

'She found me.'

'And what happened?'

Pongo moved to the mirror and inspected himself in it. He seemed to be looking for grey hairs.

'Well, that I can hardly tell you,' he said. 'The whole thing's a bit of a blur. Have you ever been in a really bad motor smash? Or hit by an atom bomb? No? Then it's hard to explain. Still, the fact that emerges is that the engagement's off.'

'Oh, Pongo!'

'Oh, Sally!'

'Oh, Pongo darling! Then we can live happy ever after.'

Pongo applied the handkerchief to his forehead once more.

'Yes,' he agreed, 'after a brief interval for picking up the pieces and reassembling the faculties. I don't mind telling you the recent scene has left me a bit weak.'

'My poor lamb. I wish I had some smelling salts.'

'So do I. I could use a bucketful.'

'Was it so awful?'

'Quite an ordeal.'

'What did you say to her?'

'I didn't get a chance of saying anything to her, except, "Oh, there you are," right at the start. She bore the burden of the conversash.'

'You don't mean it was she who broke off the engagement?'

'And how! You know, Uncle Fred ought to be in some sort of home.'

'Why?'

'It appears that he met Hermione and spilled the beans with a lavish hand. He told her so many things about me that I wonder she remembered them all. But she did.'

'Such as——?'

'Well, getting pinched at the dog races and going down to the drawing room last night to get a spot and being caught this morning in Ma Bostock's wardrobe. Things like that.'

'In the wardrobe? What were you doing there?'

'I had gone to her room to get you a lipstick, and——'

'Oh, Pongo! My hero! Did you really do that for me?'

'Not much I wouldn't do for you. Look what you did for me. Pushing Potter into that pond.'

'I think that's what's so splendid about us. Each helps each. It's the foundation of a happy married life. So Uncle Fred told her all that about you? Bless him.'

'Would you put it like that?'

'Well, he saved you from a girl you could never have been happy with.'

'I couldn't be happy with any girl except you. Yes. I suppose he did. I hadn't looked at it in that way.'

'He never minds how much trouble he takes, if he feels that he's spreading sweetness and light.'

'No. There have been complaints about it on all sides, and I still maintain that he ought to be in a padded cell with the board of Lunacy Commissioners sitting on his head. However, I agree that he has smoothed our path. I mean to say, here we are, what?'

'Here we are.'

'All our problems solved. Nothing to worry about any more.'

'Not a thing.'

'Oh, Sally!'

'Oh, Pongo!'

The embrace into which they fell was a close one, close enough, had it taken place in Hollywood, to have caused Eric Johnston to shake his head dubiously and recommend cutting a few hundred feet, but not so close as to deprive Pongo of a view of the window. And Sally, nestling in his arms, was concerned to notice that he had suddenly stiffened, as if he had been turned into a pillar of salt.

'What's the matter?' she asked.

Pongo gave a short gulp. He seemed to find a difficulty in speaking.

'Don't look now,' he said, 'but that blighter Potter has just stepped off a ladder on to the balcony.'

It was at about the moment when Constable Potter, having found the light ladder, was starting to lift it and Pongo, in the bedroom on the first floor, had begun his emotional description of the recent conference with Hermione that Major Plank turned his car in at the gates of Ashenden Manor and proceeded up the drive at a high rate of speed.

He had been progressing at a high rate of speed ever since leaving the Bull's Head. He would probably have driven fairly fast in any event, for he was one of those men who do, but what made him so particularly disinclined on the present occasion to loiter and look at the scenery was the fact that the full significance of Lord Ickenham's words in the saloon bar had just come home to him. He had remembered, that is to say, that the man whom he had known as Barmy Twistleton had told him that he was now Lord Ickenham.

There were circles in London where the eccentricities of Lord Ickenham were a favourite topic of conversation, and it was in these circles that Major Plank, when not among the alligators, was accustomed to mix. His old schoolmate's character and habits, therefore, were fully known to him, and he was able to form a vivid picture of what would be the effect on the reputation of anyone whom the other had decided to impersonate.

How long this public menace had been established at Ashenden Manor he did not know, but he felt very strongly that even a single day was too much and that anything like forty-eight hours would have caused a stigma to rest upon the grand old name of Brabazon-Plank which it would take a lifetime to remove.

There is probably no one who moves more slippily than a Brazilian explorer on his way to expose an impostor who has been causing stigmas to rest upon his name, and not even Hermione could have made better speed up the drive than did this fermenting Major. His was a large, flat, solid foot, admirably adapted for treading on accelerators, and he pressed it down with a will.

Arriving at the house, he was in far too great a hurry to ring the front doorbell and wait till it was answered. Voices were proceeding from the open French window to his right, presumably that of the drawing room, and he went thither and walked in. He found himself in the presence of his young subordinate, Bill Oakshott, and a rugged man of an older vintage who was puffing at a white moustache of the soup-strainer class. He had a feeling, looking at them, that they were upset about something.

Nor was he mistaken. Both Bill and his Uncle Aylmer had come to the tea table with their bosoms full of the perilous stuff that weighs upon the heart. The memory of his craven behaviour during that interview with Hermione had not ceased to torture Bill, and Sir Aylmer was still in the grip of the baffled fury which comes to men of imperious nature when their daughters tell them they must not bring actions against publishers, a fury which his conversation with Constable Potter had done nothing to alleviate. To say that William Oakshott and Sir Aylmer Bostock were human powder magazines which it needed but a spark to explode is not only clever, but true.

It is possible, however, that the soothing influence of tea, muffins and cucumber sandwiches might have succeeded in averting disaster, allowing the exchanges to confine themselves to harmless commonplaces, had not Sir Aylmer, too pleased to keep such splendid news to himself, chanced to mention that Hermione had told him that, her romance having sprung an unforeseen leak, he would not have to pass the evening of his life with Reginald Twistleton as his son-in-law. For this led Bill to exclaim 'Oh, gosh!' in an enraptured voice and, pressed to explain his elation, to say that the thought had crossed his mind that if Hermione was back in circulation again, there might be a chance for a chap who had loved her with a growing fervour for years and years and years: and this in its turn led Sir Aylmer to attack him with tooth and claw. There was a smile on his nephew's face which he considered a silly smile, and he addressed himself without delay to the task of wiping it off.

'Gar!' he said, speaking dangerously through a mouthful of muffin, and added that there was no need for Bill to grin all over his beastly face like a damned hyena, because whether free or engaged Hermione would not touch him with a barge pole.

'Why should she?' asked Sir Aylmer. 'You? She looks on you as a——'

'I know,' said Bill, with a return of gloom. 'A brother.'

'Not brother,' corrected Sir Aylmer. 'Sheep.'

A quiver ran through Bill's massive frame. His jaw fell and his eyes widened.

'Sheep?'

'Sheep.'

'*Sheep?*' said Bill.

'Sheep,' said Sir Aylmer firmly. 'A poor, spineless sheep who can't say boo to a goose.'

A more practised debater would have turned this charge to his advantage by challenging the speaker to name three sheep who could say boo to a goose, but Bill merely stood rigid, his fists clenched, his nostrils dilated, his face mantled with the blush of shame and indignation, regretting that ties of blood and his companion's advanced years rendered impossible that slosh in the eye for which the other seemed to him to be asking, nay pleading, with his every word.

'Sheep,' said Sir Aylmer, winding up the speech for the prosecution. 'She told me so herself.'

It was on this delicate situation that Major Plank intruded.

'Hullo there,' he said, striding in with the calm assurance of a man accustomed for years to walk uninvited into the huts of native chiefs. 'Hullo, Bill.'

It would be difficult to advance more conclusive proof of the turmoil into which Bill Oakshott's soul had been thrown by his uncle's words than by saying that the unexpected entry of the last man he would have wished to see in the drawing room of Ashenden Manor did not cause so much as a gleam of horror to come into his eyes. He regarded him dully, his mind still occupied by that sheep sequence. Did Hermione, he was asking himself, really look on him as a sheep? And, arising from that, had she a prejudice against sheep? The evidence went to show that she had none against baa-lambs, but sheep, of course, might be a different matter.

It was left to Sir Aylmer to do the honours.

'Who the hell are you?' he asked, not unthankful that here was another object on which he could work off some of the spleen induced by the chit-chat of daughters and policemen.

Major Plank had had far too much experience of this sort of thing to be abashed by nervous irritability on the part of a host. Many of the householders on whom he had dropped in in his time had said it with spears.

'Who the hell are *you*?' he replied agreeably. 'I'm looking for Mugsy Bostock.'

Sir Aylmer started.

'I am Sir Aylmer Bostock,' he said, and Major Plank stared at him incredulously.

'You?' he said. 'Don't be an ass. Mugsy Bostock is younger than me, and you look a million. Have you seen your Uncle Mugsy anywhere, Bill?'

It was at this point that Jane, the parlourmaid, entered bearing strawberries in a bowl, for they did themselves well at teatime at Ashenden Manor – cucumber sandwiches, muffins, strawberries and everything. Sir Aylmer addressed her in the carrying voice which was so characteristic of him.

'JANE!'

A lesser girl would have dropped the bowl. Jane merely shook like an aspen.

'Yes, sir?'

'Tell this son of a . . . this gentleman who I am.'

'Sir Aylmer Bostock, sir.'

'Right,' said Sir Aylmer, like the judge of one of those general knowledge quizzes which are so popular nowadays.

Major Plank said he was dashed.

'It's that ghastly moustache that misled me,' he explained. 'If you go about the place behind a whacking great white moustache, you can't blame people for taking you for a centenarian. Well, nice to see you again, Mugsy, and all that, but, cutting the guff, I came here on business. Plank's my name.'

'Plank!'

'Brabazon-Plank. You may remember me at school. I've just discovered that that raving lunatic, Barmy Twistleton – Lord Ickenham he calls himself now – has been passing himself off as me under your roof; and it's got to stop. I don't know what made him do it, and I don't care, the point is I'll be damned if I'm going to have people thinking that Barmy Twistleton is me. Good God! How would you like it yourself?'

There had been an instant, just after the words, 'Plank's my name,' when Sir Aylmer had given a quick and extraordinarily realistic impersonation of a harpooned whale, shaking from stem to stern as if a barb had entered his flesh. But as the speaker continued, this had given place to a frozen calm, the dangerous calm that heralds the storm.

'I can tell you what made him do it,' he said, allowing his eyes to play upon Bill like flame-throwers. 'He wished to be of assistance to my nephew here. We are holding our annual village fete shortly, and one of its features is a contest for bonny babies. My nephew was to have acted as judge.'

'Barmy told me he was going to be the judge.'

'That was the latest arrangement. My nephew persuaded him to take his place.'

'Very sensible of you, Bill,' said Major Plank cordially. 'Dashed dangerous things, these baby contests. The little beasts are bad enough themselves, but it's the mothers you want to watch out for. Look,' he said, baring his leg and indicating a cicatrice on the calf. 'That's what I got once in Peru for being fool enough to let myself be talked into judging a competition for bonny babies. The mother of one of the Hon. Mentions got after me with a native dagger.'

'The problem then arose,' proceeded Sir Aylmer, still speaking evenly and spacing his words with care, 'of how to introduce Lord Ickenham into my house. He was well aware that I would never allow him to enter my house, if I knew who he was. So he said he was Major Brabazon-Plank, the explorer, and my nephew endorsed this statement. What do you mean,' roared Sir Aylmer, suddenly abandoning the calm, judicial method and becoming a thing of fire and fury, 'what do you mean, you infernal young scallywag, by introducing impostors into my house?'

He would have spoken further, for it was obvious that the greater part of his music was still in him, but at this moment Bill exploded.

A good deal is always required to change a mental attitude which has endured for a number of years. From early boyhood Bill Oakshott had regarded this uncle of his with respectful awe, much as a nervous young prehistoric man might have regarded the leader of his tribe. He had quailed before his wrath, listened obsequiously to his stories, done all that lay in his power to humour him. And had this scene taken place at a time when he was in normal mood, there is little doubt that he would have folded like an accordion and allowed himself to be manhandled without protest.

But Bill was not in normal mood. His soul was seething in rebellion like a cistern struck by a thunderbolt. The interview with Hermione had left him raw and wincing. The information that she regarded him as a sheep had dropped vitriol on the wounds. And now, not once but three times, this white-moustached cuckoo in the nest had alluded to Ashenden Manor as 'my house'. At these emotional moments there is always something, generally trivial in itself, which fulfils the function of the last straw, and with Bill now it was this description of Ashenden Manor.

In the automatic, barely conscious fashion of the Englishman at teatime he had been continuing to eat and drink throughout his uncle's exposition, and for an instant a muffin prevented him expressing his views. He swallowed it, and was at liberty to proceed.

'"My house"?' he said. 'I like that. Where do you get that "my house" stuff?'

Sir Aylmer said that that was not the point, and was starting to indicate once more what the point was, when he was swept away as if by a tidal wave.

'"My house"!' repeated Bill, choking on the words like one who chokes upon a muffin. 'Of all the crust! Of all the nerve! It's about time, Uncle Aylmer, that we got this thing cleared up about who this ruddy house belongs to. Let's do it now.'

'Yes, let's,' said Major Plank, interested. A man with five sisters and seven aunts, he was well versed in family rows and thought that this one promised to be in the first rank and wanted pushing along. 'Whose house is it?'

'Mine,' thundered Bill. 'Mine. Mine. Mine. Mine. Mine.'

'I see,' said Major Plank, getting his drift. 'Yours. Then where does Mugsy come in?'

'He planted himself here when I was a mere kid, unable to do anything about it. I was only sixteen when my father died, and he barged over from Cheltenham and got into the woodwork.'

'What happened when you came of age?'

'Nothing. He stuck on.'

'You should have booted him out.'

'Of course I should.'

'That was the moment.'

'Yes.'

'Why didn't you?'

'I hadn't the heart.'

'Mistaken kindness.'

'Well, I'm going to do it now. I've had enough of this business of being a . . . what's the word?'

'Fathead?'

'Cipher in the home. I'm sick and tired of being a cipher in the home. You can jolly well clear out, Uncle Aylmer. You understand me? Buzz off. Where you buzz to, I don't care, but buzz. Go back to Cheltenham, if you like. Or Bexhill.'

'Or Bognor Regis,' suggested Major Plank.

'Or Bognor Regis. Go anywhere you like, but you're not going to stay here. Is that clear?'

'Quite clear,' said Major Plank. 'Very well put.'

'Right,' said Bill.

He strode out through the French window, and Major Plank helped himself to a muffin.

'Nice chap, Bill,' he said. 'I like a young fellow who knows his own mind. Extraordinarily good muffins, these, Mugsy. I'll have another.'

4

Emerging through the French window, Bill passed along the terrace, walking rapidly towards the spot where the drive began. His eyes glowed. He was breathing stertorously.

The appetite grows by what it feeds on. So far from soothing him and restoring him to everyday placidity, his throwing off of the shackles had left Bill Oakshott in a mood for fresh encounters. He had tasted blood, and wanted more. It is often so with quiet young men who at long last assert themselves.

He was in the frame of mind when he would have liked to meet Joe Louis and pick a quarrel with him, and as he turned the corner and came into the drive there caught his eye something which seemed to have been sent in direct answer to prayer.

It was not Joe Louis, but it was the next best thing. What he had seen was a stout young man with a pink nose and horn-rimmed spectacles in conversation with Hermione Bostock.

And just as he beheld him this young man suddenly folded Hermione in his embrace and started to kiss her.

Bill broke into a gallop, the glow in his eyes intensified, the stertorousness of his breathing still more marked. His general mental attitude was that of the warhorse which said 'Ha!' among the trumpets.

XIV

I

It is never easy for a high-strung young man whose whole future as a publisher of the book beautiful is being decided at a country house to sit in an inn two miles from that house, waiting patiently for news to be brought to him from the front. With each long minute that goes by his nervousness increases. The limbs twitch, the eyeballs roll, the illusion that there are ants in his pants becomes more and more pronounced, until eventually the urge to be closer to the centre of things grows so imperious that he yields to it.

That was why Otis Painter had been absent from the Bull's Head when Hermione arrived there. He had started to walk to Ashenden Manor. Like Edith of the swan's neck after the Battle of Hastings, he wanted to find out what had been going on.

When we say that Otis had started to walk to Ashenden Manor, it would be more correct to put it that he thought he had; in actual fact, having got his instructions twisted, he had turned to the left instead of to the right on leaving the inn, and it was only after he had proceeded a mile and three quarters through delightful country that he discovered that though he was improving his figure and getting lots of pure air into his lungs, he was diminishing his chances of reaching his destination with every step that he took.

Returning to the Bull's Head, he had borrowed a bicycle from the boy who cleaned the boots, a courteous and obliging lad of the name of Erbut with blacking all over his face, and after a couple of unpleasant spills, for it was many years since he had cycled and the old skill had rather deserted him, had found himself at the top of the drive. There, feeling that this was as far as it was prudent to penetrate into territory where there was a grave risk of meeting Sir Aylmer Bostock, he deposited his machine behind a tree, concealed himself in the bushes and resumed his waiting. And presently Hermione appeared, walking briskly.

As she drew near and he was enabled to get a clear view of her, his heart sank, for he could see that her lips were tightly set, her bosom heaving and her eyes bright and stormy. She looked, in a word, like a daughter who, approaching her father in the matter of withdrawing legal actions against publishers, has come up against something too hot to handle.

Actually, of course, Hermione's appearance was simply the normal appearance of a girl who has just been ticking off a viper. After a dust-up with a viper the female lips always become tightly set, and it is rarely that the bosom does not heave. But Otis did not know this, and it was with a mind filled with the gloomiest forebodings that he stepped from his hiding place. 'Here comes the bad news,' he was saying to himself.

'Well?' he said, uttering the monosyllable loudly and raspingly, as so often happens when the nerves are over-strained.

The briskness of her pace had taken Hermione past him, and it was from behind that he had addressed her. At the sound of a voice suddenly splitting the welkin where no voice should have been she left the ground in an upward direction and came to earth annoyed and ruffled.

'I wish you wouldn't pop out of bushes like that,' she said with a good deal of asperity.

Otis was too agitated to go into the niceties of etiquette and procedure.

'What happened?' he asked.

'I bit my tongue.'

'I mean,' said Otis, clicking his, 'when you saw your father.'

Hermione mastered her emotion. Her tongue was still paining her, but she had remembered that this man was a publisher who believed in column spreads in all the literate Sunday papers.

'Oh, yes,' she said.

The reply dissatisfied Otis. It seemed to him to lack lucidity, and lucidity was what he desired – or, as a literate Sunday paper would have put it, desiderated.

'What do you mean, "Oh, yes"? What did he say?'

Hermione's composure was now restored. She still disapproved of her sponsor's practice of popping out of bushes and speaking like a foghorn down the back of her neck, but was willing to let bygones be bygones.

'It's quite all right, Mr Painter,' she said, smiling kindly upon Otis. 'Father has withdrawn the suit.'

Otis reeled.

'He *has*?'

'Yes.'

'Gee!' said Otis, and it was at this point that he folded Hermione in his embrace and started to kiss her.

The last thing we desire being to cast aspersions on publishers, a most respectable class of men, we hasten to say that behaviour of this kind is very unusual with these fine fellows. Statistics show that the number of authoresses kissed annually by publishers is so small that, if placed end to end, they would reach scarcely any distance. Otis's action was quite exceptional, and Hodder and Stoughton, had they observed it, would have looked askance. So would Jonathan Cape. And we think we speak for Heinemann, Macmillan, Benn, Gollancz and Herbert Jenkins Ltd when we say that they, too, would have been sickened by the spectacle.

In defence of Otis there are several extenuating points to be urged. In the first place, his relief was so intense and his happiness so profound that he had to kiss something. In the second place, Hermione was a very beautiful girl (not that that would have weighed with Faber and Faber) and she had smiled upon him very kindly. And, finally, we cannot judge men who have lived on the left bank of the Seine by the same standards which we apply to those whose home is in London. If Eyre and Spottiswoode had taken a flat in the Rue Jacob, within easy reach of the Boul' Mich', they would have been surprised how quickly they would have forgotten the lessons they had learned at their mother's knee.

It was unfortunate that none of these arguments presented themselves to Bill Oakshott as he turned the corner. In Otis Painter he saw just another libertine, flitting from flower to flower and sipping, and we are already familiar with his prejudice against libertines. His impulse on seeing one, we recall, was to pull his head off at the roots and rip his insides out with his bare hands, and it was with this procedure in mind that he now advanced on the entwined pair. He gripped Otis by the coat collar and tore him from the clinch, and he would almost certainly have started to detach his head, had not Hermione uttered a piercing cry.

'Don't kill him, Bill! He's my publisher.'

And then, as she saw him hesitate, she added:

'He's doing my next three books and giving me twenty per cent rising to twenty-five above three thousand.'

It was enough. Practically berserk though Bill was, he could still reason, and reason told him that publishers of this type must be nursed along rather than disembowelled. Hermione's literary career was as dear to him as to herself, and he knew that he could never forgive himself if he jeopardised it by eviscerating a man capable of planning contracts on these spacious lines. He released Otis, who tottered back against a tree and stood there panting and polishing his spectacles.

Bill, too, was panting. His breath came in loud gasps as he strode up to Hermione and grabbed her by the wrist. There was in his demeanour now no trace of that craven diffidence which had marked it during their previous interview in the hall. Since then William Oakshott, with a victory over a tyrant under his belt, had become a changed man, and the man he had changed into was a sort of composite of James Cagney and Attila the Hun. He felt strong and masterful and in the best possible vein for trying out the Ickenham system. Otis Painter, peering at him through his spectacles, which he had now resumed, was reminded of a Parisian *inspecteur* who had once arrested him at the Quatz Arts Ball.

Nor was Hermione unimpressed. She was now being waggled about, and she found the process, though physically unpleasant, giving her a thrill of ecstasy.

Like all very beautiful girls, Hermione Bostock had received in her time a great deal of homage from the other sex. For years she had been moving in a world of men who frisked obsequiously about her and curled up like carbon paper if she spoke crossly to them, and she had become surfeited with male worship. Even when accepting Pongo's proposal she had yearned secretly for something rough and tough with a nasty eye and the soul of a second mate of a tramp steamer. And in the last quarter where she would have thought of looking she had found him. She had always been fond of Bill, but in an indulgent, almost contemptuous fashion, regarding him, as she had once mentioned to her father, as a sheep. And now the sheep, casting off its clothing, had revealed itself as one of the wolves and not the worst of them.

Little wonder that Hermione Bostock, as Bill having waggled her about, clasped her to his bosom and showered kisses on her upturned face, felt that here was the man she had been looking for since she first read *The Way of an Eagle*.

'My mate!' said Bill. Then, speaking from between clenched teeth, 'Hermione!'

'Yes, Bill?'

'You're going to marry me.'

'Yes, Bill.'

'That's clearly understood, is it?'

'Yes, Bill.'

'No more fooling about with these Pongos and what not.'

'No, Bill.'

'Right,' said the dominant male. He turned to Otis, who had been looking on at the scene with a sort of nostalgia, for it had reminded him of the old, happy days on the left bank of the Seine. 'So you're going to publish her books, are you?'

'Yes,' said Otis eagerly. He wanted there to be no mistake about this. 'All of them.'

'Giving her twenty per cent rising to twenty-five above three thousand?'

'Yes.'

'Why not a straight twenty-five?' said Bill, and Otis agreed that that would be much better. He had been on the point, he said, of suggesting it himself.

'Fine,' said Bill. 'Well, come along in, both of you, and have some tea.'

Hermione regretfully shook her head.

'I can't, darling. I must be getting back to London. Mother has been waiting for me at my flat since one o'clock, and she may be wondering what has become of me. I shall have to drive like the wind. Can I give you a lift, Mr Painter?'

Otis shuddered.

'I guess I'll go by train.'

'You'll find it slow.'

'I like it slow.'

'Very well. Goodbye, darling.'

'Goodbye,' said Bill. 'I'll be up in London tomorrow.'

'Splendid. Come and see me to the car. I left it outside the house.'

Otis remained, leaning against his tree. He felt a little faint, but very happy. Presently the two-seater, with Hermione bent over the wheel, whizzed round the corner and passed him at a speed which made him close his eyes and say to himself, 'There but for the grace of God goes Otis Painter.' When he opened them again, he saw Bill approaching.

'Why not thirty?' said Bill.

'Pardon?'

'Per cent. For her books. Not twenty-five.'

'Oh, ah, yes. Why, sure,' said Otis. 'Thirty might be nicer.'

'You don't want to skimp.'

'That's right. You don't.'

'And publicity. You believe in lots of that, I hope?'

'Oh, sure.'

'Fine. She was always complaining that her last publishers wouldn't push her books.'

'The poor fish. I mean, fishes.'

'Used to stall her off with a lot of rot about all that counted being word-of-mouth advertising.'

'Crazy saps.'

'You intend to advertise largely?'

'In all the literate Sunday papers.'

'How about the literate weeklies?'

'In those, too. I also thought of sandwich men and posters on the walls.'

Bill had not supposed that he would ever be able to regard this man with affection, but he did so now. He still had him docketed as a libertine, but indulgence must be accorded to libertines whose hearts are in the right place.

'Fine,' he said. 'Posters on the walls? Yes, fine.'

'Of course,' said Otis, 'all that kind of thing costs money.'

'Well spent,' Bill pointed out.

'Sure,' agreed Otis. 'Don't get the idea that I'm weakening. But it begins to look as if I may have to dig up a little more capital from somewhere. There isn't any too much of it in the old sock. You wouldn't feel like putting a thousand pounds into my business, would you?'

'That's an idea. Or two?'

'Or three? Or, say, look why not five? Nice round number.'

'Would you call five a round number?'

'I think so.'

'All right,' said Bill. 'Five, then.'

Otis's eyes closed again, this time in silent ecstasy. He had had his dreams, of course. Somewhere in the world, he had told himself, there must be angels in human shape willing to put money into a shaky publishing firm. But never had he really supposed that he would meet one, and still less that, if he did, such an angel would go as high as five thousand.

Opening his eyes, he found that he was alone. His benefactor had either been snatched back to heaven or had gone round the corner to the terrace. He took his bicycle from behind the tree and flung himself on the saddle like a gay professional rider. And when, halfway down the drive, he had another of those unfortunate spills, he merely smiled amusedly, as one good-naturedly recognising that the laugh is on him.

Life looked very good to Otis Painter. In the old left bank days he had been at some pains to cultivate a rather impressive pessimism, but now he was pure optimism from side-whiskers to shoe sole.

If Pippa had happened to pass at that moment, singing of God being in His heaven and all right with the world, he would have shaken her by the hand and told her he knew just how she felt.

2

Bill had not been snatched up to heaven. It was to the terrace that he had made his way on leaving Otis, and he had not been there many minutes when Lord Ickenham appeared, walking jauntily like a man whose forty winks in a field has refreshed him. At the sight of Bill he hurried forward with outstretched hand.

'My dear chap, a thousand congratulations.'

Bill gaped. This seemed to him clairvoyance.

'How on earth did you know?'

Lord Ickenham explained that his young friend's ecstatic expression, rather like that of a cherub or seraph on the point of singing Hosanna, would alone have been enough to tell him.

'But, as a matter of fact,' he said, 'I had the news from an acquaintance of mine whom I met bicycling along the road just now. Well, when I say bicycling along the road, he was lying in a ditch with his feet in the air, chuckling softly. He told me everything. It seems that he was a witness of the proceedings, and he speaks highly of your technique. You strode up and grabbed her by the wrist, eh?'

'Yes.'

'Waggled her about a bit?'

'Yes.'

'Then clasped her to your bosom and showered kisses on her upturned face?'

'Yes.'

'With the results that might have been anticipated. I told you the Ickenham system never fails. Brought up against it, the proudest beauty wilts and signs on the dotted line. It saddens you a little now, no doubt, to think of all the years you wasted on timid devotion.'

'It does, rather.'

'Timid devotion gets a lover nowhere. I was chatting with Miss Bean this morning, and she was telling me that she had a good deal of trouble at one time with Constable Potter owing to his devotion being so timid. She says that in the early days of his courtship he used to walk her out and chew his moustache and talk about the situation in China, but no real action. So one evening she said, "Come on, my lad, get on with it," and he got on with it. And after that everything went like clockwork.'

'Fine,' said Bill absently. He had been thinking of Hermione. 'Potter?' he went on, his mind returning from its flights. 'That reminds me. You haven't a bit of raw steak on you, have you?'

Lord Ickenham felt in his pockets.

'Sorry, no. I seem to have come out without any. Why? You feel peckish?'

'Elsie Bean was out here a moment ago, saying she was in the market for a bit of raw steak. It's needed for Potter. Apparently someone has been sloshing him in the eye.'

'Indeed? Who?'

'I didn't gather. Her story was confused. I seemed to catch some mention of Pongo, but would Pongo punch policemen in the eye?'

'It seems unlikely.'

'I must have got the name wrong. Still, there it is. Someone has given Potter a shiner, and he's fed to the tonsils. You see, he got pushed into the duck pond this afternoon, and now on top of that comes this biff in the eye, so he feels he's had enough of being a policeman. He's chucking it up and buying a pub, Elsie tells me. She seemed rather braced about it.'

Lord Ickenham drew a deep, slow breath of contentment and satisfaction. He looked pleased with himself, and who shall blame him? A man whose mission in life it is to spread sweetness and light and to bring the young folk together may surely be forgiven a touch of complacency when happy endings start going off like crackers all round him and he sees the young folk coming together in droves.

'Great news, Bill Oakshott,' he said. 'This is . . . what is that neat expression of yours? Ah, yes, "fine!" . . . This is fine. You're all right. Pongo's all right. And now the divine Bean is all right. It reminds one of the final spasm of a musical comedy.' He paused and regarded his companion with some surprise. 'Are you wearing woolly winter underclothing?' he asked.

'Me? No. Why?'

'You keep wriggling, as though something were irritating the epidermis.'

Bill blushed.

'Well, as a matter of fact,' he confessed, 'I'm finding it awfully difficult to keep still. After what's happened, I mean. You know how it is.'

'I do, indeed. I, too, have lived in Arcady. You would like to go for a long, rapid walk and work off steam? Of course you would. Push off, then.'

'You don't mind me leaving you?'

'Well, one hates to lose you, of course, but better a temporary separation than that you should burst all over the terrace. Au revoir, then, and once more a thousand congratulations.'

Bill disappeared round the corner like a dog let off the chain, gathering momentum with every stride. His pace was so good and his preoccupation so intense that it was not until he was out in the open road a mile away that it suddenly came to him that he had omitted to inform Lord Ickenham of the arrival of Major Plank.

He paused, debated within himself the advisability of going back, decided that it was too late and walked on. And presently Lord Ickenham and Major Plank had faded from his mind and he was thinking again exclusively in terms of wedding bells and honeymoons.

3

As things turned out, it would have been unnecessary for him to retrace his steps, for almost immediately after his departure Major Plank came out of the house, wiping butter from his lips.

'Hullo, Barmy,' he said, sighting Lord Ickenham. 'You're too late for the muffins. I've finished them. And very good they were, too.' He replaced his handkerchief. 'You're surprised to see me here, aren't you? Thought you'd baffled me, eh? Well, what happened was that shortly after you left the pub that well-nourished girl behind the bar told me the bonny baby contest was off. So along I came.'

Lord Ickenham had given a slight start on seeing his old friend, but his voice, when he spoke, was as calm and level as ever.

'Off, is it? Why?'

'Outbreak of measles. Thousands stricken.'

'I see. And have you exposed me?'

'Exposed you is right.'

'Did Mugsy seem interested?'

'Most.'

'One sees how he might well be, of course. You're a ruthless old bird, Bimbo.'

Major Plank bridled.

'Ruthless be blowed. I merely took the necessary steps to protect my reputation. And what do you mean, "old bird"? I'm a year younger than you. My idea of an old bird is Mugsy. I was shocked when I saw how he had aged. He looks like that chap in the Bible, Methuselah, the fellow who lived to a thousand and ate grass.'

'Methuselah didn't eat grass.'

'Yes, he did.'

'He never ate grass in his life. You're thinking of Nebuchadnezzar.'

'Oh, am I? Well, the principle's the same. And now I suppose you'll be sliding off. You'd have done better to start packing when I told you to. Still, you're in luck in one way. You won't run into Mugsy. He's in that room over there, holding a court martial.'

'A what?'

'Court martial. There have been all sorts of stirring goings-on here. Just as I was finishing the muffins, a policeman with a black eye barged into the drawing room with a tall, thin, light-haired young chap in one hand and a dashed pretty girl in a red jacket in the other, and said that the girl had pushed him into a duck pond and that when he was starting to apprehend her the light-haired young chap had biffed him in the eye. And Mugsy has taken them into that room there and is sitting on the case. I gather he's a magistrate or something and so is entitled to execute summary justice. I'm sorry for that young couple. It looks like a sticky weekend for them.'

Lord Ickenham gave his moustache a thoughtful twirl.

'Leave me, Bimbo,' he said. 'I would be alone.'

'Why?'

'I want to ponder.'

'Oh, ponder? Right ho! I'll go back and have some more strawberries,' said Major Plank.

He returned to the drawing room, and Lord Ickenham, left alone, lost no time in giving himself up to that survey of ways and means which the other's presence had hindered. For some moments he paced up and down, his hands behind his back and a concentrated look in his eye. The tautness of his features showed that his agile brain was not sparing itself.

And presently it was plain that it had given service. His face cleared. The lips beneath the trim moustache curved in a contented smile.

He crossed the terrace and went into the collection room.

4

Only Sir Aylmer was in the collection room when he entered. He, too, was wearing a contented smile.

For the first time that evening Sir Aylmer was feeling cheerful; as cheerful as a Colosseum lion which after a trying day when everything has gone wrong has found itself unexpectedly presented with a couple of Christian martyrs and has been able to deal faithfully with them. There is nothing which so braces up a chairman of a bench of magistrates in times of despondency as the infliction of a sharp sentence on a pair of criminals. It would be too much to say that he regarded Lord Ickenham amiably, but he did not bite him.

'Ha,' he said. 'It's you, is it?'

Lord Ickenham preserved his suavity.

'Ah, Mugsy,' he said. 'I understand you've met Bimbo Plank. How did you think he was looking? He thought you had aged. Where's Sally?'

'Who?'

'Bimbo told me she and my nephew Pongo were in here with you.'

Sir Aylmer started.

'You know that girl?'

'She is my honorary niece.'

A warm glow pervaded Sir Aylmer's system, as if he had been taking Doctor Smythe's Tonic Swamp Juice. This was even better than he had hoped.

'Oh, is she?' he said. 'Then it may interest you to know that I've just given her thirty days without the option, and your nephew the same. Potter's locked them up in the scullery while he has his eye bathed, and in a few minutes he'll be taking them off in custody.'

'A harsh sentence.'

'The only possible sentence. One of the most disgraceful cases that has ever come before me. She pushed Potter into the duck pond.'

'Well, what does a policeman expect, if he deliberately goes and stands on the edge of duck ponds? Girls will be girls.'

'Not while I'm sitting on the bench, they won't.'

'And how about the quality of mercy? It isn't strained, you know. It droppeth as the gentle rain from heaven upon the place beneath.'

'Damn the quality of mercy.'

'You'd better not let Shakespeare hear you saying that. Then you won't reconsider?'

'No, I won't. And now we'll discuss this matter of your coming here under a false name.'

Lord Ickenham nodded.

'Yes, I was hoping you would be able to spare me a minute to tell you about that. But before I begin, I would like to have a witness present.'

Lord Ickenham went to the door and called, 'Bimbo,' and Major Plank came out of the drawing room chewing strawberries.

'Could you come here a moment, Bimbo. I need you as a witness. I'm going to tell you a story that will shock you.'

'It isn't the one about the young man of Calcutta, is it? Because I've heard that.'

Lord Ickenham reassured him.

'When I said "shock", I meant that the tale would revolt your moral sense rather than bring the blush of shame to the cheek of modesty. Shall I begin at the beginning?'

'It sounds a good idea.'

'Very well. There was an American girl named Vansittart who came to London and bought a number of trinkets in Bond Street, her plan being to take them back to America and wear them. All straight so far?'

'Quite.'

'What—?' began Sir Aylmer, and Lord Ickenham gave him a stern look.

'Mugsy,' he said, 'if you interrupt, I'll put you over that chair and give you six of the juiciest. I've no doubt Bimbo will be glad to hold you down.'

'Charmed. Quite like old times.'

'Good. Then I will resume. Where were we?'

'This American wench. Bought jewels in Bond Street.'

'Exactly. Well, when she had got them, the thought flashed upon her that on arriving with them in New York, she would have to pay heavy customs duty to the United States Government. She recoiled from this.'

'I don't blame her.'

'So in her innocent, girlish way she decided to smuggle them in.'

'Quite right. Don't pay the bounders a penny, that's what I say. They've got much too much money as it is.'

'Precisely what Miss Vansittart felt. She held that opinion very strongly. But how to work this smuggling project?'

'That's always the snag.'

'She mused a while,' said Lord Ickenham, interrupting Major Plank in what threatened to be rather a long story about how he had once tried to sneak some cigars through at Southampton, 'and was rewarded with an idea. She had a friend, a young sculptress. She went to her, got her to make a clay bust and put the jewels in its head, and was then all set to take them to America in safety and comfort. She reasoned that when the customs authorities saw a clay bust, they would simply yawn and say, "Ho hum, a clay bust," and let it through.'

'Very shrewd.'

'So that was that. But . . . this is where you want to hold on to your chair, Bimbo . . . unfortunately this young sculptress was at that time modelling a bust of Mugsy.'

Major Plank was plainly bewildered. He stared at Sir Aylmer, studying his features closely and critically.

'What did Mugsy want a bust of himself for?'

'To present to the village club.'

'Good God.'

'During the sittings,' proceeded Lord Ickenham, 'Mugsy and the young sculptress naturally chatted from time to time, and in the course of these conversations she was rash enough to show him the bust that contained the jewels and to tell him that she was leaving it at my house a few miles from here until Miss Vansittart sailed. And Mugsy . . . I hardly like to tell you this, Bimbo.'

'Go on.'

'Well, you will scarcely credit it, but yesterday Mugsy nipped over to my house, effected an entrance and snitched the bust.'

'The one with the jewels in it?'

'The one with the jewels in it.'

Not even the menace of six of the juiciest could keep Sir Aylmer silent under this charge.

'It's an insane lie!'

Lord Ickenham raised his eyebrows.

'Is there anything to be gained by this bravado, Mugsy? Do you suppose I would bring such an accusation unless I could prove it to the hilt? Yes, Bimbo, he nipped over to my house, was admitted by my butler—'

'I wasn't. He wouldn't let me in.'

'That is your story, is it? It is not the one Coggs tells. He says he admitted you and that you roamed unwatched all over the premises. And, what is more, as you were leaving he noticed a suspicious bulge under your coat. Honestly, Mugsy, I wouldn't bother to persist in this pretence of innocence. It would be manlier if you came clean and threw yourself on the mercy of the court.'

'Much manlier,' agreed Major Plank. 'Whiter altogether.'

'I told you I could prove my accusation, and I will now proceed to do so. You have a nice, large foot, Bimbo. Oblige me by stepping to that cupboard over there and kicking in the door.'

'Right ho!' said Major Plank.

He approached the cupboard and drove at it with his brogue shoe. The niceness and largeness of his foot had not been overestimated. The fragile door splintered with a rending crash.

'Aha!' he said, peering in.

'You see a clay bust?'

'That's right. Bust, clay, one.'

'Bring it here.'

Sir Aylmer was gaping at the bust like one who gapes at snakes in his path. He sought in vain for an explanation of its presence. His wife could have given him that explanation, but his wife was in London.

'How the devil did that get there?' he gasped.

Lord Ickenham smiled sardonically.

'Really, Mugsy! Good, that, eh, Bimbo?'

'Very good.'

'Break that thing's head.'

'Bust the bust? Right ho!' said Major Plank, and did so. Lord Ickenham stooped and picked from the ruins a chamois leather bag. Before Sir Aylmer's bulging eyes he untied the string and poured forth a glittering stream.

Major Plank's eyes were bulging, too.

'This must have been one of your best hauls,' he said, looking at Sir Aylmer with open admiration.

Lord Ickenham replaced the gems in the bag and put the bag in his pocket.

'Well, there you are,' he said. 'You were asking just now, Mugsy, why I had come here under a false name. It was because I hoped that if I could get into the house I might be able to settle this thing without a scandal. I knew that you were shortly to stand for Parliament and that a scandal would ruin your prospects, and I took the charitable view that you had yielded to a sudden temptation. As far as I am concerned, I am now willing to let the thing drop. I have no wish to be hard on you, now that I have recovered your ill-gotten plunder and can restore it to its owner. We all understand these irresistible temptations. Eh, Bimbo?'

'Oh, quite.'

'We need say no more about the matter?'

'Not a word.'

'You won't tell anyone?'

'Except for a chap or two at the club, not a soul.'

'Then the whole wretched affair can now be forgotten. Of course, this monstrous sentence which you have inflicted on my nephew and Sally Painter must be quashed. You agree to that, Mugsy?' said Lord Ickenham, raising his voice, for he saw that his host was distrait.

Sir Aylmer gave that impersonation of his of a harpooned whale.

'What?' he said feebly.

Lord Ickenham repeated his words, and Sir Aylmer, though evidently finding it difficult to speak, said, 'Yes, certainly.'

'I should think so,' said Lord Ickenham warmly. 'Thirty days without the option for what was a mere girlish – or, in Pongo's case, boyish – freak. It recalls the worst excesses of the Star Chamber. The trouble with you fellows who have been Governors of Crown colonies, Mugsy, is that you get so accustomed to giving our black brothers the run-around that you lose all self-restraint. Then let us go and notify Constable Potter immediately to strike the gyves from the young couple's wrists. We shall find them, I think you said, in the scullery.'

He linked his arm in Sir Aylmer's and led him out. As they started down the hall Major Plank could hear him urging his companion in the kindest way to pull himself together, turn over a new leaf and start life afresh with a genuine determination to go straight in the future. It only needed a little will-power, said Lord Ickenham, adding that he held it truth with him who sings to one clear harp in divers tones that men may rise on stepping stones of their dead selves to higher things.

For some moments after they had left, Major Plank stood where he was, regarding the African curios with the glazed look of a man whose brain is taking a complete rest. Then gradually there came upon him a sense of something omitted, the feeling which he had so often had in the wilds of Brazil that somewhere there was man's work to be done and that it was for him to do it.

Then he remembered. The strawberries. He went back to the drawing room to finish them.

THE END

DIVE INTO THE HILARIOUS WORLD OF WODEHOUSE

'The purest kind of comedy'

Independent

WHAT HO!

For more gloriously witty goings on,
join the P. G. Wodehouse community.

Visit the official website
www.wodehouse.co.uk

Follow on Twitter
@wodehouseoffice

Become a fan on Facebook
facebook.com/wodehousepage

Revel with fellow aficionados as a
member of the P. G. Wodehouse society
www.pgwodehousesociety.org.uk